Rock My Heart

Cover Photo by by Robert Bejil Photography

Cover by S. Warren

ISBN-13: 978-1514199824

ISBN-10: 1514199823

Rock My Heart

Jean Haus

To all those alone in the dark...

Chapter 1
April

Once upon a time, I used to be a music fanatic—breathed, lived, and luuuved it. Now music is background noise, a popular radio station to fill in the silence while studying or cleaning my apartment or driving in the car. I don't have playlists, songs to pump me up or remind me of a past affection, at least not since high school. Back then, music was my life and connected to every emotion. These days I try to stay emotionless. Yet here I am again in a dingy bar to see a local band.

This bar might be the dingiest.

Even in the dim light, the tiles overhead are a dark, stained yellow. The walls brown, battered paneling. The stage is tiny, and the 'dance' floor in front of the stage much smaller. As I walk across the room, my shoes stick to the dirty carpet. There are five tables occupied on this Thursday night. Not exactly hopping. I spot Romeo sitting in the back.

Fine, six tables.

Yet a band is currently setting up on the small stage, speaking in hushed tones as they arrange the drum kit, speakers, and microphone stands.

At his table, I tug out a chair and Romeo says with a warm smile, "Hey, April. I already got you a drink. Thought you could nurse at least one." He nods to the tall glass on the table.

"Hey, thanks." I sit and lift the pinkish orange mixture waiting for me. "What is it exactly?"

"Um a…some concoction with fruit juice, the bartender says it doesn't taste much like alcohol," he says with a slight grin. His dark hair is messy and he's wearing his usual black shirt and jeans.

I return the grin. Romeo knows me rather well—he was the only one in my small circle of friends who didn't insist I go out for my twenty-first birthday last winter—at least compared to most people. I'm not much of a drinker. Besides the taste, I don't like losing control. I take a sip of the fruity smelling drink—huh, not too bad—then lean toward Romeo. "So have they finally decided on a band name?"

"Yeah."

"Well?"

He grimaces before spitting out, "Shush."

"Shush? Like be quiet?"

He shrugs.

"Really? Knowing Riley they have to be loud, so…"

"Riley got out voted. The singer thinks it's ironic, since they are so loud. And you know Riley."

"She doesn't really care."

He smiles. "Nope."

We both say together, "She just wants to play," then laugh.

As I watch them finish setting up on the little stage, I ask, "Why would Riley want to play here?"

All of a sudden serious, Romeo glances across the room at his girlfriend. "She wanted a small venue. It's just a short practice round before the U-Palooza. The singer and guitar player have never performed in front of a crowd."

I inspect the small half-filled bar. U-Palooza, a concert the fraternities and sororities of our university put on every autumn, is huge compared to this. "Not much of a crowd here."

He shrugs. "Riley didn't want a big crowd. Too much pressure for the singer."

"Is that why it's just you and me?" I'm guessing Riley didn't want Romeo's bandmates, who recently finished a national tour with two major bands less than a month ago, from Luminescent Juliet making her bandmates nervous.

Romeo gestures with an index finger toward the bar. "And Gabe. He knows the owner. Hooked Riley up."

Gabe Reed, the drummer for Luminescent Juliet, leans on the bar, talking with the older, female bartender. Tall and lean, he looks like a mix between a biker and a surfer with his brown and sun streaked jaw length hair, five o'clock shadow, old tatty jeans, white T-shirt, and permanent scowl.

"Ah, this venue is making more sense by the minute." I take another sip of the fruit mixture.

Romeo raises a brow.

"Seems like Gabe's type of place."

"He knows the bartender. His father's girlfriend…I think. Gabe's never very forthcoming."

The band finishes setting up and Riley comes over to our table. Her and I look like complete opposites, me in white capris, silver flats, and an aqua polo—that my mother bought because she claimed it perfectly matches my eyes—her in tight jean shorts, combat boots, and a black tank. My light brown hair is pulled back in a low ponytail at the base of my neck. Her dark hair with its dyed blonde streaks is in a ratted out ponytail.

She gives me a quick hug. "Thanks so much for coming."

Hugging her back, I say, "Wouldn't miss your debut. I'm super excited to see your band play."

She lets out a nervous laugh. "Hope we don't suck too much."

Romeo drags her onto his lap. "Drummer extraordinaire and suck don't go in the same sentence."

Gabe shows up, his presence and scowl as usual intimidating, sliding a tray of shots on the table, but then he smirks at Riley. "Liquid courage?"

"Hell yes! Thanks." Riley grabs a shot with shaky fingers. "One won't hurt."

I've never seen her so nervous. Actually, I don't think I've ever seen Riley nervous. Even her ever-present ponytail is bobbing with obvious apprehension.

Gabe pushes the tray closer for Romeo and me to grab a shot glass. I take one, trying to be polite.

Riley lifts hers and we all follow suit. "To not sucking!"

I nearly spit the stuff—tequila?—out, but somehow choke it down. Yuck. I haven't done a shot since high school. I found the taste of pure alcohol awful then too.

Romeo takes the shot glass from Riley's shaky fingers, gives her a quick kiss, and shoves her off his lap. "Go get em'," he says and playfully slaps her butt. She glares at him furiously before marching toward the little stage.

Unfortunately, Gabe grabs a chair, turns it backwards, and sits at our table. Though across from me, his hard profile faces the stage and he rests his lean muscled forearms on the back of the chair.

I take a huge gulp of my fruity drink. I've never been popular with Romeo's band. He and I dated a few years ago, but decided to be just friends. While we dated, the rest of the band kept their distance. Though Justin, the singer, did call me an ice princess, behind my back *and* to my face. When Romeo and Riley started getting together, both Sam, the bass player, and Justin resented me, thinking I was still after Romeo. Yet, they've slowly come to the realization that we are just good friends and have been more tolerant of me. And though I never would have let them come between our friendship, it's nice not to get the evil eye all the time.

But Gabe is different. Although he rarely speaks to me, or is even near me, I can almost feel his irritated indifference toward me. It has nothing to do with Romeo or Riley. He simply doesn't like me. Usually, I take dislike with an air of acceptance—few people really know me— but for whatever ridiculous reason—and it is ridiculous—Gabe's dislike puts me on edge, which is probably why when he handed me a shot, I didn't decline like usual.

He leans over and murmurs something low to Romeo, who's setting out his phone on the table to record Shush's performance.

Ignoring Gabe's rudeness and refusing to contemplate if he is talking about me, I scoot my chair, facing it toward the stage.

I'm here to see the band.

That's it.

Riley has settled behind the drums. The guitar and bass player are looking back at her. The singer clenches the microphone stand in a near death grip. They're all dressed in black or dark tones. One of the girls even wears fishnet stockings. Riley nods to the guitarist, the lone male in the group, and he faces forward, eyeing his guitar stem before twanging out the first riff.

And in seconds—without any introduction—they're banging out Zepplin's "Communication Breakdown." The music roars through the little bar, and I almost laugh. First, because Riley would pick this song. It's heavy drumming would appeal to her. Second, the lyrics remain the same except for 'girl' changed to 'boy', and the song from a female perspective is a bit sexually empowering. Unsurprisingly, the few patrons, most who are older, instantly recognize and pay rapt attention. However, none of them seem to notice the changes made to the guitar solo to make it more simplistic.

Once the song and some surprised clapping is over, Gabe turns to Romeo. "They changed the guitar solo."

Obviously, I wasn't the only one who noticed. I'm sure Romeo being a guitar player noticed too. But Gabe plays the drums, so I'm surprised he spotted the changes.

"He's working on it." Romeo shrugs. "Most people can't tell."

Before Gabe can reply, the next song starts with the singer screaming out, "I miss the misery!" The band kicks in at the end of scream into a heavy tune I don't recognize. Between the angry lyrics and loud music, the song is rocking, on the edge of metal, and obviously the title is, "I Miss the Misery." The entire band head bangs for an added effect. How fun.

Out of the corner of my eye, I notice Gabe with his arms crossed over the back of the chair, tapping his thumb to the rhythm and paying close attention to the performance.

When the song is over, he turns to Romeo. "That one was better, but they're not staying with Riley."

I take a long sip of my drink. I'd been thinking the same thing. They're just a touch behind her with the rhythm.

Romeo shrugs again. "Riley isn't going for perfection, merely sounding good enough to do a few gigs here and there. They'll get better eventually."

The start of the next song, which is "I'm Just a Girl" by No Doubt, cuts their conversation off. I'm instantly thrown through a time loop. I used to love, love, love this song. The memories, various flashes of my past filled with music, it evokes makes it hard for me to pay attention to the performance, especially after a shot and half a drink. Imaginary notes dance across my brain and fingertips. Until the emotions become too much. I guzzle the rest of my drink, hoping to kill the overwhelming nostalgia with alcohol.

Luckily, they practically roll right into "Been Caught Stealing" by Jane's Addiction, which is purely a feel good song to me.

Both Romeo and Gabe watch the band intently as I get my emotions in control. Once the song is over, the singer shouts out a,

"Thank you!" amid a few claps—I clap wildly—then the band heads off to the side of the stage for a pow wow.

Gabe and Romeo lean toward each other discussing the performance. It's mostly about the guitar player and how Riley is leading perfect but the band needs to keep up. Then Gabe takes off toward the bar.

"So what do you think?" Romeo asks, turning to me.

I glance at the band in discussion. "Well…I agree. They're not keeping up with Riley and the guitar player, while proficient, needs to work on the solos. A lot. Yet the songs, I'm assuming Riley picked, work for the singer and the band as a whole. Though they're not perfect, they have a great energy and judging them as a local band, they'd be one of the better ones."

Romeo nods. "Finding a good guitar player has been a challenge, but the dude is willing to work at it, so Riley finally settled." His look at me is pointed. "She's not out to make an album or write originals, so she's not after that type of talent."

I nod, understanding Riley's goals. She simply enjoys playing.

Gabe suddenly returns with a huge tray of shots, a beer for Romeo, and a drink for me.

Ugh. I'm already feeling light headed, but I'm shocked that he even thought about me. He sets the tall glass in front of me. Before I can thank him for the unwanted drink, Riley and her band are surrounding the table.

"Well?" she asks hopefully, looking between Romeo and Gabe. The other band members watch them too.

Romeo grins. "Two more songs, and I think you're ready for the U-Palooza."

Though that didn't sound like approval, it was quite the compliment. While only a local venue to raise money for our university's sororities and fraternities, Romeo takes every public performance seriously.

Riley laughs, jumping in Romeo's lap. The rest of her band beams. Gabe hands out shots. He raises his and everyone else follows, including me.

"Congrats," he says with a smirk. "Getting Romeo's approval ain't easy." He downs his shot and we all follow suit.

Yuck. I'm not sure what the clear liquor was, but I'm getting light headed. I usually watch Luminescent Juliet perform, then take off after the show. Even when I dated Romeo, we didn't hang out much at the after party. I take a gulp of my drink to get rid of the awful shot taste.

The band members grab chairs and a long discussion about what their other two songs should be commences. I'd choose something with the grittier vocals that the singer excels at and hardcore drums since Riley is their best musician. Maybe something like "Violet" by Hole. Yet, I don't say anything, just listen and take small sips of my second fruity concoction. And feeling strangely mellow, I don't bat an eyelash at the offer of a third shot.

Not really part of the conversation, I glance around the bar at the drinking patrons, people playing pool, and the empty stage. Maybe I come to these things to get a taste of what I'm missing. And perhaps the booze is allowing me to be more honest with myself. I push the last quarter of the drink away.

15

When the discussion ends, Riley jumps off Romeo's lap and heads toward the stage. One by one, we all follow and begin dismantling the stage. In my foggy state, I'm not much help. I only take two microphone stands to Romeo's van waiting out back.

Once the van is full, I realize—seeing as how everyone is leaving—that there is no way that I can drive in my current state.

"Um, Romeo?" I ask as he shuts the back doors of the van. "Could I get a ride?"

His expression is stunned. "You drank too much?"

I nod vigorously and hold up three fingers. "Three shots and almost two full drinks."

He grins. "How you feeling?"

"A little dizzy," I say and let out a laugh.

He laughs too. "Well, that's a first. Of course you can ride with us. I can bring you to your car in the morning" he says, and tosses the keys over my head. "But Gabe's driving."

I turn to Gabe as he catches the keys. "Weren't you drinking too?"

His expression is flat. "Just two shots."

Romeo shakes his head. "Gabe's like you, not much of a drinker, unless we're on tour," he adds under his breath, then tugs me to the side of the van and opens the door.

"April!" Riley happily yells and scoots over next to her bass player.

As we head toward the direction of Riley's house, the conversation stays on the topic of the performance. Giddy with excitement, Riley bounces in the middle of the seat. I try to keep the interior of the van from spinning. I don't feel sick, just very disorientated.

At her house, Riley hugs me quick, then bounces out of the van. Romeo and the bass player leave too, which means, I'm alone with Gabe. Feeling lightheaded, I lay across the back seat, while Romeo explains that I live in Sam's—their bass player—apartment complex across from the university.

The van is silent as Gabe drives across town and into the township where the local university is located.

I'm almost asleep, when Gabe asks, "What's your number?"

I push up. My number? Is he going to call me? About what I don't know, but whatever. "Nine eight nine four—"

"Your apartment number." His tone is flat and dry.

"Oh, sixty two," I say while my body over sways with the movement of the van. Whoa. Grabbing onto the back of his seat, I try to figure out where we are. I point to the right, about to tell him to turn, but he figures it out without my directions.

He pulls in front of my building and I start scooting across the seat. Before I can open the side door, he's somehow outside, opening it for me.

"Thanks." I step out and trip right into him.

Gabe catches me by the arms.

"Sorry," I mumble on his chest, breathing in the clean laundry soap scent of his shirt.

Without responding, he sets me upright. The strengthening of his perpetual frown deepens the cut of his cheekbones.

I wobble into a stance. "Okay, um, thanks for the ride." I take a step, sway, and draw in a gulp of much needed fresh air. The night is lusciously warm for September in Michigan.

He grabs me by the arm, right above my elbow. "Let me help you."

"No, s-okay," I say, trying to wrench my arm from his grip while swaying.

"You're on the second floor. I'll just walk you to your door."

"S-okay," I repeat and try to take another swaying step and almost fall against him again. "Ugh, I'm like on a boat!" I giggle at that, recalling the famous SNL video. I used to watch that show religiously, not only for the comedy, but also for the plethora of up and coming musicians. Sadly, I'm not into funny or music anymore.

A sigh escapes him. "Come on."

With a strong grip on my arm, he slowly helps me up the stairs. I mumble and laugh about being on a boat. Though I can sense his normal dislike, I find the boat thing too funny to care. I never laugh like this anymore. Never let go. It's kind of refreshing.

Okay, it's very refreshing.

When we get to the second floor, I wrench my arm from his grip, then lift my arms and sway. "I'm on a mother bleeping boat!"

I'm laughing and falling toward the wall as Gabe mumbles something about preppy girls not being able to hold their liquor, which takes me from giggly to angry.

"Hey!" I whip around, my finger pointing in his direction. I over whip and fall on him. We crash into the wall and slide down. He ends up sitting against the wall. I end up straddling his long body while weaving.

I'm about to tell him off—preppy girl!—but I'm suddenly caught by the light above us illuminating his lower jaw and lips. I'm not sure if it's because he's always scowling or that I rarely look his way since his dislike is almost tangible or the fact that I don't really check out guys, but I'm suddenly noticing his lips. Big time.

They're lush and full, the upper one just as full as the lower one. Very sexy.

I reach out and trace that upper lip with my index finger. "You have nice lips," I say in a surprised tone. His skin feels nice under my finger. Like hot, soft silk.

The silence in the walkway is suddenly filled with a harsh breath from him. I'm about to trace his lower lip when he grabs my wrist and hauls me up.

"Where's your apartment?" he growls.

I point two apartments down. "Over there."

He practically yanks me to my door.

"Sorr-e-e-e-e, I didn't mean anything. You just—"

"Key?" he demands.

I dig my key ring out of my pocket. "Look—"

He snatches the keys from me. "Which one?"

Swaying again, I point at the correct key. "Listen, your lips just caught me unawares—"

He unlocks the door, whips it open, and hands me the keys. "Try not to hurt yourself."

Then he's gone.

I roll my eyes and stumble into my dark apartment.

I'm on a dark boat…alone.

Chapter 2
April

I'm learning how to become more detached while in group therapy. Role reversal that is what I tell myself. That's the mind ticket out of this insanity. That is why I'm sitting in this circle of people. One day, I'll be the facilitator in a similar situation, helping people too. Now, I'm learning what it's like to be on the other side of things, gaining precious knowledge.

Jeff, our fearless leader slash counselor, drones on about goals, his voice a monotone whine into the uncomfortable silence. He likes to open with a long and dry commentary. No one ever listens. When I'm the leader, I plan to keep the commentaries to a minimum.

As in none.

I take a deep breath through my nose. Okay, I'm here every Tuesday afternoon because I have issues. Tons of them. Most people do. I'm just far, far better than most at hiding them. The root of my issues, the real reason, the burden I live with every day, will never come out. Not in this group. Not in the future. Just not ever.

Misha, the tattooed and pierced self-proclaimed slut, stares at me from across the circle. Her spiked pink hair flutters as she grasps the edges of her metal chair as if the tight grip holds her back from attacking me. Her stare is intimidating. It speaks a wealth of silent words. The strongest is dislike. Each week she stares with a hate that pinches her face. Most times, since I'm fairly sure she hates every other female on the planet, I feel sorry for her. But sometimes, if I'm in a rotten mood like today, I can't find the will to care, although I want to care.

As usual, I avoid confrontation and appropriately keep my face devoid of any emotion, cross my khaki clad legs, and glance away to stare at the fake, dusty flowers on the shelf by the window before returning my attention to our counselor.

I've grown into this, a calculated personality that fluctuates between emotionless, friendly, understanding, and sometimes compliant. A premeditated chameleon of sorts. The instances of genuine reaction are becoming far too rare, even for me.

When a knock sounds at the door, Jeff holds up a finger and closes the binder on his lap. His green corduroys are a loud swish in the silence as he moves across the room. He opens the door a crack and commences on conversing with whoever is on the other side. Misha gives me the devil glare, causing the diamond in her eyebrow to practically point at me. Chad, the blond guy to her right, stares at her chest, which, as usual, is on display. Jason, the guy next to me, picks at a fray in the knee of his jeans. I hold in a sigh.

This is such a waste of time.

Jeff opens the door all the way and I'm shocked—one of the few emotions I haven't been able to control— like grasping the edges of my chair and blinking in confusion at the person who walks in.

21

No. No. No. This cannot be happening. I'm thrown back in time. Five days ago. Once again waking with a pounding headache and a mortification that had me blushing in my own bed.

Tall and lean, Gabe strolls across the room, his freshly shaven face is hard lines devoid of emotion, his black boots stomp on the office carpet, and his russet, sun-streaked hair brushes his jaw.

Oh, crap. The embarrassing memory of my drunk ditziness along with touching his lips has me mortified all over again. I'm trying to control the hot flush of my cheeks as the rest of my group mates stare wide eyed and slack mouthed at Gabe while Jeff makes room for another chair.

Once Jeff gets the chair situated, he puts a hand on the newcomer's shoulder. "I'd like everyone to meet the newest member of our group, Gabe."

Misha purrs a hello. Chad gives Gabe the stink eye. Jason waves without looking up. And I sit frozen, still stunned. I agreed to this group because it was discreet being almost thirty minutes from campus and in another township. I blink at Gabe. Was is the key word.

He barely looks at any of us as he deposits his whipcord lean body in the chair between Jeff and Misha.

Calm. Internal hum. Calm. Internal hum. Calm.

I. Will. Not. Freak. Out.

"We were discussing the importance of goals, Gabe," Jeff says, sitting and opening his binder.

Deep breath.

Sadly, we weren't discussing anything. Jeff had simply been droning. More important than Jeff's illusions though, is the sudden burst of the real world into what was my own private dimension of hell.

Jeff smiles warmly at Gabe. "We'll get back to goals at the end of the session. I don't want to pressure you, however if you'd like to start by sharing something about yourself, the floor is yours first."

Cocking his head on an angle, Gabe regards Jeff through strands of sun-streaked hair. It's not a hateful stare like Misha's at me, more of a *You're an idiot* stare. Then he glances around at the rest of us. He doesn't even pause on me. And I'm suddenly very aware of his dislike.

Great. Another person in this group who detests me.

"All right," he says, crossing his arms over his plain, white T-shirt and glaring at Jeff. "I'll keep it simple. The first time my old man gave me a full ass whipping was fourteen years ago when I was age eight. By age eleven, the beatings became more frequent fueled from his alcohol rage. At age fifteen, I started fighting back. Now when I get angry, I fight. Knowing the reason doesn't change anything. I'm like a lit fuse, and yeah, I'm here because the court ordered it. Probation but no jail time. Yet." His crossed arms grow tense, daring any of us to comment.

The sound of Jason picking at his frayed jeans fills the silence.

Oh, well, wow, Gabe just won the crappy life award. Seriously, my heart squeezes at the thought of him being abused, especially at the age of eight. As Misha nearly pants over bad boy Gabe and Chad sizes him up, I faintly recall Romeo coming late to the Community Center, where we both volunteer for their suicide hotline, last winter because he had to bail Gabe out of jail first thing in the morning.

Jeff is clearly stunned from Gabe's sharing because for once he's quiet. He sits, clutching his binder while opening and closing his mouth like a fish.

"Dude, that story sucks," Chad says, breaking the silence. "Your dad sounds like a dick." Obviously, Chad sized Gabe up and decided not to make an enemy.

Though he glances at Chad, Gabe doesn't comment.

Chad turns to me. "Isn't that something?" He nods toward Gabe. "It's his first day, and I know more shit about him than I do about you after a month."

Though distressed by Gabe's induction into our group, I look calmly at Chad, instead of flinching, keeping emotion devoid from my expression. Jason doesn't say much either, but Chad is trying to impress Misha by being a jerk to me. "I'm sorry you fee—"

"Chad," Jeff says, finally gaining his wits. "We've talked about respect extensively, so let me repeat, April may share when she's ready."

Chad lets out a harrumph. "Then why is she here?"

"Yeah," Misha says, ganging up on me. "What is her purpose?"

Her tone insinuates there is no purpose to me. Lovely.

Though usually robotic, Jeff can't stop a soft sigh. "Not only do we need to respect our fellow group members, we need to care about them too."

"Like she gives a shit about me," Chad sneers.

I shake my head. Chad is an immature jerk, but I hope he gets his life straightened out and grows up.

"Of course, she cares about you, Chad. Isn't that right, April?"

"Why wouldn't I?" I say in an innocent and soft tone.

"See?" Jeff says, making me wonder for the umpteenth time where he got his license.

Chad lets out another harrumph.

Jeff ignores him and turns his attention to our newest member. "Gabe, I'd like to thank you for being upfront and honest with us. And I hope that through some shared wisdom, maybe a few revelations, some goal setting, and working to understand each other, we can help you understand and control your anger."

Help? With Jeff as the leader, this group is nothing more than one long session of complaining, either by Chad or Misha. Jason and I are about as cooperative as the chairs, and I'm getting the sense that Gabe has said his piece and will stay at the point of peace out.

Jeff opens his binder and looks at me. "Would you like to share anything, April?"

Instead of answering, I shake my head and glance at Jason's fingers picking at what has become a hole in the knee of his jeans.

"Jason," Jeff asks. "Would you like to share something?"

Anything? I imagine Jeff saying in a whine.

Pick. Pick. Pick. Jason shakes his head too as we both stare at the hole slowly growing in his jeans.

Jeff asks Misha to share, and she's soon relating one of her customary sexcapdes with a stranger. She is pouring it on thick today. Most likely for our newest member.

I take a peek at our newest member. Arms crossed, muscles bunched, and large boots crossed out in front of him, he seems to be bored, appearing to not listen as Misha describes performing oral sex in a bar bathroom. Chad is transfixed. Jeff tries not to appear shocked as usual. Jason picks. And I wonder if I can keep doing this, especially with Gabe here now.

Less than three more months, I tell myself.

Next it's Chad's turn. He goes on and on about his stepfather who is ruining his life with chores and the demand of getting a job. I'm pretty sure Chad is here via his mother who had created the self-indulgent monster and doesn't know what to do with him anymore. So this group is stuck with him.

Obviously bored with the never ending complaining, Gabe glances around every now and then, but his view never stops on me, which is relieving. I'm still attempting to get over the shock of seeing him across our little circle.

After twenty minutes of Chad whining about his evil step dad, Jeff goes back to droning, mostly about goals. However, as soon as he says, "Your first goal will be the simplest. Next week I want you all to think of something new to share. Whatever you want. A great memory, a favorite family member, a time when you felt down…anything. You have a whole week to think of something, therefore be prepared next week," he says, his regard shifting over Jason and me.

Oh, how manipulative, a new way to force Jason and I to share. I'm already planning on something mundane.

"Well, gang,"—Jeff's reference to us as a gang is so nerve grating it even causes me irritation—"we'll meet next week same time and same place," he says with a goofy smirk as if he's being funny.

I grab my purse and escape out into the hall, then past the receptionist's desk.

26

Jason, as usual, is right behind me.

As I step into a warm autumn afternoon, my hand on the logo, New Hope Center, in the middle of the glass, I turn and ask, "Need a ride?"

After seeing him walking away the first time, I ask Jason if he wants a ride following every session.

"No thanks," he quietly says like always and turns toward the sidewalk.

"All right, see you next time." I sigh and head into the parking lot of the medical facility, which is mostly doctor and dentist's offices. Apparently everyone, except me, and Gabe, live in the area.

I had done a ton of research before I agreed to join this group. Partial insurance coverage and discreet were my top priorities when it was recommended to me. Mainly, I didn't want anyone to know I was in a therapy group. People tend to think I'm perfect. Not that I am perfect—quite the opposite—but it's a persona I've learned to cultivate. It keeps me on the straight and narrow, or more specifically, aiming toward fake perfection keeps from losing it, as in becoming depressed to the point of won't-get-out-of-bed.

As I near my car and click unlock, I wonder how Gabe ended up here. Since we're all close in age? Wanted discreet? The partial insurance? Probably not. His joining was court ordered and I'm sure he didn't have a choice. Not that I had much of one.

Opening my door, I recall my vow five days ago to stay away from Luminescent Juliet. Just my luck that the person I wanted to stay away from is in my therapy group. I go to shut my door, except someone outside, specifically the grip on the door handle, stops me.

I glance up and meet a pair of hard, mahogany colored eyes partially hidden by wisps of hair. Gabe looks anything but indifferent now.

I let the handle go and he stumbles back a bit. "Can I help you?" I ask innocently, though my heart is beating wildly in my chest. He scared the crap out of me.

With a scowl growing on his face, he leans down. "Why are you here?"

His tone has me wanting to shut the door on him. "In the parking lot?" My tone is sarcastic as I turn toward him as much as the steering wheel will allow.

His brows lower and his scowl grows. "No, in the group."

For several long seconds, I stare at his scowling, contempt-filled expression—ignoring the lips that brought me so much embarrassment. Until rapid, chaotic anger, like a tornado shoots inside me from both his question and his demanding glare. My mortification about acting like a drunk ditz is gone.

"Really? Did you just sit in there? I don't own you any explanation," I say without thinking, without curbing my response, which is unusual for me. And although I always try to see the best side of a person, Gabe is making that habit super hard.

"What could someone like *you* need to come *here* for?" he asks through clenched teeth.

"Someone like me? Someone like me!" I repeat, before a wild laugh escapes me. "You know nothing about me."

He glances at the front of my car. "You drive an Infiniti, and"—his gaze roams over my short sleeved sweater and khaki pants—"and dress like a prep."

Angry tornado gaining power. "The car is eleven years old. It was my step-father's. And your reference to my clothes? Are you still in high school?" I push myself up, and if I were as tall as him, we'd be nose to nose. "Furthermore, if I were some rich...snob? I think that's what you're getting at. Are you saying that rich people don't have problems? Aren't depressed or lose loved ones or their rich fathers don't beat them?" I'm getting angrier with each word I speak. "Just what are you saying?"

His expression tightens to the point that his cheekbones slash across his face, but his tone is level when he says, "I'm saying that I have to go to this shit, and you don't. It's weird enough, much less with Romeo's ex-girlfriend who tried to hit on me the other night, sitting across from me."

The tornado goes wild in my head. "I. Did. Not. Hit. On. You." I draw in a deep breath. "I would never hit on you. I'm not like that. I was drunk and giggly." And though I'd love never to come to this group again, it's not an option. "And I'm not quitting," I practically snarl, then slip back in my car and face forward. "Let go of my door."

Across the parking lot, Misha leans against the building, waiting for a ride and watching us. Great.

Gabe bends down, his hair swaying forward, and says in a pacifying tone, "There are tons of other groups, probably better groups for you and your problems."

"Right now, my problem is you. Let go of my door and get away from my car."

He doesn't let go.

Misha shades her eyes with hand to get a better look at us arguing.

"Now." I jam the keys in the ignition. "Or I will make a scene."

He reluctantly steps back.

I slam the door shut and drive off, almost squealing my tires on the way out of the parking lot.

My hands tightly grip the steering wheel yet shake. Though I can't control shock, I rarely get angry. More than Gabe demanding I leave the group, more than his insinuation that I'm a rich snob, more than his assertion that I hit on him, even more than him being in the group, I'm shook up over the swift loss of my control.

I do need to get out of that group and away from Gabe. I don't like losing control like that.

Ever.

Chapter 3
April

In over two short weeks since the start of school, Wednesday afternoon lunch with Riley has become an official tradition. Since we both have class in the morning—me, Community Psychology and her, Probability and Statistics—we always meet at the Market, a little shop in the university's main building that serves sandwiches and soups.

I didn't warm up to Riley at first. Honestly, I was jealous of her. Not of her budding romance with Romeo—though he and I dated, a real romantic connection between us never materialized —instead, I was terrified she would damage our friendship. Romeo had become one of my closest friends, out of very few friends. Once I realized how much he truly liked her, I let go of my jealousy, and overtime Riley and I became friends. Riley is hard not to like. She's upbeat, a bit quirky, and an incredibly genuine person.

"So you're coming next Friday, right?" Riley asks as she crumples her empty sandwich wrapper.

Recalling the upcoming party, and the fact that I already agreed to go, I almost choke on a gulp of water. "Um…"

Dang.

I want to let out a number of expletives. I'm quite sure Gabe will be there given that the reason for the party is the band signing with a label. Besides the fact that his dislike is almost tangible, I don't want to be anywhere near him since my strange reaction to him twice, but I want to go to the party for Romeo and show my support.

"April?" Riley asks, her forehead scrunched. "You're coming early to help me get ready, right?"

My mind is stuck. I can't come up with a legitimate excuse that won't have me feeling guilty. "Yes, of course," I say, forcing a slight smile. I can do this. Gabe just caught me off guard in the parking lot, and the time previous to that I wasn't myself. I won't lose control again.

"It's not going to be fancy or anything. And it will be only our close friends. Romeo was irritated I even wanted to have a get together." She rolls her eyes. "But come on. They're getting signed!"

"It's very exciting," I agree, then take another sip of water, forcing myself to think of the conversation instead of being in close proximity to Gabe. I want to get off the topic of the party. It's making my insides jittery. "Do you wish you were in the band now that they've signed with a label?"

Not many people know about the label's offer. Romeo is keeping it under wraps. Even before they went on tour and opened for two nationally known bands, they'd been celebrities on campus. If the label thing got out, life on campus would totally suck for the members that go here—meaning not Gabe.

Riley pauses lifting her bottle of tea, then slowly sets it on the table, obviously collecting her thoughts. "I miss playing with people

32

who are at the top of their game. My band's coming along, though it's obviously nowhere near Luminescent. But the touring? The possible fame? The interviews?" She shakes her head. "No thank you. Seriously, I don't think I could deal with all that."

Her response doesn't surprise me. She's wonderfully in tune with herself. "It seems like Romeo would feel the same way about the fame part."

She tilts her head and taps her cap on the table. "He wants…the full experience. He doesn't let things go to his head, whether it's fame or stress. And yeah, one day he might step in the background and become the producer or the manager or the songwriter, but for now he's learning. Romeo's always learning."

I smile genuinely for once. Riley understands Romeo more than I ever could. How lovely it would be to have such a connection with someone. Not that I ever could. I glance at the clock. "I need to get going, need to get in three hours of filing today. Do you need me to bring anything on Friday?"

"No, I've got everything. I'll just need some help pulling it together."

"Okay, I'll be there by five," I say with a quick wave, heading over to the psychology wing.

Inside the wing, I pass a few people I've had classes with in the past, but only offer a slight wave. The whole Gabe in group therapy, along with the addition of the party, has me feeling like I'm stuck between a rock and a very hard place. I enter the department offices, greet the secretaries, store my bag under the community desk, jot down my time, and begin filing papers—my fifteen hours a week job. When I started this job freshman year, there had been five of us. This year I'm the sole paper filer. Other students work on computers, putting the information in databases. After a half hour, I find myself in Dr. Medina's office, knocking on the open door.

She looks up from her desk and smiles. "Hello, April. Do you need something?"

Dr. Medina is the department head of Psychology. I've had her for three different classes in the past. Most importantly, Dr. Medina refers students for the Clinical Counseling Graduate Program. Though my GPA is a four point, she has been hesitant to refer me to the program. I've never told her about my past, but the woman has psychological x-ray vision because she can see right into me. She believes I need to accept whatever is in my past before I can counsel others. Thus the group therapy prior to the recommendation, and although Jeff can't tell her anything specific, he can tell her if I'm making progress or not. What I need to do is get my head out of my behind and open up about something soon or he'll deem me progress-less. What I want to do is get out of that group.

I nearly bite my lip off before I blurt, "Do you think it's too late for me to find another group?"

In the mist of writing something, Dr. Medina's pen pauses hovering over the paper she is grading. "Why would you want to switch groups?" she asks in a cautious tone.

Her tone has me wanting to take the question back. "Well," I say slowly. "I'm not sure the fit is…um, right."

"Jeff tells me that the group is comprised of all young adults, it should be a perfect fit. People at the same place in life tend to see and understand things the same way." She puts her pen down. "Plus, you told me that it was going great a few weeks ago. Why this sudden change of heart?" Her expression is thoughtful and a bit suspicious.

Crap! I should have never opened my stupid mouth. "I…the last session felt extremely uncomfortable," I say, trying to be honest because I respect Dr. Medina very much.

A soft smile curves her mouth. "Then that is exactly where you belong. Your boundaries need to be pushed, April. A little discomfort may do you good."

Yup, a rock and a hard place.

I have to get into the program. And Dr. Medina holds the key. I draw in a deep breath so I can force out the words, "You're probably right. I'm sure you're right. I'm just being a coward."

Her head shakes. "Not a coward, just human."

I force a smile. "Thanks for listening to me."

She picks up her pen. "Anytime, April."

I go back to filing papers. While I work, I try to calm myself and tell myself I can handle Gabe.

But I'm worried.

I haven't reacted to anyone like that in years.

Actually, I don't think I've ever reacted that way to anyone.

Chapter 4
Gabe

Riley watches me playing the drums, foot tapping to the beat, forehead wrinkled in concentration, and hands gripping the edges of the chair. She ignores Romeo, her boyfriend, playing the guitar to the left of me. I used to find her intense attention unnerving. After a while, it just became part of practicing. Also, beyond finding her stare uncomfortable, my dislike for her used to border on hate.

Though I'd never admit it, she intimidates the hell out of me. She beat me out over a year ago for the drumming spot in Luminescent Juliet. They offered me the job when she quit. Because drumming is my addiction, a calm in the storm that is me, I swallowed my pride and took the job. Without the release of playing, I probably would have landed in jail or prison long ago.

I learned how to play the drums by ear and practice, practice, practice. I didn't know the proper lingo, how to read music, or even the fractional way music is broke down. I simply learned how to copy to the point of perfection.

Once Romeo had taught me all he could, I had to swallow my pride again—which was shit ass hard, since there are times pride is all I have—and take lessons from my nemesis. Though I cling to pride like a motherfucker, I'm not stupid. So when he brought Riley in, I swallowed pride like a heroin addict prostitute swallows in a back alley—without a blink of an eye, even as their insides have to be retching like hell. Drumming is my heroin, Romeo my pimp, and Riley my pusher.

I roll into a drum fill, adrenaline and anger pushing my energy, then bring down the energy as Romeo strums out the ending riffs of the new song.

Riley smiles wide. "Perfect! You finally toned down the intro and ending."

Yeah, pounding lightly is a problem for me. Over the last three rounds of the song, I've forced myself to ease up a bit more each time through.

Romeo places his guitar on a waiting stand. "I'm going to go get some food before practice. You two finish the sheet music."

Romeo is a bossy dick, and if he weren't the driving force that keeps our band on track, along with the hours he has spent helping me hone my skill, I would have beat his ass long ago. He could piss off a saint, and I'm the furthest thing from a saint.

He murmurs something in Riley's ear—that has her smiling wider—then he takes off down the stairs that lead to this second floor dungeon above an old antique shop.

Riley waves a clipboard at me. "Finish this up, so I can head out."

I tuck my sticks in a back pocket and go over to her. Now that we have a label, every instrument needs to be composed on paper before we head into the studio over the next couple of months. And though

Riley taught me how to read music, writing it is difficult. Therefore, she sets it up, I finish it out, and she checks it over.

Swallow fucking swallow.

I am getting better at this shit though, even though it's only been a month since we got back from the tour. Plus, Riley helps me swallow my pride by always being gone before the other members of the band come for practice. I'm honest enough to admit I'd be humiliated if the other band members knew how much she helps me.

Sitting next to her, I grab the sheets attached to the clipboard and start working on the drum notation.

She waits and texts while I start filling in the drum keys.

After a few minutes of silence, I nonchalantly say, "Can I ask you something? If you don't want to answer, feel free to tell me to fuck off if you feel like it."

She pauses texting to look at me like I've grown another head, then she nervously presses her lips together before blurting, "I don't want to be in the band. I can't work with Romeo on a regular basis like that. It put a huge strain on our relationship. The idea of touring, living on a bus for weeks, sounds like hell. You're pretty much as good as me now and—"

"Whoa," I say, raising my hand. "I wasn't going to ask that."

She blinks at me.

I'm not surprised at her response. Working with her at first, I probably was noticeably resentful, and yes, I used to agonize about her coming back into the band and leaving me high and dry until I talked myself into not giving a fuck, or at least trying not to give a fuck. Between her starting her own band and Luminescent going on a major tour, I began to lose that worry. With the worry mostly gone, I'm still all work and little conversation. Talk is cheap. But her response isn't unexpected. The question she supposed I asked has been silently sitting between us every time we practice.

I force a close lipped smirk. "I'm glad you're not planning on taking over my spot, and ah…thanks for the compliment, though you're a better player than—"

"No," she says, shaking her head. "Not really. I do have an edge as far as mechanics, but you have an edge because of your intensity. Thus it all evens out in the end."

This time I blink at her. I try not to compare myself to this girl. She's that good.

"So what were you going to ask?"

I let my shock over her evaluation of my skill go. "I wanted to ask about April…" I don't give a shit what Riley or anyone else thinks about my mental state. It's fucked up. End of story. I'm just not comfortable sharing that April is in group therapy. I don't snitch on people to the cops or their friends. That shit was pounded in me at the age of thirteen during a two-month stint in juvie. Got caught stealing tennis shoes—my second shop lifting offence—that I truly needed. I also learned how information could prove to be the scale tipper while in juvie, and I need information on April. Usually I don't care enough to play games, yet I'll do just about anything at this point to get rid of her.

Riley's face constricts in confusion. "April Tanner?"

"Um, yeah, she's your and Romeo's friend, right?"

"You're interested in April? I thought you were dating...that one blonde girl," she finally says, obviously not able to recall the name of my last girlfriend.

"Ah, Kristy and I haven't really connected since I got back from tour." I don't have time for clingy Kristy's drama between all my probation demands, working at the garage, and writing a new album.

Riley's eyes grow huge. "So you want to ask April out?"

A harsh laugh escapes me. "Ah, no," I say, thinking people like April don't date people like me, or vice versa. I'm on the other side of several tracks from her. I'm on the real side of life. She's on the lucky side, with her nose stuck in the air so far I'm surprised it doesn't have wings. Sometimes her side slums on my side for some adventure, but that shit never lasts.

"I just want..." *Her to quit group and never touch me again.* I've been trying to quit or get myself moved into another group for the last three days. My probation officer refused to move me. Since he'd already spent a huge amount of time finding me the "right" group due to my new semi-fame—his words not mine—he determined that I was trying to get out of any group therapy. But people rarely recognize me, unless I'm with the band. Usually, I'm low key or working at my job at the garage. Yet, even though I told him this, he refused to change my group.

Riley's expectant and confused stare has me looking at the drum notation and mumbling, "I might be a little interested in her." I internally punch myself in the face. I hate lying, but nothing else to do. I plaster a forlorn look on my face and meet Riley's wide smile. "So what is she like?"

"Well…" Riley tucks her phone in pocket. "She can seem a bit standoffish. Justin used to refer to her as the ice queen. She's just very private and usually quiet. Kind of like you…" My brows rise in unbelief. Yet she just draws a knee up and wraps her hands around it. "Anyway, when Romeo and I were going through some problems, she pulled me aside and bitched me out. So she's not shy or anything, but she doesn't date much," Riley says with a frown, slouching in thought before perking up. "She'll be at the get together Friday. You could try talking to her there."

I nod like that's the best idea ever. "Anything else I should know about her?"

"Well, I'm not going to tell you anything super personal. I can only tell you she's very driven. She's going to college to be a counselor. She'll be graduating this year, a semester early. College takes up most of her life, which is probably why she doesn't date much…"

Counselor? Maybe that's why she's in group, part of her education, which makes her being there worse. Like I'm a caged animal to be poked and prodded and dissected.

The fucking cherry on top of this mess is that I want therapy to help me. I never buy into hope, but when we got offers from several labels, a different future than the shit I always anticipated flashed in my imagination. Now I need therapy to help me. Yet I'm beyond uncomfortable bearing all my shit to some chick I see from time to time out of therapy, who used to screw Romeo, and who is still friends with Romeo and Riley. Like I said to her, it's just too weird. And beyond the weirdness, I don't think I can admit all my dirt with her sitting across from me. The wannabe slut, the jean picker, and even the spoiled douche bag I can handle, but the princess?

Nope.

She's so calm, cool, and collected, gazing down her nose at the rest of us. With her back stiff, her hands clasped, and her expression smooth, she makes me feel dirty merely looking at her.

Yet, out in the parking lot she lost some of that cool, her blue eyes flashing angrily, her mouth twisting in fury. She didn't look like the ice queen then. And my previous assumption, that her icy, cool beauty was a turn off, changed in an instant. Cracking her cool, bringing out that fire, became a hot, sexual fantasy in an instant.

And fuck that.

Fuck my dick and its fantasies. I will never go there. I force my features to smooth and glance back at the music sheet. "Yeah, I'll definitely have to talk to her at the party."

Chapter 5
April

Although I loathe group therapy, following my little talk with Dr. Medina, I left myself with the only option of participating more. It doesn't matter that Gabe stoically sits across from me or that people may find out about me being in therapy. I have to make it appear that the therapy is working to some degree because I have to get into the program. Therefore I sit in my chair, listen attentively, and wait to participate.

After his usual introduction monologue, Jeff asks Chad then Misha to share. Apparently, he wants to get the usual crap out of the way in the beginning. Next, he turns to Jason. Thumbs tapping on the sides of his thighs, Jason tells a short story of his mother giving him a surprise birthday party when he was ten. We're all intent on listening since Jason never says more than two words. And even with the shortness of the story, it's apparent that the memory is a fond one.

"I always wanted to give someone a surprise party, so that was a great memory, Jason," I say, wanting to participate with a bit of honesty.

Jeff waits for other comments until the stale silence has him giving Jason an exuberant thanks before he asks Gabe to share.

Gabe's eyes flick to me so quick that I almost miss it, making me wonder if I missed any glances last week.

Though he casually leans back in the chair, his long body is ridged steel. "When I retaliated against my father that first time"—there's no need for him to elaborate given that we all clearly remember him announcing that he beat his father's ass—"it wasn't because I was defending myself. I never tried to defend myself. It was because he hit his girlfriend who had been living with us since I was thirteen. She'd been taking care of me more than my father did the moment she walked through the door. After he hit her, I lost it, snapped, and jumped on him, fists going wild." He crosses his boots. "He hit me from time to time after that, but he never hit her again."

Misha looks at him with wide eyes. "And you were only fifteen?"

Gabe nods.

"Did you ever beat his ass again?" Chad asks.

Gabe shakes his head. "He turned to threats more than fists after that."

"How much?" I blurt out in a demanding tone.

Gabe's brow rises in question.

"How much d—did he hit you?" I almost said does.

His shoulders shrug. "Every now and then."

"Well," Misha sneers at me. "For someone who doesn't say much, you're awfully intrusive."

I actually agree with her. The question had come more from the future counselor in me. I'm betting that Gabe has grown to consider getting knocked around every now and then as acceptable. And as usual when Misha is being aggressive, my gaze finds the floor. I mumble, "Just curious."

I glance up to find Gabe watching me, most likely wondering why I backed down from Misha and not him. I wonder too—it's always simpler to back down—but for some reason, I spontaneously responded to him.

Jeff asks Gabe a few more questions about how he felt before and after the confrontation with his dad. Gabe's one word responses are "angry" and "pissed." Then Jeff swivels in his chair toward me. "Ready to share, April?"

Dread fills me, but I nod and grab for my purse—some designer brand my mother got from an outlet store—from the floor. I shuffle inside for a few moments, buying time, even though the pamphlet is neatly folded inside my planner. After a deep breath, I yank the folded paper out, then set my purse back on the floor.

"This"—I wave the pamphlet in the air, unfolding it and the thick paper flutters from my nervousness—"is the program from the church service for my...my cousin's funeral. She—she committed suicide." I don't pay attention to anyone just flip the program over. "Her—my aunt had her bucket list printed on the back. I'd like to share that." Though my voice is even, almost monotone as I read, the paper shakes. I can't control my voice and my hands.

Speaking low and slow, I somehow get out the first item. "Release a paper lantern, get a tattoo, kiss at the top of a Ferris wheel, get belly button pierced, meet Michael Thomas, ride on the back of a motorcycle, slow dance in the rain, walk through a drive thru, share a bottle of strawberry wine, and sleep under the stars." I fold the program with trembling hands, my throat tight with the urge to cry. Done, I raise my gaze to find everyone staring at me, even Jason.

Gabe's gaze is unexpectedly thoughtful.

To my surprise, Misha asks, "When did your cousin…" She lets the question hang in the air like a clap of thunder inside of our circle.

I clear my throat and let all the tangled feelings inside of me go— actually, I shove them deep down like I always do. "Almost four years ago."

"Four years ago?" Chad echoes. "I mean the whole thing sucks, but four years… that's a long ass time."

It's actually been three years seven months and eight days since Rachel passed.

"Chad," Jeff says in a warning tone. "You—"

"Need to shut the hell up," Gabe says, glaring at Chad.

Chad sinks onto his folded chair.

"I'd like to sleep under the stars," Jason says softly, breaking the tension.

"I'd like that too, Jason," Jeff says, latching on to the calmness Jason's soft announcement brought to the tension filling the circle.

As Gabe sits back, Jeff turns to me. "Thank you for sharing, April. That took a lot of courage. And whenever you'd like to share more, we're here waiting to listen." He then starts his closing monologue, a long explanation of how sharing and listening to each other helps us understand and respect others. I liked it better when I tuned him out, but I'm determined to participate. He ends the session with not only telling us that we need to think of something to share again for next week, we also need to think of someone we could do an act of kindness for. Merely decide on an act kindness at this point, worry about the doing later.

Two assignments for next week. Great. Let the healing begin.

I grab my purse and make it out into the hallway in record time. Passing the receptionist, I offer a quick goodbye, then step outside. On the sidewalk, I ask Jason, "Would you like a ride?"

"No thanks," he says, pulling his hood over his shaggy black hair.

"All right, see you next week," I say, moving into the parking lot. After last week, I practically run to my car. I'm pulling out when I notice Gabe marching across the lot toward me.

I'm not sure if he's going to his car or coming to demand I quit again, but I drive past him without looking, staying calm, cool, and collected.

Well, except for the tremor in my hands.

Chapter 6
April

Since the warm weather is holding out, Riley decided to have dinner on the patio in her backyard. Her mother took her little sister to a movie, so we have the house to ourselves. Riley made chicken enchiladas, while Allie—Justin's girlfriend—and I cut vegetables, like a million tomatoes, onions, and peppers, for fresh salsa. Peyton—Sam's new girlfriend who I just met this evening—brought dessert: spicy chocolate cupcakes. Sam and Justin brought stuff for margaritas—I stick to water. And Romeo brought the entertainment in the form of a fiddle, an acoustic guitar, and a thin drum or precisely a bodhrán.

Though being in close proximity to Gabe puts me on edge, especially after he claimed I hit on him and my revelation in therapy, the night has gone smooth. The discussion about Luminescent Juliet signing with a label dominated most of the dinner conversation. Plus I made sure to sit on the opposite end of the table from Gabe. Then I spent as much time possible clearing the table.

Now the band sits across from us on the stairs connected to the deck for the above ground pool. Surprisingly, Gabe has been pleasant and easy going. But after quietly arguing—I'm guessing about who would play—with Riley off to the side of the patio, his expression is rigid and intense as he holds the thin drum. Actually, if memory serves me correct, Gabe is always intense when he plays the drums.

Riley comes over and plops in the chair next to me. "Ah, Romeo playing the fiddle," she says with a wistful smile that has me smirking. Riley is whipped but then so is Romeo.

They start "In the Pines" by Nirvana. Actually, it is Led Belly's version of an American folk tune that has been done by numerous artists. I've heard the band play it in an acoustic version—and each time they play it, the sad song brings on memories that I strive to forget about —yet this is slower, sadder, somehow more melodic with the fiddle added to Sam's guitar playing and the slow booming beat of the antique drum.

As Justin lowly sings, "Don't lie to me, where did you sleep last night. I stayed in the pines where the sun never shines, and shivered the whole night through," a shiver inches along my spine. This new version is stunning. It's a mix of rock and folk that's deep and dark and soul touching. My favorite kind of music.

Or at least it once was.

And though I try to ignore its melancholy appeal, I can't help being transfixed as the music tries to fill the hole inside of me left from the absence of it. As Justin's voice rises, the dark space within me lightens a touch. Romeo is in deep concentration with the fiddle stuck under his chin. Sam strums and watches Peyton. Sitting on the top stair, Gabe looks at the ground, the drum between his spread knees. Suddenly, he does glance up and I'm caught in his intense gaze until I have to look away.

The song ends and Riley elbows my arm. "Didn't Gabe do great?" she whispers.

"Yeah, great," I slowly say, bewildered at her asking me about him.

"He's gotten really good this past year," she adds in another whisper as they begin another soft melodic tune.

This time I keep my eyes from Gabe. Across the table, Peyton and Allie sway to the rhythm. I don't know the song—it must be newer—but Sam's light strumming combined with the melancholy tone and the refrain, "My heart's on fire," has me wishing the song would end, though they play it beautifully.

Finally, the song does end, and as soon as Romeo sets his fiddle in the case, I grab the remaining dishes on the table and head into the house. We had left all the dirty dishes on the counter per Riley's instructions. Now I'm a dishwashing loading machine.

Through the window above the sink, the energy around the table as everyone talks and smiles and laughs is nearly visible. The music leaves me melancholy and wistful at the same time. I wonder if I'll always be stuck on the other side of the glass, left alone. Shaking the water from a dish, I shake the thought off.

I belong on the other side of the glass.

I'm rinsing a plate when I notice Riley bending toward Gabe and gesturing toward the house. Brows low, he nods at her. Recalling her elbow and words earlier, I'm suddenly suspicious the girl is playing matchmaker. Once the suspicion settles, I almost laugh. Other than a few dates, anyone and me is a stretch. I went dead to romance a long time ago, but Gabe and me is preposterous. Whatever Riley has got going on her head, it's a waste of time. He obviously doesn't like me, and I'm not much of a Gabe fan.

Unsurprisingly, within minutes Gabe is in the kitchen. "Getting a little too gushy out there," he nonchalantly says, reaching for a bottle of hot sauce and sour cream. Face impassive, he opens the fridge. "Thought I'd come in and help."

I turn toward the sink and pick up a dirty pan along with a sponge. "No need. I'm almost done."

The fridge shuts and I sense him leaning on the island counter.

"Listen, April," he says in a wary tone. "I shouldn't have demanded you quit therapy. It was a dick move. I was just shocked at you being there. I tend to get pissed, let off my steam, and think later."

He wasn't the only shocked one.

"Honestly, I still don't want you there." He lets out a sigh of frustration. "After this Tuesday, I get that you probably need to be there but…"

The pan in my hand bangs against the sink as I stare at the loving couples outside.

"I would think we'd both be uncomfortable, especially after you—"

"I didn't hit on you." The words come from behind clenched teeth. "I rarely drink, and obviously drank too much. I was just being silly."

"Okay, maybe I should have said because we share the same circle of people or some shit, but come on, you have to be uncomfortable too."

Now I let out a sigh and start furiously scrubbing the pan. "You don't seem to take it serious. I have a hard time taking that therapy group serious. What's the big deal?"

Dang. Why am I so honest with him?

"It is hard to get serious with Jeff and the clowns in that group"— I hear him shuffle along the island behind me, then tap on the counter in a quick roll that echoes a drum fill—" yet this label thing is big. Big enough that I want to get my shit together. I need to get my shit together."

The plea in his voice has me turning around. His eyes are pleading too, his expression so desperate I want to reassure him.

But I cannot.

I slowly shake my head. "I can't quit. I would if I could, but the head of the psychology department has made group therapy an unofficial hoop to get in the graduate program for Clinical Counseling."

His jaw tightens as he runs a hand through his hair dragging it back and revealing black barbell hoops in both of his ears. "Funny, how you can't take it serious, but it's what you want to do."

I can't help a scowl from forming on my lips until I finally nod. "I want to help people but it's probably easier leading, easier helping— you just have to have patience to help. With the other you need…courage."

Gabe is studying me with what appears to be speculation and I'm gnawing on my lip, trying to overcome a wave of guilt, as Riley bounces into the kitchen.

Her smile stiffens at our expressions, mine tense, while Gabe's is still contemplative, but she cheerfully says, "All right, enough with the dishes. I can finish later." She shuts the dishwasher.

Gabe continues staring at me with that weird speculation as Riley drags me by the elbow outside.

His look sends a tinge of nervousness running through me.

Chapter 7
April

Jeff has done his monologue. Misha has announced she will be helping her current boy toy become a better lover. Chad is going to help his mother with the dishes. Jason is going to help his neighbor with yard work. Now it's my turn.

Jeff looks at me expectantly.

I clear my throat. "I'm going to volunteer at the Child and Family Services." I already volunteer for their suicide hotline on Sundays, but I have less credits at school this semester. I can volunteer more than one day at the center.

Misha and Chad sneer at me while Jeff smiles—perhaps a bit too wide. "That sounds like an excellent plan, April."

I force a curt nod. With his constant praise, Jeff sometimes reminds me of my grade school teachers. Problem? I'm not in grade school. Gabe's only reaction is the slight rise of his eyebrows. Jason stares at his hands clasped in his lap.

Jeff shifts toward Gabe. "And who have you decided to help?"

Gabe stretches his legs then crosses his ankles, his gaze settling on me. "I'm going to help April complete her cousin's bucket list."

A loud gasp rings out in the room.

It takes me several seconds to realize the gasp came from me.

"That sounds like a wonderful idea, Gabe." Real bone a fide enthusiasm fills Jeff's voice.

Misha's lip curls so far the hoop in the center of her upper lip almost touches a nostril. Chad appears stupefied. Jason stares at his clasped hands. I gradually shut my mouth, as confusion rolls around my brain. Why would Gabe want to help me? That he'd announce such a thing is rather presumptuous. Oddly, I've never thought about completing the bucket list, and suddenly the idea is very intriguing. But with Gabe? That thought is intimidating, as in shaking hands with the enemy intimidating.

Confused and irritated with Gabe's arrogance, I work hard to keep my face neutral for the rest of the session. I barely acknowledge Jeff telling us that the assignment next week is to report any progress on our act of kindness. Finally, he does his final monologue and dismisses us.

Still in a fog, I wander out of the building. On the sidewalk, I absently ask Jason if he'd like a ride home. He declines like usual as Gabe passes us. I follow him to a beat up, old pickup truck.

Numerous thoughts, words, and rebuffs swirl in my head, but as he reaches for the door handle, "What are you up to?" comes out of my mouth.

He lowers his hand and turns, cocking his head, giving me a picture of his harshly lined profile. "Up to?"

"Why would you want to help me? You can't stand me."

Those full lips turn down as he turns around. "I never said that."

"And now you want to help me?" I say incredulously, ignoring his response. "Is this your new ploy to get me to quit?" There's a desperate whine to my voice that has me internally cringing.

He shakes his head and draws in a visible breath. "I'm truly trying to help… and deal with the issue of you being in group head on. I like to deal with issues head on, and maybe gain some courage for myself," he admits in a sullen tone.

Though I realize his idea for courage came from me the other night at the party, I'm still confused. "Maybe I don't need your help."

"So you don't want to fulfill your cousin's list?" he softly asks.

"She was—fifteen," I say, feeling out of my element more than ever from the gentle timbre of his voice.

"Fifteen year-olds-can't have dreams?"

"Of course they can."

"But they're too immature for you?"

"Seriously, I'm going to meet Michael Thomas?" My tone drips with cynicism due to the fact the man is a famous actor.

"Maybe. Nothing is impossible. The band is going to California over the next few months. Plus most of the list is easy."

"Several of them are ridiculous!"

He looks over my shoulder. "You might want to tone it down. We have an audience."

Glancing behind, I notice not just Misha but Jeff on the sidewalk in front of the counseling office, watching us. At this point, I could ignore Misha, however Jeff, the sunny counselor and reporter to Dr. Medina, I cannot.

I turn back to Gabe, drawing in a deep gulp of air.

He spins his keys on his index finger. "You have somewhere to be? Work? School?"

"No," I slowly say. "Why?"

"I'm heading to Allie's shop."

It takes me a few seconds to put two and two together. Allie owns a tattoo parlor. A wild laugh escapes me, a laugh that Jeff will hopefully read wrong. "I'm not getting a tattoo."

He stops spinning his keys. "You could just check her place out."

I can't help an eye roll.

"Just look for something small and hidden?"

"I'm not getting a tattoo," I repeat, just thinking about a needle piercing my skin gives me the willies.

His lips twitch. "Scared?"

"Yup."

Geez, my honesty around him is astounding. I'm an open book without one obscure metaphor.

"Well, don't be. Allie won't stab you for looking."

My eyelids drop as I glower at him. "Are you trying to goad me in to going?"

"Maybe a bit," he admits with a grin.

The grin is what does me in. "All right," I say, letting go for once. It's a foreign sensation, but I like the freeing feeling of it. "This doesn't mean I'm agreeing"—I take a step back toward my car—"to anything."

He opens the truck with a nod. "Point taken. See you in twenty."

On the sidewalk, Jeff pretends to be in deep conversation with Misha as I walk to my car.

I call bull crap.

I'm aware he paid total attention to Gabe and me. I keep a slight smile on my lips as I move between cars. Slipping into my front seat, I realize Gabe's idea might actually help me con Jeff in to thinking I am making progress. The notion has me smiling for real as I slip into the car.

Though I've never been to Allie's shop, I know it's on the far side of our small downtown. While I drive, I'm preoccupied with the idea of Jeff buying into my progress by completing the bucket list. The entire scenario is almost perfect.

There's just one catch.

Can I handle the emotion of it? Or more accurately can I distance myself from the emotion of it? That is the million-dollar question on my mind as I park behind Gabe's empty truck in front of Allie's shop.

Chapter 8
Gabe

Though April looks out of place, she appears calm and cool in her preppy, white sweater and pressed pants as she enters the shop. I'm always expecting her to pull out a tennis racket from somewhere with the clothes she wears. It's kind of shocking that she even dated Romeo. Though somewhat tame compared to the rest of us, he is the extreme wild side for her. I'd expect her to date some rich, prick named Edmond or some shit. The two of them sucking on silver spoons and flipping back their hair.

Allie, who is handing me the key to the upstairs apartment, pauses to glance at the newcomer. "Hey, April," she says in a surprised tone.

Yeah, I'm betting she never imagined she'd see Romeo's preppy ex in the shop.

April smiles and returns the greeting. Forgetting the key and me, Allie asks if she can help April with anything.

I pluck the key from Allie's open palm. "She's here with me." Both women's eyebrows shoot up. "But she might be interested in some of your tiniest masterpieces."

"Is he messing with me?" Allie's look to April is questioning since April is scowling at me.

April tones down her scowl. "I'm just looking, maybe interested. And I'm not anything with Gabe."

That has me laughing. April scrunches her nose and Allie appears confused. But within seconds, Allie does show her the smaller designs on the wall above a glass case, then several photographed custom designs in binders.

I stand to the side, watching mostly April. She seems intent on paying attention, which has me hoping that she'll agree to my help. Selfishly, my offer is not so much about helping her but myself. The idea of it empowers me, makes feel in control, makes the distress of opening up around her less invasive. As soon as the idea hit me the day after the party, I couldn't let it go. Witnessing the shaking of her hands and the soft timbre of her voice while reading the list, I felt like such a prick for wanting her gone. But I am a prick and I still wanted her gone. But me helping her, her needing me, helps me somehow feel equal to her.

And if that's going to help me deal, then I'm going to push.

Carefully.

Allie closes the binder and asks April if she has anything custom in mind.

She shakes her head, pointing to the jewelry in the case below the binders. "Are these for belly buttons?"

Fuck. I should be excited that April's asking such a question—and I am—since it points to the fact that she might agree to my proposition, but what has most of my attention is the image of prim and proper April with a belly button piercing. That would be beyond hot.

Allie points to the far end of the case before moving around it to remove jewelry. She shows April several pieces while I lean on the other end of the counter and watch them. Auburn haired Allie is sexy with her eyebrow and lip piercings paired with a sleeve tattoo that covers most of her arm. Very dramatic compared to April with her long, light brown hair, aqua colored eyes, naturally flushed pinked cheeks, and matching pink lips. April is pretty in a wholesome, angelic way. Someone like me, should find Allie more attractive. Even though it pisses me off to no end, it's April who continually catches my attention. I try to tell myself it's because Allie is taken—and quite caught by Justin—but I'm lying to myself. It seems April grows more gorgeous each time I see her.

"You like that one?" Allie asks as April holds up a silver dangling music note.

The image of it hanging over her belly button has my throat dry.

April frowns at the jewelry. "Yeah…I'm not sure."

Oh, I'm sure, it would be totally fucking hot.

"Well, Todd, our piercer, should be done any minute," Allie says, cocking her head and watching the dangling note too. "If you do decide you want the piercing, he has the next hour or so open."

April gnaws on her lip.

"You could do it another day too," Allie says, obviously aware April is going through some sort of internal dilemma, which I'm thinking is more about the list than the piercing. "Why don't you take a look at the apartment upstairs with Gabe and give yourself some time to think about it?"

"Yeah, okay," she says with a forced smile, her eyes glued to the silver note as Allie puts it back in the case.

Allie glances to me. "The stairs to the apartment are around the corner of the building. Shay will be fully moved out in a few weeks."

April continues to be transfixed by the jewelry, so I brush her shoulder with my arm as I stride past her. "Come on. Let's see if this apartment is classy enough for me."

She absently follows me outside, around the building, and up the stairs. She follows me inside too but waits by the door as I take a walk around the one room apartment. It's small with a kitchen on one end, a couch in the middle to divide the room and space for a bed on the other end. Yet remodeled a few years ago, everything is new—not that I care—from the tile in the kitchen to the carpet on the other half of the room to the small appliances in the kitchen. Plus Shay—Allie's employee—is leaving the couch along with a small dining table and chairs, since Allie's friends gave her the stuff. So I won't need to buy any furniture. I just plan to take my bed from my dad's house whether he likes it or not.

More importantly, I need to get out of my dad's shithole. Prior to the tour, though I technically lived there, I rarely stayed there. Instead, I had spent most of the time at my current girlfriend's. Like the prick that I am, I made sure to date women who could accommodate me for overnight stays. In the mechanic program at our local community college, I couldn't afford my own place. Plus, I didn't want to leave Sharon alone with my dad too much. And although I did graduate, the garage I work for couldn't hold the full time position I had lined up while I was on tour, but they're offering me two to three days a week. Now with a mechanic certificate, I can live on those three days of work with somewhere cheap to live, unless I want to dip into the money from the tour and indie album sales that I put away, and I don't.

I glimpse into the small, but clean, bathroom off the kitchen. "Compared to my pop's, this place is a castle."

As I expected, that declaration jerks April from the cloud of deliberation she seemed to be stuck inside. She glances around the room with a frown. "You still live with your father?"

I shrug. "He may be a dick, but he has never asked for rent to live in his shithole."

Her frown grows. "No, he just probably used you for a punching bag."

I shrug again. "A slap upside the head keeps me in line sometimes."

Her eyes grow wide and her mouth twists in outrage.

"Relax. I'm messing with you. After this long, I know when to stay away from him."

She stares at me, worry lining her face. Her concern hits a nerve. I hate people feeling sorry for me. I come from a shithole and a shithead. Feeling sorry for me doesn't change shit. It just belittles me and pricks at my pride.

And yeah, I've learned to hold on to my pride like a motherfucker.

I stalk across the room until I'm feet from her. "I'll admit I'm screwed up, emotionally scarred, whatever …but I'm a man now and my old man doesn't mean dick."

Most likely sensing my hit nerve, or maybe understanding my position from all the shit she has learned about me, she nods.

I let out a breath. "So what about you?"

She blinks in confusion at me.

I force a light grin. "Are you going to let this screwed up asshole help you?"

She draws in a deep breath. "You'll report everything to Jeff?"

It takes me a second to put two and two together. She wants to do it for show, not to help her. What does it matter? She'll be indebted to me either way. "Sure, if that's what you want."

She wraps her arms around her waist and sort of rocks on her feet. "I mean we don't have to do all of them, just enough for him to think I'm trying. I mean the Thomas thing, going to L.A. that's a bit farfetched. And the kissing ones…" She lets out a nervous laugh. "You freaked out when I merely touched your lips…"

Fuck. Fuck. FUCK. I hadn't let my head go there, even while contemplating the offer, but now that she has said it, my head is full of visions. Pushing her against the back of the door. Covering her mouth. Tasting her. Again and again as things go further. Much further. Dirtying up her wholesomeness. And she'd like it. They all like it. At least for a little while.

Staying calm on the outside, I let out a low laugh. "I'm not glass. A few pecks won't shatter me."

She winces. "Still, we can do only the ones that you're comfortable with."

"Whatever works," I say nonchalantly, moving toward the door and out of this space that is suddenly filled with images of touching her. "So you taking the plunge downstairs?" I ask and gesture for her to exit.

She winces again as she steps outside. "Suppose, it's something to report, right? And I probably won't have the courage to come back."

I follow her down the stairs, trying to ignore the curve of her ass and failing miserably. If she knew my deviant thoughts, I'm sure even the bonus of me reporting to Jeff would cancel our agreement.

In the shop, it takes seconds for a smiling Allie to whisk a nervous April and a bellybutton barbell with a dangling music note to a back room. Once Allie comes back to the counter, we discuss the apartment. She gives me paperwork to fill out, but in my mind, I'm visualizing Todd lifting April's shirt, checking out her smooth skin, and touching her. The rage that always simmers under my skin feels like it's about to boil over.

I struggle internally to talk myself down. Todd did the barbells in my ears. He's a good guy. This reaction is about a chick I don't even like. The rage continues to simmer at the thought of him touching her until I grab the paper work, tell Allie I have to get to work, and get the hell out of there.

Before I lose it and let my fists loose.

Chapter 9
April

I nearly trip over the long box in front of my door, coming home from work on Thursday. A quick glance at the return address confirms my suspicion that it's from my mother. The woman needs to go to shoppers anonymous, if such a thing exists. Her 'sale' purchases each week could probably feed a family of four. My stepfather could have already retired as a real estate broker if it wasn't for my mother's spending habits, but then he doesn't do much to control her. And really, I suppose it's none of my business.

After unlocking the door, I shove the box inside with my foot.

Though I've lived in the one bedroom apartment for over three years, it is sparsely furnished with a loveseat, a coffee table, and a small dining table. And the walls are completely bare. I've always taken at least eighteen credits and always stayed tremendously busy with tons of homework. With only three classes left to take this final semester, I have a meager ten credits right now. The new extra down time I have isn't welcome. It leaves me with too much time to think.

I set my bag on the desk and commence opening the package. It contains two polo shirts—I have a collection of polo tops in every brand and color that would rival a tennis champion—a pair of gray dress slacks, a black sleeveless blouse with silver beads around the neck, a silver purse, and low-heeled silver sling backed shoes.

The sight of the matching outfit with purse and shoes has me rolling my eyes. Between the endless polo tops and the 'grownup' outfits she sends, I'm aware that my mother dresses me like a country club debutant. When I was a teenager, we'd argue nonstop because I refused to wear her selections or get my nails or hair done. As an adult who doesn't care what she wears, and an aspiring counselor, I understand that my mother's vision works. I just don't need fifty million polo shirts or outfits. Nor can all the crap she sends me fit in my closets. And that's with donating clothing on a regular basis.

I snatch my phone from my backpack on the table, hit my mother's number, and start pushing the box toward the bedroom.

My mother answers with, "Aren't those shoes adorable? I found them first and matched everything else to those shoes." Her tone is gushing.

"Yeah, their great, Mom." I fish for empty hangers in the closet. "But I thought we agreed that I have enough clothes." Other than the car, my mother and stepfather's only donation to my college career is clothes. My real father pays for my rent and tuition along with depositing money in my account every month. Though my parents were never married, my father is the furthest thing from a deadbeat dad. And I'm very, very appreciative of him.

"I just sent one outfit and a few shirts."

This is true. The box did contain a lot less than usual. I start hanging up the new clothes.

She lets out a wistful sigh. "I didn't get to look at gowns for homecoming this year."

I wince. I haven't had the heart to tell her that I've never gone to homecoming in college. Freshman year I even put on the dress—some ridiculous pink thing—she sent, did my hair, and sent her selfies of myself, before donating the dress. She'd been so excited about her purchase I didn't have the heart to tell her that I wasn't going.

My mother is a true Southern Belle. Born and raised in Kentucky, she came in second for Miss Kentucky when she was nineteen. And though we lived in Ohio while I grew up, she had me, from age six to eleven, in every pageant possible until I refused to do any more. She's still a stunning beauty, and while people say I'm her spitting image, I'm a pale comparison.

I've been told enough about how pretty I am that I believe it, yet I could truly care less about my looks. I don't want to be like my mother. She has a good heart, but a nearly empty head. Clothes, makeup, hair, and house decoration are what dominate her brain cells. I'm not sure if she was always this way or if centering her entire self-esteem and self-worth on her appearance produced her airhead. Though she has always tried, I'll never be like her.

Attempting to be a bit honest, I say, "Good. I won't need a dress. I'm not going this year."

"Why ever not?" she says in a stupefied tone.

My mother never went to college, but she imagines it as an extension of high school. Perhaps for some people it is, however I'm here to get an education, start a career, and above all, eventually help others.

"Too busy with my last semester," I say, lying through my teeth and dropping a few things in a waiting donation bag outside the closet. The bag stays there, since my wardrobe is replenished almost constantly.

"April," my mother whines. "A four point isn't worth giving up a social life."

I stroll toward the kitchen. "I have lots of friends, Mom. I went to a dinner party this weekend." Of course, I don't tell her about the piercing that is now making my belly button itch like crazy. She'd pass out from mortification, if I told her about that.

"Did you have a date?" she asks her voice full of excitement.

Grrr. She never lets the dating thing go. I'm aware she hopes I leave college with a degree and an engagement ring on my finger. She has been planning my wedding since the day I was born. "No, but I met someone nice, so maybe," I say, lying for a second time as I open the fridge. It's as empty as it was this morning.

"Did he ask you out?"

I shut the fridge, ignoring my hunger pains. "Um, no, but he got my number." It's not that I want to lie. I just spent most of my teenage years in conflict with my mother, and now in guilt over my younger stubborn self, I over appease her.

Someone knocks on my door. Probably the girls in two apartments over. They have a habit of starting to bake something without all the ingredients. They're forever borrowing eggs, sugar, or flour. Or at least trying to borrow them. I usually only have half the stuff they ask for.

"Has he called yet?"

"Mom, my neighbor's at the door. I need to go. Thanks for the clothes, but I really, really don't need anymore."

"You can always use them for work eventually, you know."

"Mom," I whine as I open the door.

"I'll try…"

I don't hear whatever she says next because I'm shocked at the person standing outside.

"Got to go. Bye," I say, trying not to stare bugged-eyed at a grinning Gabe, his white teeth a triangular slash in his face. He's dressed in all blue, a mechanic's outfit I realize. "Um…" I peek past him around the corner, looking for Riley or Romeo or someone. "What are you doing here?"

"An unexpected opportunity," he says in a carefree tone.

Confused and feeling lost, I repeat his last word. "Opportunity?"

He leans his long body on the doorframe, crossing his arms. "A friend, well, more like an acquaintance, loaned me his bike for a few hours."

"Bike?" I repeat, sounding like an idiot parrot.

He pushes off the doorframe, stretches out curled hands, and twists his fists, saying, "You know, vroom, vroom as in motorcycle."

My brows lower and my fingers clamp around the edge of the door. "What? A motorcycle?" Rachel's list lingers in my brain until I put two and two together. "I'm not…I couldn't…I don't have a helmet. Plus I need to go grocery shopping. So um…"

He grins fully. "I brought an extra helmet, but are you that scared?"

"A bit, maybe a lot," I add out of the side of my mouth, always so damn honest with him. I force myself to let go of the door. "I really do need to go shopping."

"Well, then let's go. The bike is a real bike as in a Harley. There are two side compartments for your"—he slowly looks me over from head to foot—"two bags of groceries."

"Three," I say, through clenched teeth. "I usually have three bags of groceries."

"Three will fit fine." As I stand there silent, trying to think of another plausible excuse, he says, "Think of how impressed Jeff will be when I tell him you accomplished not one but two items off the bucket list."

Well that does it. Progress, even fake progress, is a motivator. "All right, I'll be down in five. Give me a few minutes to change."

He smirks and I shut the door in his face. Inside my bedroom, I find the thickest pair of jeans I own, a heavy sweatshirt, and low winter boots. For a warm September day, I look like an idiot, but the fear of my body skidding across the cement is worth the extra perspiration and out of season look.

In the parking lot, I'm a bit shocked at the sight of the bike. He said it was a Harley but the spectacle of all the chrome wows me a little. "An acquaintance borrowed you this?" I ask Gabe, who waits on the side of the bike with the extra helmet in hand.

Gabe shrugs. "Dude who works at the shop."

"The shop?" Apparently, I have to parrot him since he never speaks in complete thoughts.

"The garage I work at part time," he says, lifting the helmet over my head.

Okay, yeah, given his outfit I should have put that together I realize as he clips the strap on the side of my chin. I'm beyond nervous.

He puts his helmet on and gets on the bike. I'm having a hard time making myself move. The questioning and pointed look over his shoulder gets my feet going. With a deep breath, I'm on the bike behind him and wrapped around him. "How many times have you driven one of these things?" I squeak out.

"Maybe ten?

"Maybe?" I practically screech as he reeves the engine.

And then we're off. Way. Too. Fast. I hold on to his abs like they're safety handles and bury my face in his back for most of the ride. When he slows or stops for a light, I do peek at my surroundings. Those little glimpses are few and far between. Finally, he pulls into the lot of a grocery store. Not my usual store, but at this point I just want off the bike.

Once I peel myself from him and stand on safe ground, he nods to a hardware store at the end of the small shopping center. "I need a few things. I'll catch up with you in a few."

My hand trembles as I unclip the helmet, then hold it up to him in question.

"Just take it with you," he says, un-straddling the bike.

"Okay," I say weakly, turning toward the store on legs that feel like rubber. Inside, I grab a cart, set the helmet in the seat, and begin to find my usual purchases in an unknown store. Between the unfamiliar store and brain fog, it takes me forever to shop. Irritated with myself, I open a box of granola bars and precede to eat one, hoping missed nutrition is the issue with my head.

I'm in the last section—dairy—when Gabe finds me.

He glances at my half-filled cart. "You're not the quickest shopper, huh?"

"Do you need to be somewhere?" I ask, ignoring the remark and grab a carton of eggs.

"No, I just assumed you'd be in line by now." He grasps the back of the cart and leans on it as I set the carton by the helmet.

"Never shopped here before," I say in an apologetic tone.

He nods, inspecting the items—whole grain bread, dry pasta, granola bars, veggies, and fruit—in my cart. "Don't think a diet is necessary for you."

"I'm not on a diet," I snap, dropping in a brick of cheese.

He shuffles through the cart. "Not one ounce of junk food in here."

I snatch a bag of fresh carrots from his hand. "I like to eat healthy for…other reasons than what I look like," I say defensively.

His brows go up.

"Poor eating habits and depression have been linked," I stammer, then yank the cart from him and go to the yogurt section.

He follows and leans sideways at the end of the yogurt cooler. "So are you worried about becoming depressed or are you depressed?"

Am I depressed? Fruit flavors, blueberry, lemon, cherry, and strawberry swirl—a colorful kaleidoscope—in my vision. I never confront the depression question, even to myself, just skirt around it. Most people go through bouts of depression. It is normal to a certain degree. And no matter what, I have to keep going, so there is no point fixating on the question. "That's none of your business," I say, grabbing whatever yogurt flavors are in front of me, then spin away from him.

Luckily for me—or maybe for him since he hit a nerve—he quietly follows me to the cashier. Surprisingly, he carries the three bags out for me.

Outside, he shoves—hello, eggs!—the bags into the leather pouches on each side of the back wheel while I nervously clip on the helmet. Gabe mumbles a "Ready?" Then without waiting for an answer, he gets on the bike, facing away from me. After a deep breath, I force myself behind him and once again clamp onto him.

This time, I try to take in the moving scenery, try to see why Rachel would have wanted to do this, and try to find some enjoyment from it, but being on the back of the motorcycle makes me queasy and anxious. And way, way too aware of Gabe, specifically his six-pack, even I can admit the man has some serious wash boarding going on.

Finally, we stop below my apartment. Gabe offers to take the groceries up for me, but I grab the bags from his hand. "That's okay. I'm pretty sure I can handle three bags. Um…thanks for the ride, for doing this for me, and telling Jeff," I add, reminding him about our deal.

He settles back on the bike, looking me up and down. "How's your piercing doing?"

Between his gaze and the reference to my itchy bellybutton, I'm suddenly excessively self-conscious. "All right." I take a step back toward the stairs and the honestly he usually produces in me has me admitting, "A bit sore, other than that, its fine."

He hits the kickstand down. "Not going to show it to me?"

"Ah…that would be a definite negative," I say, trying not to imagine raising my shirt and him bending to check out my midriff. I turn around and go up a few stairs. Over my shoulder, I say, "Thanks again, see you Tuesday." Then I practically run up the stairs because I'm losing the battle with my imagination and all sorts of odd things are happening in my brain, like Gabe's hands on the bare skin of my midriff.

The entire image is unsettling and bizarrely exciting.

Chapter 10
April

I don't rush out of group in my usual frenzy because for once group had gone well. Misha and her lap dog Chad were rude as predictable, but Jeff beamed at me when Gabe shared the two items we did to 'complete' the bucket list. I could practically see the report of progress he'd give Dr. Medina written all over his face. The expectation kept me giddy through group.

In fact, I'm so slow leaving the building I miss offering Jason a ride. He's already going around the corner of the building as I exit. I'm two steps into the parking lot as Gabe catches up with me. Strangely, being around him has become somewhat normal. Or maybe it's that I feel normal around him. The shield of flawlessness I usually wear is refreshingly absent when we're together.

"Got a favor to ask," he says as he matches my shorter stride. "My truck's in the middle of getting fixed. Think I could get a ride?"

"Um…sure," I say, a little startled at the request. "How did you get here?"

"Sharon, my father's girlfriend, drove me."

I frown, thinking of someone going half an hour out of their way. "You should've got my number from Romeo or Riley and rode with me."

"Thought about it. I didn't know what to say." He splits away from me, going around the back of my car to the passenger's side. "Wasn't sure you wanted them to know you're in group therapy."

I'm annoyed and startled that he can read me that well, but as usual, I'm all honesty with him. "I'd rather they didn't know I'm in therapy, so thanks."

He nods at me from across the car's roof before we both get into the car.

As we buckle our seatbelts Gabe says, "Don't want to ruin that Little Miss Perfect image?"

I push the keys in the ignition and turn toward him, my expression flat. "Nope, I don't."

His brows rise the slightest bit.

I shrug and shift into drive. "It's not that I really want them to think I'm perfect or that I've ever been perfect...it's just that this perfection image thing keeps me"—I pause, searching for acceptable ambiguous words—"keeps me going sometimes."

I sense Gabe staring at me while I drive. The highway keeps my attention, but my fingers tighten on the steering wheel. I finally ask, "What?"

The seat creaks as if he's sitting back. "Sorry, you're telling me you weren't always Miss Perfect?"

A boisterous laugh escapes me. "Hardly. I used to be normally imperfect."

I sense his continued stare.

"I'm having a hard time believing that."

"Don't really care."

This time he laughs.

The car is silent until he switches on the radio. A popular pop song by some teenybopper pervades the space with its bubblegum beat.

"Seriously?" Gabe asks with an incredulous tone. "You listen to this shit?"

"It's just background noise."

He's soon pressing buttons, searching for a rock station. In less than a minute, loud guitar riffs and hard drumbeats fill the interior of the car. The song must be newer. I don't recognize it.

At the commercial break, Gabe turns down the radio. "Hey, pullover."

Seeing nothing but fast food places and a gas station, I ask, "Why? Where?"

"Burger joint."

"Seriously? You eat that stuff?" I whine, copying his opinion of the radio station.

"I'll pretty much eat anything. Cupboards were rarely full as a kid."

Well, that has me turning into the restaurant. "Can I just go through the drive-thru?"

"Of course not, pull into a parking space," he says in an authoritative tone.

My brow rises. Instead of arguing, I do as he instructed. The argument isn't worth the time.

He reaches for the door handle, then glances at me expectantly. "Well, come on."

"I'm not hungry. I'll just wait in the car."

"This isn't about hunger."

My look at him is quizzical.

He grins wickedly. "It's about completing the list."

Ugh. I should have guessed his intentions. "How can you remember every single thing on that list? It's like you have a photogenic memory or something."

He taps an ear. "It's because I heard it as you read it. I would have remembered only half if I read it. Now come on."

I keep my internal grumbling, recall Jeff's beam, and get out of the car to follow Gabe around the back of the building and the drive thru speaker.

"This is not going to work," I whisper.

"Never know until you try," he whispers back, then clears his throat. "Hello?" he says loudly.

After several long seconds, the intercom comes on. "Um… can I help you?"

The male voice sounds young and confused.

"Sure can," Gabe says. "We'll take two fries, two cheeseburgers, a coffee, and a"—he gestures to me.

When I stand there, he nudges me with his elbow.

"And an ice water," I blurt out.

The confused voice on the intercom repeats the order while Gabe smirks.

As we walk to the window, I dig in my purse.

"Oh, no," Gabe says. "This one is on me."

I keep digging. "I'll pay for my therapy, thank you."

"Put it away, April," Gabe says in a harsh tone.

A glance at his harsher expression has me closing the purse. "Fine."

The teenager at the window eyeballs us over, his face flushing with each second. "You're not supposed to walk through the drive thru."

Gabe puts his elbow on the window ledge. "It's a bet dude. She"—he tilts his head my way—"didn't think I'd go through with it. So I had to, right?" He holds out a twenty-dollar bill. "I mean look at her."

The boy glances at me, blushes and nods before taking the money. "You're lucky the manager's on break," he grumbles.

"Oh, yeah," Gabe says. "I'm one lucky son of a bitch. Been lucky my whole life."

His sarcasm and the 'look at her' comment, mixed with the fact that I'm standing at a drive thru window has me shuffling forward. I move onto the sidewalk past the window as a car comes around the corner.

Gabe waves at the car.

Finally, after what feels like the longest three minutes of my life, the boy hands over the drinks and a bag. I move to round the restaurant toward my car, but Gabe decides we need to eat at a picnic table on a little patio in front of the place.

I plop on the bench across from him. "We could have just ordered drinks. The point was to walk through the drive thru."

He pushes a burger and fries across the table toward me. "True, but I missed lunch."

I consider his grease stained T-shirt, then recall the also grease stained pants now under the table that Misha sneered at during therapy. "Fixing your truck?"

He unwraps a burger. "Yeah, then there was the ride thing that took some time." He takes a huge bite of burger.

"Your father's girlfriend who gave you a ride," I say, pushing my cheeseburger toward him. "Is she the same one…from when you were fifteen?" I pluck out a fry, attempting to make it appear like the question is small talk. I'm not sure if I want him to think I'm not that interested or convince myself that I'm not that interested.

He nods.

"So she's like a mom to you?"

He swallows, his Adam's apple a bob. "Suppose so, don't know what it's like to have the real thing."

"Oh crap, I'm so sorry. Your mother passed?"

"Not that I know of. My mother left when I was six."

The fry in my hand drops to the table. "You haven't seen your mother since you were six?"

"Maybe six and half."

My mouth hangs open until I say, "And she left you with your father?"

He pauses unwrapping the second burger. "You know, once people hear that my father was abusive"—I continue to question the was—"that's all they can see, but he never left me."

My mouth becomes a flytrap again. "You're defending him?"

81

Gabe sighs. "I know I make it sound like it in therapy because that's what people want to hear, but it's not like the man is just a fist. It's not like I wasn't a little shit. It's not like he hit me out of the blue." He lifts the burger, then sets it down. "Well, most of the time."

"Really?" The word rolls out of me in a dry incredulous tone, thinking no one, but especially a child, deserves to be hit.

"Really," Gabe says in a confident voice, but his hands grip the edge of the table. "Though an asshole, my dad has had a rough life too. His mother was an alcoholic, and he has become one too—which is why I'm not in to drinking much. He never graduated from high school, never even got a GED because he started working at sixteen to support her. A shit job six days a week that he is still stuck in. I think he met my mom at the diner he's a line cook at. He doesn't talk about her much because yeah, she walked out on him and never looked back. And I could be a lazy, non-listening shit. Tried to get out of chores. Stayed out way past the streetlights coming on, even as early as the age of nine. Did stupid shit like light firecrackers in the basement…"

"Gabe," I say softly, patiently. "No matter what you did, your father didn't have a reason, or an excuse, to abuse you."

"I know that." He lets go of the table only to tap on the wood with his index fingers. "Trust me, my psychologist has brainwashed that into me. But I don't want to remember only the bad. I don't want my past to simply be belts and knuckles and the bottom of a boot."

My eyes grow large as he continues, "There were other things." Tap. Tap. Tap. Like a slow drum roll on the table. "A bicycle next to the Christmas tree when I was ten. A bicycle he couldn't afford. Fishing from the river docks during the summer. Teaching me things like how to change the oil in a car. I'm not going to brush all the good away. I'm not going to ignore the shit life he has lived. I can't"—his voice becomes hoarse as he stops tapping and glances down—"I don't want the sum of me condensed to a mother who abandoned me and a father who beat me."

At first, I assume this is about people pitying him. As I slowly take in his intense expression and clenched jaw, I realize he wants, maybe needs, to have a parental bond. Turning his father into solely a villain negates that connection. And perhaps having—even if imagining—the bond allows him to deal with his past.

"Yet you want to move out," I add, truly trying to understand the connection to his father.

"Most of the time I can't stand the mean, old bastard, and he can't stand me, but more than that, I have to get out the cycle. When I'm there, I'm too close to my fifteen-year-old self. But for the six weeks during the tour, the first time I was gone for more than a few nights here and there, I felt like a different person. Calmer and freer somehow. Perhaps from the never ending worry of what's going to happen next. So I'm hoping moving out will bring that sense of calmness and freedom back."

Surprised at his awareness of the cycle he's caught in, I stare at him in contemplation until I blurt my next thought out. "Will you go back to visit him?"

He shakes his head. "I don't know…" He looks at the parking lot. "Damn, why am I telling you this shit? Some of it I don't even tell my shrink. It's like you ask, and my mouth spouts shit. Are you Jedi shrinking me for practice?"

A loud laugh bursts from me.

He cocks an eyebrow.

I reign in my iconic chuckle. "I'm not shrinking you. But it's kind of the same for me."

His eyebrow remains up.

I straighten my collar, feeling a bit anxious being so honest. "I can't keep up my pleasantly polite, even keeled front around you. I'm either angry and blurt stuff out or curious and blurt stuff out or strangely honest and blurt out the truth." Sighing at my own lack of control, I reach for another fry.

"Pleasantly polite?"

"Nice ring to it, eh?" I pop the fry in my mouth.

He lets out a grunt. "More like boringly stuck up."

I throw the next fry at him. He flicks it away before it beams him in the eye. "That's not true."

"Maybe not," he concedes, prying the lid from his coffee. "But I recall hearing that you bitched out Riley once. So you're not always Ms. Pleasantly Polite."

"That was pre-meditated. She was hurting Romeo with her indecisiveness."

"And you needed to be the one to set her straight?"

My look at him is sharp. "I didn't like seeing him hurting."

His gaze over a gulp of coffee is wry.

"I wanted her to get back with him. Romeo and I are just friends. Very good friends."

"You dated."

"So what?"

"People are going to assume."

"Don't care. I don't have many friends like him, so people can think whatever they want."

"You know, you're like a walking dichotomy."

My brows rise.

"You want people to think you're perfect, yet you don't care what they think."

Suppose it seems that way. I take a sip of water, collecting my thoughts. "I don't care. I keep up the perfect image for me."

"Why?"

"So... so I keep going."

His fingers drum a slow steady beat on the rough wood of the bench as he leans back, studying me. He opens his mouth to say something, but then slightly shakes his head and sits up. "I've spilled my guts. Tell me about your parents."

I don't like talking about myself. Maybe because I tend to hide too much, but after him sharing so much, it seems more than discourteous to brush the question away. Instead, I push the fries away.

"They're not very exciting. My mom lives in northern Ohio with my stepdad. My dad lives in California." I was born in Malibu, but when I was two, my mother took a job in Ohio, hoping my father would beg her to stay and propose. "My parents never married—"

"You're a bastard," he says in a shocked, high-pitched tone and clutches his chest.

"Takes one to know one," I say in a sassy tone.

"You're right," he says with an uncharacteristic wink. "Guess it's something we have in common."

"Are we supposed to be ashamed or something? What is this? The fifties?"

"No." He laughs. "But I'd guess people who grow up with dysfunction, though I suppose some kids with unmarried parents are fine, recognize it better than others."

I slowly nod, realizing that not only is he probably right, but he is also very intuitive. Though the dysfunction of my father living on the west coast and dealing with my moody stepfather are not even comparable to what he has dealt with.

He picks his coffee back up. "What doesn't kill you makes you stronger, right?"

"Okay, Nietzsche."

"Who?"

"Um, the German philosopher you just sort of quoted."

He shakes his head. "Must have heard it somewhere and it stuck. I'm not in to that college shit. Life has given me enough lessons. I'm a drummer then a mechanic. Probably wouldn't have even got that skill, but since I'm good at figuring things out, a high school teacher pushed me"—he shrugs—"made me apply for a scholarship and go to tech school."

His tone is very nonchalant, but I read through the lines and find a mix of pride and humiliation. Obviously, between the skill set of music and mechanics, Gabe is quite intelligent, but I'm guessing that someone has repeatedly told him that he isn't. I don't even want to imagine the plethora of names his father has called him over the years. My heart aches for him as a boy, but as he lifts his chin and almost dares me to comment, I realize this man does not want my pity. And in a way, I know how he feels. Though my not wanting pity isn't about pride; it's about me not deserving it.

I crumple my fry bag, trying to appear indifferent. "Lots of people are successful without college. It just depends on what you want to do, I guess. I want to help people, be a counselor, so to college I went."

He watches me as if judging my words, while the tilt of his chin remains prideful.

And suddenly, outside a fast food restaurant, under his perusal, I finally notice—on a conscious level—Gabe from a female perspective. His fierce pride, especially after his history, is the spark that leads me to become aware of him physically.

Practically every single—some not single—female at our college has gushed about one of the band members, Gabe included. I'm not a blind idiot—though sometimes I am just a plain old idiot. Like a connoisseur of art, I understand the female admiration. Each band member is attractive in their own way. Romeo with his dark good looks. While blond Justin looks like a tatted up model. Then there's Sam with his blue eyes and curly dark hair. But pretty male faces do not make my heart, or other body parts, flutter. My mother's beautiful. The sculptures in the university's art gallery are beautiful. A 57' Gibson-B acoustic guitar is beautiful. Beauty has never made me all google eyed and wistful.

Until now.

Harsh masculine beauty hits me hard. Winged brows over russet coffee colored eyes. A flared but defined nose. Full sexy lips. Cheek bones that slash across each side of his face. Sun streaked, brown hair extending past a hard jaw line lined with his nearly ever-present, sexy scruff. He is a tsunami of male brilliance that rolls over me in wave after wave. I'm a sunbaked, parched island shocked at the sudden drench.

Butterflies flutter in my stomach—I never understood the reference until now—while words build in my conscious, trying to form lyrics to his beauty. Longing pounds in my chest—thump, want, thump—and desire curls my fingers around the edge of the bench. I feel dizzy, like I'm about to fall backwards off the bench and into another world. My grasp strengthens until my fingernails cut into the wood. I don't want to fall.

His gaze turns speculative as I attempt to control the blast of longing hitting me. "Your cousin's death really messed you up, huh?"

The question breaks the spell that my sudden awareness of him spun.

I instantly let go of the bench. "Yeah, it did," I agree, as grief and guilt twist and tear throughout me, their thorny vines cutting and slicing. As usual, I run from the old wound that never ceases to feel freshly open if faced. "I need to get going." I jump up and quickly smash all our trash in the burger bag. "I have homework to do." Both statements are honest. At least separately.

"Sorry," he says, standing, running a hand through his hair, and wearing a contrite expression. "I'm guessing you don't like to talk about it."

I pause in the middle of pushing the bag in the trash. A sad laugh escapes me. "That would be an understatement." I step away from the trash bin, reaching for my purse on the table. "Really, I have to get going." I don't wait for a response, just march to my car.

Once Gabe gives me directions to his house, the ride is quiet with the blare of rock music. Luckily for me, Gabe seems to sense my mood. Though I suppose it isn't too hard to perceive how I just shut down—the only way I can deal with the past. Once I faced my wrong, accepted it, and decided to make amends, I had to move on or the guilt would have destroyed me, and most times I fear it still could.

I pull in front of Gabe's house, my mind in tumult.

He breaks the silence by saying, "Piece of shit, huh?"

Confused, I look at him then the house. Small with a sagging porch, peeling white paint, and cracked windows, the house is old. The weeds and overgrown bushes in the yard don't help improve the broken down appearance of the house. Obviously, it screams poverty, and apparently this is some kind of test. *How horrified will she be?* I'm not in the mood for his test.

I shake my head a bit. "It's just a house. It's not like it's a sneak peek into your talent or soul or something."

He stares at me for a long moment, as if trying to gage the authenticity of my words. "Well, I'm almost out of this shithole," he says, tugging the door handle. "Thanks for the ride."

Caught in the perfection of his face for a quick second, I quickly snap forward. "No problem. Thanks for…lunch, and for sharing with Jeff."

And with that, he is out of the car. I shift into drive and let out the breath I'd been holding in. Between my weird reaction to him and his bringing up Rachel, I feel like I've been through the wringer.

Too bad I don't have a ton of homework instead of just a six page paper to write.

I love homework.

It keeps me busy.

And sane.

And until now, oblivious to the word lust.

Chapter 11
April

Fridays. No work. No classes. No group therapy. Nothing to eat the time away. I've cleaned my living room and kitchen top to bottom, and they both needed it. Finished my reading for the next week and completed the rough draft of my final paper for Clinical Psychology which isn't even due until December. Re-read some parts of my old psychology textbooks. Enjoyed two hours of crap TV. It appears the only thing to do is go to bed. At nine-forty at night.

My ten measly credits are killing me.

With boredom.

After brushing my teeth and washing my face, I fill and set the coffee maker. On my way to the bedroom, a knock at the door almost has me tripping and running into the wall. Who would come to my house on a Friday night?

I groan, realizing who is most likely on the other side of the door.

Besides my weird, sudden attraction to his looks—which was the pinnacle of superficial since he annoys me most of the time—I'm aware he makes me feel too much, remember too much, and be like the old me far too much.

He pounds harder.

I don't want to be the old me. I need to be the now me.

His pounding becomes too loud to ignore.

I march across the room and whip the door open.

Yep. There stands Gabe in all his grunge looking glory. If it were the nineties, Gavin Rossendale of Bush would have lost a few—a ton—of female fans.

I wish I was physic, but no, I'm being tormented. By a hot looking jackass in loose jeans, long hair, a hoodie, and strangely a jean jacket. Who wears those anymore?

Before I can chastise him and his loud banging, he asks, "Pajamas? At ten at night? On a Friday?"

I cross my arms over my tank top and braless chest. "I'm tired."

"From what?"

"From none of your business." I don't want to admit the tortuous boredom that plagued me all day. That admittance may have me pitying myself.

His brows rise.

"Why are you here?"

"It's raining."

"What?" At first, as usual, I don't put two and two together, but of course, the list. "It rains a lot."

"Yeah, but it's going to get cold soon."

"It's late September. We have at least three more possible weeks of mild weather," I retort.

"Don't want to tell Jeff you did another two?"

My jaw clenches. I hate group therapy. "Fine. Let me get a jacket or something."

A grin curls his full lips. "Nothing wrong with what you're wearing. In fact, it's perfect for a little dancing in the rain."

I glare at him. White tank in the rain. Yeah, right.

"Give me a minute." Instead of inviting him in, I shut the door in his face. That's what he gets for making such comments. And for his hot, seductive grin.

Digging inside a dresser drawer, I tell myself to get it together. This is just another check on the list. This is just a way to get Jeff to give a positive report to Dr. Medina. This is just two strangers swaying in the rain for a few minutes.

That is all.

Done with my inner pep talk to keep me from being an idiot, I drag an old flannel—the only one left of the ten or more I used to wear—out of the drawer, tug it on, and slip on a pair of flip-flops. When I yank open the door, he's leaning on the frame, looking out over the parking lot. I almost run into him.

He catches me by the waist. "Slow down. We'll get to the dancing soon enough."

"Ha, ha," I say, moving out of his grasp. "Where were you planning on doing this?"

He tilts his chin, his glance speculative. "I'm thinking the basketball court would be romantic."

Um, no, but that is good. "Very," I agree, and start moving toward the stairs.

"Is that flannel from an ex?" he asks, following me down the stairs.

Ha, my ex list is rather short. "No. It's mine."

"Really?"

"Really."

"Like you bought it?"

"I did."

"To wear?"

"No, to practice doing laundry," I say in the most sarcastic tone possible then add, "Yes to wear."

"Like to bed?"

"Like in an ode to grunge rock."

"You're into grunge rock? Like Nirvana and Pearl Jam shit?"

I step off the last stair and into the dark night full of misty rain. "Yeah, like STP and Alice in Chains and Screaming Trees, but more like I used to be, and it's not crap."

He chuckles, a light muffle trapped in the rain, as he catches up to me on the sidewalk. "Always full of surprises aren't you?"

"Me surprising?" I push back damp strands of hair already sticking to my face. "I'm supposed to be sleeping right now, not getting pneumonia."

As we turn the corner, he leans near my ear. "I've been told I'm worth it."

My side-glance at him is flat. "So you usually give girls an illness?"

This time the rain can't muffle his loud laughter. "Oh, I give them something, but it doesn't make them sick. It leaves them…satisfied," he says in a tone over dripping with sexuality.

I'm aware he's laying it on thick, trying to make me uncomfortable, and I refuse to appear as uncomfortable as his teasing is making me. "Oh, really?" I put a finger on my wet chin. "Usually bragging stems from some sort of inadequacy."

"It isn't bragging when it's pure fact."

"Says who?"

"I could give you some phone numbers if you'd like to conduct some interviews."

"No thanks," I snottily say as we cross over a length of wet grass.

The basketball court is dark with only porch lights illuminating it and out in the open where a breeze mixes with the mist. At the center, I turn to him. "All right let's get this over with."

His brows rise. "Why am I getting the impression you're not excited about this?"

"Oh, I dunno? Maybe because I'm already sopping wet."

He chuckles s at that.

It takes me a few seconds to realize he's being perverted. I wipe the water from my forehead. "Oh, shut up and start dancing."

He hunches over, messing around with something tucked in his inside left pocket. When he stands and holds out a hand, music, a soft acoustic guitar strum, mixes with the pitter pat of rain on the cement. Suddenly, a guitar slide, then sharp notes ring out in the dark. It takes me a few seconds to recognize the tune.

A laugh escapes me. I've heard the song many times. My father loves the Rolling Stones. I used to be more of a Beatles girl. And we have argued for hours about which band is better more than once.

Hand still out, Gabe patiently waits.

"Come on. Wild Horses?" I put my hand in his warm one. At least it's the acoustic version.

He yanks me closer until my hips bump his thighs.

The contact has my breath catching as Mick Jagger's voice joins the rain.

A soft, closed mouthed smile forms on his lovely lips. "Rock's not known for slow dancing."

Stop thinking about his lips. "Can't listen or dance to anything but rock, huh?"

"It's only rock and roll but I like it," he says with a grin.

I shake my head at him using a Stones song title, yet before I can retort, he starts swaying.

We shuffle and move together in some strange circular pattern, reminding me of middle school dances. My hands on his shoulders. His on my waist. Our feet scraping on the cement. Yet unlike middle schoolers, we sway and step with a precision that is in perfect rhythm to the song.

The rain, along with the wind, picks up.

I try to remain irritated with the rain, with the chill, with the pervading wetness. I try to stay outside of the moment. I try not to think of why Rachel would find dancing in cold, wet rain romantic. Yet, the coolness of the rain doesn't touch me. Instead, Gabe's body warms me with each sway when my chest or thigh or hip comes in contact with him. Even when inches apart, the space between us is a raging fire. The space around us is a muffled bubble filled with rain and music and the sway of our bodies.

And I get why she would crave this.

It is strangely romantic. The music mixed with the pitter patter of the rain. The feeling that the need to dance against one another overrides the ugly weather. The sense of being alone in the cocoon of the rain. All of these things elevate the experience.

Halfway through the song, I forget about keeping my wits. I just enjoy. His shoulders under my palms. His fingers digging into my waist. His breath on my forehead. The perfect rhythm we make.

And I fall into the unthinkable.

I imagine for this flash in time that this is real. That we want to dance together out in the rain. That he wants me to press closer. That he wants me to lay my head on his shoulder.

And imagination becomes reality as I do each of those things.

And just feel.

Him.

The song nears the end as we sway glued to one another. My head turns. My cheek scrapes the wet fabric of his jean jacket. My nose catches the soapy scent of him, tips closer. Draws in and holds soap and rain and man in.

And even the smell of him warms me.

The music ends but we continue to hold each other. We move. We pretend this is real.

And I'm not me.

I'm a sponge soaking in his warmth, his smell, the sensation of him under my hands. Floating on a rain cloud of sensation, I can't get enough. Yearning for more, desperate for more, I lean forward pressing my lips to the skin where his collarbones meet. I drag my lips across his skin, adding the taste of him to the sensations overwhelming me, adding the tang of cool rain on warm skin.

And he tastes more wonderful than I could have ever imagined.

He stops swaying in an instant.

I suddenly wake up, yank out of his grasp, and stare at him with wide eyes. My hand covers my aggressive mouth but I gasp, "Oh, no," from behind my palm. Even in the rain and shadows, I can see his lips curling in disdain. Somewhere between the rain and body heat and my imagination, I forgot about Gabe's dislike of me.

"I'm sorry," I say from behind my hand. "I don't..." I take a step back. "I don't know what came over me. I..." Those lovely lips curl into an all-out sneer. "I'm sorry," I whisper one last time, backing up before racing to my apartment.

With shaking hands, I unlock the door. Inside, I lean on the nearest wall, drawing in huge gulps of air. I'm embarrassed, shocked, and mad at myself all at once.

What is wrong with me? Why would I do such a thing? Loneliness? Boredom? Desperation?

Like I'm drunk again, I stumble over to the couch.

Okay, okay, okay hitting on Gabe—twice—is not the end of the world.

I just touched his lips and kissed his neck—eek! Yet, it's not like I tackled and dry humped him. At least not yet.

After several more deep breaths, I admit to myself that I am attracted to Gabe—maybe because I can be honest with him, maybe because he's stunningly attractive, maybe...it doesn't matter why, but when it comes to men, I've always been reserved, now and back when I was normal.

I rub my temples. It has to be a mix of loneliness and boredom, driving me to act insane. I need to get over this and move on. Pushing myself off the couch and heading to the shower, I decide I need more of a social life.

Or else I may end up tearing off Gabe's clothes.

Or something worse.

Chapter 12
Gabe

We wait in a small cement room behind an outdoor stage downtown by the river. Across from me, Sam is practicing a new riff, plucking silently on his bass. Justin stands on the far end texting—most likely to Allie, knowing his whipped ass. Romeo and Riley stand on the other far end of the long room. They're practically nose to nose, and she appears as giddy as a groupie meeting her long time rock crush. Her band just finished, and though they weren't perfect, they were better than the night I saw them in the bar. Yet, they have an energy that transfers to the crowd and negates their imperfections. Plus Riley is one hell of a drummer.

The stage is being changed over for the final act—us—of U-Palooza, a concert of local bands put on by the sororities and fraternities of the local university. They give half the proceeds to charity and split the rest. We're donating our portion this year too, since we got a nice check during the summer, touring with two major bands and made—actually are currently making—a nice lump of cash on our indie album. Fans know we went on tour, thus the crowd is bigger than usual. But very few know we've scored a record deal.

Romeo has been keeping that hush. He wants to finish out as much of college as possible prior to becoming a real star.

We're all dressed in our stage clothes. Jeans, dark shirts, boots, and leather accessories. Actually, I'm wearing a fitted black T-shirt and jeans. During the tour, I reluctantly agreed to dress with a little more style than just long shorts and an old white T-shirt, but I refuse to wear the studded bracelets and belts bullshit.

I've been to the U-Palooza before. As a spectator. Two years ago. Luminescent Juliet blew my mind that night. Their talent, especially in our little corner of the world, seemed unreal. I never imagined I'd play with them in a million years. First, my style and music preferences were harder rock than they play. Second, my skill was more at the level of garage band at the time. Almost a year later—after I'd become addicted to drumming—I heard about their all call for a drummer. The thrash metal band I was in wasn't serious, so I tried out, made it to the second round, and didn't get the spot for drummer.

Riley did.

Which is why my pissed off ass didn't go to see them at last year's U-Palooza. Pussy, folk, blues, and rock mixing band could fuck off as far as I was concerned.

Over three months later, they called. My band was obsolete by then, and Riley had quit—personal reasons or some shit. I needed to play. Drumming helps release all the pent up aggression that always boils under my surface and keeps me stable. Or at least as stable as someone like me can be.

After swallowing my pride—when it comes to Luminescent Juliet I've done a shitload of swallowing—and joining the band, I never imagined in a trillion years that we would cut an indie album, sell over ten thousand copies, and land a spot on a national tour with two other known bands.

But the truth is I'm more nervous about playing here, where I know the people, than a sold out arena. Just my luck, I think spinning a drumstick. Shit is always back asswards, upside down, and screwed up in my head.

College students dressed in jeans and black T-shirts, playing at being roadies, come into the little cement room behind the outdoor stage. The pretend roadie leader tells us the stage is ready.

I take a deep breathe, yank my other stick from my pocket, and line up behind Romeo and Sam.

Go. Fucking. Time.

Nerves or not, I deliver.

Every time.

As planned, Romeo leads us out. Justin waits behind. The crowd goes wild as we stride onto the stage. I heard one of the fake roadies telling Romeo earlier that they reached capacity this year, something they've never done. But the crowd is a lot smaller than what I got used to over the summer. Sam gives the cheering and whistling and clapping crowd a wave. Romeo and I are stone faced as we go to our positions. Him, because he is Mr. Fucking Professional. Me, because that's how I deal.

I wait for them to strap on their instruments. I don't look at the crowd, trying to ignore my nervousness about playing in front of people who know me. Or think they know me. Actually, they don't know shit, so fuck them.

Once Sam and Romeo stand and wait, I hit my sticks together four times and we break into "At the End of the Universe." Arms flying, foot thumping, and head matching the beat, I let the music suck out my aggression and nerves as I concentrate on kicking ass and pounding the shit out of my set.

Seconds before the vocals start, Justin runs across the front of the stage. The crowd goes wild as he belts out the first line.

I belt out a drum fill before he rolls into the chorus.

And then, for the next forty minutes or so, it's just me and the drums.

We play songs from the indie album, one following the next.

After being on the road for over six weeks, the songs aren't much of a challenge, but drumming is like the best drug to me. Energizing. Exhilarating. Freeing.

The lights, the crowd, even my band members can't break the vibe. I move around the kit like it's an extension of my body. My mind and body are a drum machine. There is no bass drum or floor tom or crash cymbals. Just me and the kit.

The second to last song is a cover. The Offspring's raw and energetic "Hammerhead" is the perfect mock last song, and it was my pick. Though not thrash metal, this song comes pretty close. I roll through it with an on point intensity.

When we finish, the crowd goes crazy. Romeo, Justin, and Sam bow at the edge of the stage and the crowd goes more nuts. I start walking off. I'm not into all this pseudo shit.

Back in the long, cement room, Sam exclaims, "That went fucking perfect!"

Justin fist bumps him. "We have landed on another level."

"Don't get cocky," Romeo says but grins. "Always room to improve."

I spin a drumstick.

A fake roadie passes out bottled waters.

The crowd's chant for more reverberates in the little room while we wait for the customary five minutes. This time Justin leads us out to the stage. The crowd is like a roar as we step back out.

We end the night with our biggest hit thus far, Justin's pussy whipped song, "Inked My Heart." I actually like playing the song. It has a progression of slow to fast then back down again that was a challenge at first. Speeding up then slowing down is probably more of a challenge to me than most drummers. I like to beat the shit out of my drums when I play. At the end of a set, the song is like a work out cool down. The perfect calm after the storm of kicking ass during the set.

At the real end of the set, I go to the edge of the stage with the rest of the band and bow too. I've always found this weird—like I just performed Shakespeare or some shit—but Romeo always has us do the bow thing if we're the closing act.

Swallow fucking swallow.

After the last bow, I throw my sticks out into the crowd. One to the left and the other to the right. A tall brunette in the closed off sorority section catches the one I threw to the right. She watches me with eager eyes.

Yeah, right.

On the road, I wasn't too particular about who I hooked up with as long as they were hot and willing. A night of sex tends to fill the empty void, for a few hours at least, that is part of me. But the concept of anything long term was obsolete on tour. Here at home, I stay away from her type. Been there. Done that. No uppity bitch ever broke my heart, but several have stomped on my pride. They like the bad boys. For a night or two. Not that I had been expecting anything long term. But I don't like being treated like trash after fucking someone. Even if it is true.

The crowd still chants for more as we head to the back. We're in the cement room, waiting for out gear to be brought back, when the girlfriends and their entourage, including April, rush in. Hugging and kissing commence as if we just came back from a war instead of the stage. Riley's friend Chloe, April, and me are left standing amid the romantic congratulations.

Cheeks faintly pink, April leans on the wall and looks away from me. She appears embarrassed but ready for battle with her shoulders thrown back—which inadvertently pushes her high breasts out.

Damn. I want her. Badly. Though I admitted my attraction to her internally, I kept the actual possibility of being with her as a not-going-to-ever-fucking-happen. Until she dragged her hot mouth across my rain wet skin and turned me on so hard, I wanted to screw her in a puddle on that wet basketball court. The beauty of the situation is that she wants me too. She may not be willing to admit it—might even be horrified by it like she was the other night—but her fingers on my mouth, her lips on my skin, tell the truth. I'm just going to have to ease her into her horror—into the truth.

And yeah, I'm not good enough for her, and it will be a quick one or two nights with the bad boy for her. But screw my pride.

I want her that bad.

She glances at me and her eyes widen at my intense stare, as if reading my thoughts through my gaze. Her head snaps as she looks away again.

Good. I brace a foot on the wall, lean back, and spin a stick. Her aware of me is the first step toward those two hot nights.

Chapter 13
April

I've been to one U-Palooza after party at Sam's house. I stayed about a half hour before hightailing it to my apartment. There had been people wall to wall. So many people were in the apartment, some spilled out of the sliding doors onto the back lawn. Music had blared so loud talking wasn't possible. Beer and booze had been everywhere. And the skunky smell of pot hung in the air. I'm not against people partying. It's just not for me.

This time, Sam didn't announce the party for weeks ahead of time. In fact, he didn't announce it at all. Therefore, it's only the band, Riley's band, and some close friends. A few more people trickle in, most likely having been to the previous parties, but Sam's apartment stays far from full. Most people hang in the kitchen and dining room area, talking and drinking. Some of the guys are in the living room playing video games.

It's nothing like the craziness I witnessed the last time, so I'm shooting for an hour before I head home. Riley and her band are celebrating their debut, and she personally invited me. I couldn't say no. She is practically bouncing off the walls with excitement, at least in between shots. That girl is going to be feeling the booze tomorrow, even with declining every other shot. I've declined all shots and sip on a lukewarm hard cider while everyone keeps talking about the performances. Luminescent Juliet sounded awesome while Shush did a good job. They definitely sounded better than they did the other night at the bar.

Gabe is in the other room, which allows me to collect my thoughts especially after his intense angry look behind the stage, which led me to suspect he is still upset about me hitting on him then running away. Surprisingly, the fact that I upset him is upsetting me. It seems like we've been becoming friends, and I don't want to mess that up with my attraction to him.

I'm almost out of cider when Gabe waltzes into the kitchen. Almost everyone is gathered around Chloe's phone, watching Riley's band's performance. I shuffle near the edge of the crowd where Gabe stands. He is a bit overwhelming in a fitted T-shirt and jeans.

I bend a little closer to him. "I want to apologize again for the other night."

He slowly turns, mahogany eyes appearing weary.

"I'm not sure what came over me." I force a feeble smile. "Guess dancing in the rain is more romantic than I expected."

At first, he appears angry. The lines of his face harden before his expression softens and he grins crookedly. "You sure it was the dancing in the rain? Maybe it was dancing with me?"

My mouth falls open. I'm immediately embarrassed, until I decide to screw it. So what if he thinks I'm attracted to him? It is the truth. It's not like anything is going to come of it. "Maybe it was the combination," I concede, grinning too.

His eyes narrow the slightest, then he lets out a laugh.

Smiling, I take the last sip of my cider, thinking that was easier than I had imagined.

Sam breaks up the crowd around Chloe's phone by bringing out his laptop and an adapter. Everyone moves to the living room and within minutes we're watching Riley's band perform on the big screen T.V. mounted on the wall. In all honesty, the band is better live. The video doesn't capture their energy, while the flaws are more obvious on the recording, at least to me.

The singer of Riley's band scoots closer to Gabe. In between fishing for compliments on her singing, she flirts and giggles. Gabe doesn't seem to mind her antics. He even lets her lean on him.

How lovely.

I pretend to watch the show with everyone else, but I'm watching rock chick put her hand on his stomach, right above his belt. When she draws back his hair to check out a tattoo on the back of his neck—a tattoo that I didn't know he had and am now wondering about since I can't make it out from this angle—I decide my hour has to be up. In the kitchen, I set my empty bottle on the counter and slip out the back sliding glass door.

The night air is a bit cool as I walk home. It doesn't bother me. I'm too wrapped up in chastising myself over the twinge of jealousy I just experienced.

Not cool.

Not realistic.

Not going to happen.

I have to get my head on straight, and soon. Before I make a complete idiot of myself.

Shaking my head at my stupid jealously, I unlock my door. Inside, I go to the kitchen and make my lunch for tomorrow. I have an eight hour shift at the Family Center on Sundays. I make an extra sandwich because I missed dinner. Riley was adamant I come over her house while her band got ready. Her best friend Chloe, a hairdresser and makeup artist, went to town on the three girls in the band. Riley tried to get Chloe to make me up and even tried to talk me into a little black jersey dress. I stayed with my sweater, jeans, and flats. My hormones might want attention from a certain guy, but my brain doesn't want attention from any guy.

I have one more semester, and then I'm on to grad school. If I put my mind to it, I can get grad school done in a year and a half. And even though I'm quite sure Gabe doesn't share even an eighth of the attraction I have for him, me getting involved with someone for more than a few dates doesn't fit into my plans. Other than Romeo, I've dated a bit—like three dates in over three years—but I've never been over the top attracted to anyone like Gabe.

I need to get over my attraction, and quick.

Working hard at keeping myself together, I have gotten resilient, even tough, over the last few years. So I'm thinking this Gabe thing will take a little time, but I will get over it. In fact, getting over a silly infatuation will be one of the lesser challenges I've had to deal with.

A knock sounds at the door.

My hands pause lifting the sandwich.

You've got to be kidding me.

 A louder knock sounds.

Maybe it's Riley, drunk and upset I left her party.

I set the sandwich on a paper towel as a third set of knocks clatter on the door.

Of course, it's Gabe.

"This is getting a little weird," I say, my hand on my hip, though I am elated—like idiotically giddy inside—that he left rocker chick to see me. The feeling of elation is not good, and so not a way to get a handle on my growing infatuation.

"Maybe you shouldn't have run off," he says, stepping forward, which forces me to step to the side and let him inside my apartment.

"Well, why don't you come in?" I shut the door just short of a slam.

"Huh," he says, moving farther into the main room and looking over the apartment. "I expected something more swanky."

Behind him, I roll my eyes. Half of my furniture, like the loveseat and coffee table, is cast off items from my mother that were in our basement. The other half, like the end tables and TV stand, came from Walmart. "I don't need swanky. I need some where to sit and eat."

He passes the kitchen counter, glancing over the note cards organized in order for my power point presentation on Wednesday, and swipes the half-eaten sandwich from the paper towel. He takes a bite and continues onto the bookshelves behind the couch, his lean body graceful with his precise movements. And I'm suddenly fully aware of his body. Though lean, he's all muscle, wide shoulders, and a slim waist. I need to fix my eyeballs. They never notice this kind of stuff. But they're noticing him. Big time.

Munching on my sandwich, he peruses through the different academic titles. Bending over, he begins to read titles. "*General Psychology, Adolescent Psychology, Behavioral Psychology, The Psychology of Addiction...*" He stands and glances at me, his eyes twinkling with sarcasm. "I'm getting psyched out just reading the titles."

"Ha, ha," I retort, keeping my eyes on his face since I seem to be way too aware of his body. "Understanding people and their motives takes a lot of knowledge."

"Yeah," he says in a patronizing tone. "Humans can be wrapped up in the pages of books."

My gaze becomes a glare. "We're taught to take environment and circumstances into account also."

"Well then, aren't you Little-Miss-Figure-everyone-out." He pops the last bit of sandwich in his mouth and moves toward the hallway, his jean clad sexy butt defined with every step.

Trying to ignore the shape of his backside and not interested in his views on phycology while more interested, as in fearing, the direction of his roaming curiosity, I snap at him, "Ever heard of privacy?"

He pauses reaching for the bathroom light. "Privacy?" he repeats, flicking on the light. "Hmm...don't think I have ever heard of it."

My glare boils simmered rage at him. He gives the bathroom a quick glance, then heads to the bedroom. Part of me is quite upset at his intrusion. Another part of me is ecstatic, wondering why he's interested in my apartment. But really, my bedroom is off limits.

"All right, this is getting ridiculous," I say, following him. "You need to go back to the party."

He stops just outside of my bedroom, turning part way toward me, his profile sharp with a devilish grin. "You hiding something?" His brows slant in suspicion. "Just what am I going to find? Dirty mags? Sex toys? A half written poem about me?"

"Oh, shut up," I say, then let a laugh out that I can't contain at the thought of writing a poem about him.

He flicks on the bedroom light.

My laughter dies. There's only one thing that I don't want him to see.

Gabe steps into the room, scanning the space. "Hmmm…unmade bed. Dresser covered with stacks of clothes and other miscellaneous crap. Dirty clothes on floor. Books piled haphazardly on the night stand…"

Jaw tight, I stand in the doorway.

He turns to me, eyes wide with obvious fake shock. "Why, April, you're a slob."

"Yup," I agree. "You've found my secret out. Now, if you're done invading my privacy…" I sweep an arm toward the living room and the front door.

He studies me in contemplation before he turns back to the room. Dammit.

His gaze stops at the far corner.

Damn. Damn. Dammit. That's exactly what I didn't want him to notice.

"What is that?" He marches over to the corner.

"It was my father's," I say in the most offhand tone I can muster. "He gave it to me years ago."

Gabe grabs the guitar case and sets it on the bed. "He plays?"

The case free from its corer fills my vision even more than Gabe. "Um, yeah, he used to be in a band."

"Like a bar band?" Gabe flicks a clasp open.

The click of the clasps releasing echoes in the room like a gun blast to my ears as a constricted knot forming in my chest stops me from answering him. He lifts the lid, and the wonder in his expression has me picturing what he sees below.

I recall the smooth, pale, blonde wood. The dark, glossy neck inlaid with mother of pearl. The lovely Brazilian wood sides. And the sharp, tight strings. It's easy to imagine since I periodically dream of playing the instrument.

"What the hell?" he mutters, reaching inside the case. "Your dad gave you this? To gather dust in the corner of your bedroom?"

At the sight of the guitar—the gleaming beauty of it—I swallow. The air joins the knot in my chest. I haven't laid eyes on the instrument in over three years. Leaving it in the case in the corner without taking it out or touching it had been a small victory. Now my palms sweat with the desire to hold it and my fingers itch to play it. I want to fall to my knees and beg him to give me the guitar, even though my fingers can't perform the magic they once did.

Gabe studies the guitar, his expression full of wonder. "I actually know what this is. McPherson guitars have this hole to the side."

I finally find my voice. "Yeah, I think that's what my dad said it was."

His face perplexed, he studies me like he did the guitar. My stiff stance. My hands clenched in fists at my sides. My strained features.

I put my hands behind my back before blurting out, "My dad used to be in an eighties hair band." I lean on the doorframe for support. "They had a few songs that made it into the top one hundred. I think the highest they charted was just in the top forty. But it opened other doors for him. He went on to write music for other people and produce stuff too," I say, keeping the facts vague. I don't tell people about my semi famous father or the super famous people he is connected to. I don't like the weird attention it brings. This time it explains—to somewhat of a degree—why I'd have such a guitar sitting in the corner of my bedroom.

Gabe's gaze turns thoughtful. "What was the name of his band?"

"Hanged Man."

"Hanged Man," he repeats slowly, then shakes his head. "Never heard of them."

I shrug, keeping my attention on him instead of the guitar. "Like I said, they weren't very big."

"Hmm," is his only response as he studies the guitar in his hands. He adjusts its position, raising a knee and placing his fingers on the neck.

"Please don't mess—"

Standing there like a rock god come to life, he strums. The clear, sweet notes fill the room, beckoning me toward the instrument. He obviously does know a few cords at least. During the second strum, he watches me.

Even with my clenched hands behind my back, my body language is pure tense. "Why did you come over?" I snap, then add, "To torment me?"

His brows rise. "Whoa. I didn't know this equated to torment."

I'm about to start shaking. I want the guitar. I want him. I don't want him touching the guitar. Except for my father, no one has ever played it but me. Before I lose it, as in have a ridiculous tantrum, I force myself to calmly say, "It's just that my dad gave the guitar to me, and I may be a bit over protective of it."

"All right," he says, studying me. Again. Then while I hold my breath, he puts the guitar in the case, snaps it shut, and sets it back in the corner. I'm enjoying breathing when he asks, "Better?"

I nod, though my body is still wound too tight.

He steps toward me, a sly smile on those lips. "I did come over for something specific."

My heart starts pounding as he gets nearer. With the guitar away, all I can see is him. His hard profile. His muscled arms and shoulders. His full upper lip. "You did?" I squeak out.

"Oh, yeah." He comes closer, his gaze suddenly intense. "I wanted…"

I tip my chin in question while my entire body hums at his nearness. "You wanted?" I practically breathe the words instead of saying them while my body hums like an electrical tower at his nearness.

Those brown eyes somehow smile at me. "I wanted to see how your piercing is doing."

"My piercing?" I repeat caught in the mirth of his gaze.

He nods, and now his mouth smiles.

Oh, he has the prettiest mouth! I think before understanding what he is asking. Part of me, the newly awakened hormonal part, is hyperventilating at his obvious flirting. The other part, the part of me with a brain, realizes I need to get control of myself and the situation. I sweep my arm toward the living room again. "Not going to happen, so…"

He crosses his arms. "Not leaving until I perform a full inspection."

"What is this? Invade April's privacy night?" I say, my voice rising with each word.

The arms across his chest tighten and bunch. "I could be gone in the next thirty seconds."

I glare at him.

He grins back.

"Is that thirty seconds a promise?"

"Yup."

"Fine." I yank my shirt up, planning to drop it as quick, but I'm not expecting Gabe to fall to his knees and fold his hands over mine. His palms on my hipbones are hot. His thumbs on each side of my belly button are scalding. The intensity of his gaze is an inferno. As he brushes his thumbs along my skin, tracing the shape of my belly button, my knees tremble.

His attention is locked on my stomach, on the little silver note hanging over the center of my belly button. "It looks good, real good," he says in a hoarse tone. His thumbs keep circling. My knees keep trembling.

What the heck is he doing?

Then while my body is turning into a puddle of goo and my hands are shaking with the desire to wrap in his hair, he bends forward and places his open mouth on me, right around the piercing.

I fight to keep a moan from escaping. When his tongue touches the dangling note and my skin, I lose the fight, and a long whiney breath of air escapes me.

He leans back, rolling into a squat. With the rise of his dark lashes, russet eyes meet mine. "I think that makes us even," he says in a light tone, and though it's his usual flippant tone paired with a grin, his expression is taut to the point that it looks as if he's in pain.

As I stand there frozen in desire and distress, he releases my shirt and bounces up. "Guess I gotta go if I'm going to keep that thirty second promise." He stiffly moves past me and into the living room. "See you Tuesday," he calls before exiting out of the apartment.

At the sound of the door shutting, I plop on my bedroom floor.

The tingling rush of yearning he evoked slowly dissipates and I can think again.

Well sort of.

What the heck just happened? The tingle that lingers a bit has me ridiculously hoping that Gabe was seriously flirting. My brain tells me he had been teaching me a lesson, getting me back for my behavior in the rain. Yet the rush of emotions he brought out leaves me confused and hopeful while embarrassed and fearful.

I brush a hand over my slightly quivering stomach.

One thing is for sure. My body wants him.

It wants him real bad.

Chapter 14
April

In one eight-hour shift, the average number of calls we get working the suicide hot line is three. Three people too many. Three people alone in the dark. Three people that are on the brink of giving up. One call can last hours. The longer the better. We offer words of encouragement and understanding, but mostly we simply listen.

Romeo and I trained together over three years ago, and we've worked a lot of Sundays together. Yet, he was gone for half of the summer on tour, so I worked with a variety of other people, mostly teenagers and college students. The hotline prefers teenagers and young adults because those ages are the highest bracket for suicides. Rachel's suicide brought me here. Romeo's own past demons brought him.

Since there are usually long lulls between calls, we were kind of destined to become friends. Over the last three years, we have talked about everything from music to Riley to classes. And although he didn't admit it right away, he knew who I am, as in who my father is, from the moment we sat in the first class.

A fan and student of guitar, he had read several articles and interviews over the years in various guitar magazines about my dad, and he'd even read that one. During my sixteenth summer, Guitar Page had done a five page story on my dad. I'd been at the house, so they not only asked questions about me, but included me in some of the photos. Once Romeo finally admitted he knew who I was—even though my mother changed my last name to Tanner, so it matched hers and my stepfather's—he agreed to keep mum about my father. And he has kept that promise. Riley doesn't even know my connection to music.

Yet, while Romeo and I are close, I've kept my perfection mask pretty much in place around him since we met. Perhaps that's why we never connected when we tried dating for a couple of months. But we've stayed friends, good friends actually.

Its mid-afternoon and we sit in a tiny room with two desks facing each other and two phones across from each other. He pushes a pile of mini candies onto my desk. I always bring the sandwiches, veggies, and dip. He brings the chocolate.

"So," he says, plucking a mini peanut butter cup from the pile. "I was leaving Sam's last night, practically dragging my buzzed up girlfriend to the car, when I noticed what looked like Gabe leaving your apartment."

He says it all nonchalant like, but it's as if he's dropping a bomb. Only I would be so lucky that they would both leave at the same time.

"Well, it was Gabe." I lean back in my chair, playing nonchalant too, though I do try to be as honest as possible around Romeo.

He pauses unwrapping the chocolate, shock lining his face. "You think that's a good idea? Hooking up with Gabe?"

I pluck a mini candy bar from the pile. "It's not what you're assuming. We're not hooking up. We're just friends." I tap the chocolate on the desk. "It kind of started the night of your label party when Riley pushed us together, so blame it on her."

"Huh?" he says, continuing to appear skeptical as he chews. "You and Gabe friends?"

I shrug. "You know the saying, opposites attract."

"Exactly. Gabe has come a long way since joining the band, both in attitude and drumming, but he is too messed up for you."

I drop the candy bar. "Are you implying that he's not good enough for me?" My tone drips with incredulity.

Romeo's dark eyes widen. "No. Of course not. It's just that you're you and he's him."

My brows rise.

"You have a four point, a planned future, an organized life, and rarely date. He goes through girlfriends by the month—by the day on tour—he works as a part time mechanic, and is on probation for assault and battery times two. It's not a question of good enough. He is just screwed up."

"Wow. You make me sound like the biggest bore on the planet. And people do make mistakes."

"You're mature. He's getting there, but it might take years."

"Again boring. And there are reasons for Gabe's mistakes. Perhaps not excuses but reasons. And we really are just friends."

He watches me as if judging my words and tone. "Just be careful. You may be more mature but he's jaded."

"All right then." I roll my eyes. "And you may be more business savvy, but Riley has more soul."

"No shit. Why do you think I'm with her?" He plucks another piece of candy from the pile. "I'm more boring than you."

"And stubborn."

"And talented."

"Pfft."

"Prove it then. Join Riley's band." His stare challenges me.

Oh, not this again. He has been trying to talk me in to playing guitar for Riley's band from the moment she began forming it. "Not going to happen."

"Not going to give up."

"Wasting your time," I say, unwrapping a piece of candy.

"Then I am the most talented."

"Pfft." I pop the chocolate in my mouth.

He shakes his head. "You may not be at my level"—he smirks—"but you've got to be better than what she has currently got."

I give him a narrowed look as I finish chewing. "If I ever removed that thing out of its case, it wouldn't be Luminescent Juliet. It would be Luminescent April."

He laughs. "That name suck—"

The phone rings and we instantly stop harassing each other.

Since it's his rotation, he picks up the phone and I begin filling in the log. Though I listen to his side of the conversation, we're just friends faintly echoes in my head, and strangely that echo saddens me.

Chapter 15
April

"She should dive into the shallow end of a pool," Misha says, staring at me.

I keep my appearance void of anger, irritation, or even pity as I glance around the circle. No matter how mean she gets, I refuse to lower myself to Misha's level. And though sometimes it's hard for me to believe, I'm aware the girl is a witch because of whatever pain she is hiding.

Jason stares at the floor. Gabe sits with his arms crossed and wears a bored expression. Chad stares at Misha's chest.

It's the same old same old.

Though everyone in the group is aware that Gabe and I hang out—at least to conquer the bucket list—group has not gotten better. In fact, Misha is worse than ever, obviously hoping that being a monumental witch will get Gabe to join her side—the hate April for no apparent reason side.

Jeff clears his throat. "Misha, lashing out at others won't help you, and breaks the respect inside our circle. If something has happened that recently hurt you, please share that with us instead."

She lets out a huff then draws in a breath. "Something did happen." She scans Gabe's stretched out legs. "I met a man, an older man. He comes in every Thursday for a lap dance," she says, dragging out the last two words.

Now that Misha's stripping, there is no bounds to her ego. Sadly, I'm pretty sure her ego is a front. For what I haven't totally figured out—though I'm guessing it's connected to her lack of self-esteem. However, she definitely uses sex as not only a way to get attention, but also as a shield.

Chad practically drools. Jason keeps his eyes on the floor. Gabe looks bored. Jeff's brow wrinkles in a scrunch.

"After, he waits for me until closing, takes me for a drive in his corvette, and I blow him off," she says low and seductive, before she slams into the back of her chair. "But the asshole won't tell me his name!"

"Well," Jeff says slowly, as his hand curls tightly around his binder. "Perhaps—"

Gabe sits up and interrupts with, "Do you enjoy being slutty?"

Misha whips toward him, a snarl growing on her red mouth.

"Gabe!" Jeff says.

"No, really," Gabe continues. "If you enjoy it, then more blow job power to you, and who gives a shit if he tells you his name? And who cares what people think? But if you're looking for more from these guys, then you need to stop blowing men off in bathrooms, cars, parking lots, and walk in coolers, because they aren't going to give you more. They're just going to take from you without an ounce of respect."

Misha's hands clench around the edge of her seat, as if she's ready to attack. "Fuck you. Maybe I'm a sex addict. Did you think of that, asshole?"

Gabe sits back, crossing his arms once more. "Then once again, you don't need to know his name."

"Sex addicts can feel guilty," she huffs.

He nods. "Still don't need to know his name."

Chad glances between them, mostly likely deciding if his lust for Misha outweighs his fear of Gabe.

The air cracking with tension, Jason quietly says, "If you don't respect yourself, no one will."

"Fuck you too, freak." Misha looks like she is going to jump across the room and throttle Jason.

I scoot to the front of my chair, ready to intercept her.

"Leave him alone," Gabe says in a low tone.

"Okay, everyone," Jeff says, attempting to take control. "I think Gabe is actually trying to help you, Misha, though he should have used kinder words."

Misha's top lip curls at Jeff before she points to me and spits out, "Just like her"—the girl never says my name—"what I do is my business."

Gabe leans forward putting his elbows on his knees. "Then quit bragging about blo—"

"I think that is enough," Jeff says quickly in a fake chirpy tone. "I'd like to share a positive story about…"

As Jeff drones, I tune him out, watching Gabe out of the corner of my eye. Though he should have been more polite, I'm impressed that he had the balls to call Misha out.

Soon my watching turns into admiring. He is dressed in his normal jeans and white T-shirt. The muscles of his arms appear tight and smooth. His long legs are stretched out to the middle of the circle. Sun streaked hair brushes the hard line of his jaw scruff. Studying him, I feel like one of the fan girls who swoon over Luminescent Juliet. I want to lean across the circle and touch him, see if all that sexy appeal is real or a figment of my imagination or newly awakened hormones.

Gabe looks up and I realize I'm not watching him from the corner of my eye anymore. I'm full out staring at him. He smirks at me as I snap away. I keep my eyes adverted for the rest of the session, through Jeff's long story and through his assignment—sharing a happy time for the next session.

Outside in the parking lot, Gabe catches up with me. He's still wearing that darn smirk.

"You busy tonight?"

I almost trip because it sounds like he's asking me out. He can't be asking me out. "Why?"

"During a break this week, my manager was talking about where he took his kids last weekend. It gave me an idea for the next item on the list."

I hit unlock as I come to my car. "What item?"

His smirk expands. "Why not let it be a surprise?"

I open the car, trying to ignore his closeness. "Why not just tell me?"

"You busy?" he demands, grabbing hold of the top of my door.

I slip into the front seat. "Homework."

"It's a bit of a drive. You can do it on the way."

Brows lowering, I wonder what he could possibly be planning.

He lets go of the door. "I'll pick you up around six." He steps away, but over his shoulder says, "Dress warm."

As my brows lower more, I watch him walk across the lot and wish my heart hadn't picked up speed at the thought of being alone with him.

Chapter 16
April

We've been in Gabe's truck, rolling down the highway for almost forty minutes. I pretended to read and study most of the time, but so close to him, it's a bit difficult to concentrate. The last time I felt this way—breathless and giddy and brainless—around someone was at the age of twelve with my college aged piano teacher. Infatuations are immature. I know this, yet I can't stop the bubbling emotions he produces. Well, at least internally. Outwardly, I try to stay as cynical as possible.

Finally giving up on reading and closing my clinical psychology book, I ask, "Is this an overnight trip or something?"

Gabe nods toward the green sign we're about to pass. "This is our exit."

I search the signs on the side of the road as we come closer to the exit. None of the restaurants or 'attractions' makes sense with the items left on the bucket list. At the end of the ramp, he turns away from the businesses and we roll along a highway with farms on each side. Across the cab, he smirks again, as my anticipation laced with dread grows.

He slows, then turns, near a large sign titled Cross Historical Village.

I'm stumped as he parks in a half-filled parking lot, not only about why we're here, but also about what here is exactly.

He hops out of the truck. "You coming?"

"Ah, yeah," I absently say, releasing my seat belt.

At the entrance, he pays for our tickets while I peek across the gate. The sight of little old houses and barns and a church has me realizing we're at a museum of sorts. He hands me the ticket and I ponder the remaining items on the bucket list: release a paper lantern, get a tattoo, get over stage fright, kiss at the top of a Ferris wheel, meet Michael Thomas, share a bottle of strawberry wine, and sleep under the stars.

As we pass a train depot, along with an antique train chugging steam into the orange streaked sky, I'm thinking that they must release paper lanterns here. Or maybe hoping because there better not be a stage where tourists can participate.

A lady wearing a long dress and bonnet, hands me a map from a basket on her arm, but before I can open it, Gabe snatches it out of my hand.

"The suspense won't kill you."

"It might." I glare at him reading the map held out of my reach.

He scans it, then tucks it in his back pocket. "This way," he says, gesturing toward the right. We walk the length of a narrow dirt road lined with houses, a barbershop, a blacksmith, and a windmill. Other people, mostly families, fill the path or wander into the buildings.

"Did you want to check anything out?" he asks, his tone purposely polite.

I glare. He knows the anticipation is killing me. "Maybe later."

"Sure you don't want to stop for some cider and donuts?" He nods toward a barn like structure as we round a corner.

"No thanks," I say in a false light tone.

He chuckles. "I am a bit hungry."

"You can wait for once." My teeth grind as I imagine possibilities. Me on a stage with a guitar? Fearless. Even if I suck. Me on a stage without an instrument? Terrified.

A large building looms ahead of us, as we come closer, I read the plaque at the edge of the path. Dance Hall. My heart pounds a bit faster. The hall would be the perfect place to put on an impromptu play. I force my legs to keep moving, instead of turning and jogging away. Much to my relief, we pass the hall.

Gabe seems to be on a mission toward the back of the park. He walks so fast, I nearly do have to jog. Keeping his pace, I squint past a log cabin and a church steeple. I'm almost sure I glimpse water, but the sun is almost set. It might just be the reflection of light. However, a small lake would be a perfect place to release a paper lantern.

Please, please, please be a lake.

We turn another corner and a carousel comes into view. Beyond and above that is a—I stop cold at the sight—Ferris Wheel. Large and old looking with basket like cages, it looms above us. I peel my wide eyes from the sight of the wheel to see Gabe standing a few feet ahead of me. He is watching me, a smirk etching his face.

I back up. "You can't be serious."

His steps closer as the smirk grows. "Are you scared?"

"Just one month ago you couldn't stand me." Confusion fills my tone.

He stops moving closer and crosses his arms. "It's just a kiss, April."

My stomach does a back flip at the k-word. Funny, as much as I have been lusting after him, as much as I swoon over his lips, I'd never imagined us kissing. Until now. Hot images and sensations fill my brain.

He grabs my hand and tugs me inches from him. "Afraid you'll find me more irresistible after just one peck?"

Yes, I am. My eyes narrow. "More?"

He nods and caresses the top of my hand with a thumb. "It's a known fact. The first girl I kissed"—he pauses, tilting his head in contemplation—"back in junior high, wrote me… love letters, poems included, for the entire year."

"Oh, please," I say, laughing and yanking my hand from his grip. "I'm not scared of you or your magic lips. I just—you—well…I don't want the list to make you do anything you don't want to."

"Ah, yeah, I think I can survive it somehow." He gestures to the wheel. "Shall we?"

I march past him. Past the carousel, we join the line. A bright star twinkling in the center of the wheel casts shadows as people are slowly unloaded and loaded into the baskets. I'm trying to pay attention to the surroundings instead of the ridiculous anticipation running through me. Amid the lights and circus like music, I try to tell myself that Gabe is right, it's just a kiss, and maybe it will be so lifeless that my newly awaked hormones will go back to sleep. But then maybe I will find him more irresistible than ever and pine for him like so many female fans of

Luminescent Juliet. As we move up in the line, the spinning star feels like it has become a roulette wheel with my hormones at stake.

When we come to the front of the line, the attendant dressed in a striped red shirt and bow tie gestures for me to enter the basket. I almost smash myself into the corner, but with a deep breath decide that I'm going to face the inevitable and stop thinking like an idiot.

It's just a kiss.

Gabe slides in beside me, his thigh pressing against mine.

"Still scared?" he asks, as the man locks the basket gate.

"Of heights? Yes, I am."

"Do you want me to hold your hand?" he asks, his tone light and teasing.

My expression is forcefully wry. "I think I'll be okay."

The wheel moves and we're soon a quarter of the way up. Are we doing this right away? As soon as we hit the top? My mouth is suddenly dry. *Idiot. Idiot. Idiot. Stop thinking about it and it won't be a big deal.*

Though I do have a healthy fear of heights, I peek out over the edge and attempt —maybe pretend—to watch the people milling about below.

"You going to Riley's gig this weekend?" Gabe asks.

The wheel shifts and we're at the halfway point. I feel my skin whiten. Whether from the height or the upcoming liplock, I'm not sure. "Of course. You?"

"Yeah." He shifts his weight so that his legs are stretched out to the far corner in front of me. "You know, there was a time that I almost hated Riley. Now she just worries the hell out of me."

Surprised at the revelation, I turn to him. "Why would you hate Riley?"

He studies the people below like I had been. "She beat me out in auditions. She could come back at any time."

"Riley, even Romeo, wouldn't do that to you, especially since you guys have signed with a label."

"But what if I fuck up?"

"How would you screw up that bad?"

He shrugs, his shoulder brushing mine. "Lose my temper. End up in jail. Maybe even prison."

I almost say, *Well then don't f-up*, but that's not easy for someone raised like he was. "I could…I mean I know some breathing techniques and imagery exercises that can help you learn to keep control."

"My psychologist has probably shown, taught, explained, you name it, everything possible. Yet when I get angry like that, I snap. The last time I got in trouble, I saw Allie's ex smack her and I lost it. It took the entire rest of the band to peel me off him."

Gabe is so intense that scenario isn't too hard to imagine. "Well, maybe—"

He nods his head toward outside. "We're at the top."

I look around to find that we are indeed at the top. Our basket precariously swings in the breeze. I hadn't even noticed us moving. "Did you do that on purpose?"

"What?"

"Steer my attention from the…height?" I refuse to refer to why we're up here.

"Maybe," he says, his gaze on my face.

Gabe shifts closer, and my heart starts hammering all over again, and it's definitely not because we're in a little basket at the top of a high wheel.

He leans forward, his eyes intense. "You ready for this?"

At the touch of his palms on my jaw, anticipation pounds through me, so much that a wild bubbly laugh escapes me. I feel like I could jump out of my skin. "Sure. Lay those magic lips on mine."

He smiles, authentically for once before he lowers his lashes and head.

Those lovely lips cover mine, and I'm frozen at the feel of him. The press of his firm, soft mouth. The slight scrape of the scruff on his chin. The tip of his nose brushing my cheek. His lips caressing mine, back and forth, nipping and almost sucking, drumming up desire from the storm in my stomach, making me remember all of these sensations from my teenage years, but not like this. They were never like this. So sharp, so acute, so bone melting that I may dissolve onto the antique seat and drip into the autumn night.

Magic lips. The man really does have them.

He presses closer, both his body and mouth.

The desire that had been slowly building in my stomach explodes as a gasp from my mouth into his, and that sound changes everything. The hands that were clasped in my lap grip his shoulders and pull him closer. Instead of just experiencing, I'm all in, moving my lips over his, touching his tongue with mine, and grasping that hair in my hands.

He changes too, from gentle and coaxing to demanding and forceful, pushing me back against the metal basket weave, crushing my mouth under his, digging his fingers into my jaw.

We become a tangle of mouths and hands and lust until the basket lurches forward and shifts downward.

Gabe gradually draws away and sits back.

Smashed in the corner, I stare at him, trying to get my brain back. I'm a blob of pulsating hormones. He stares back at me. Now dark, the lone light illuminating our little world is the star on the wheel. It's hard to read, nearly impossible, his face in the shadows.

"Um…" I say desperate to break the silence, specifically break the spell of lust that hangs inside the cart before I jump on him, since my entire body pulsates with the need he invoked.

"Relax, April. It was just a kiss," Gabe says in an oddly light but tight tone. "One more check off the list."

The list. I almost bang my head on the metal weave of the basket. I should be thinking of Rachel, maybe imagining her in this situation. Instead, I'm thinking of attacking Gabe and going for round two. I'm sure Rachel would have imagined something like part one of the kiss, but I liked part two much better. Maybe being with Misha once a week is rubbing off on me. One kiss and I'm on my way to becoming a wannabe sex addict. Or probably since it's Gabe, a real one, but just for him.

"Bit quiet over there," Gabe says. "Still in shock? Don't tell me you're going to become obsessed with me. If so, try not to write any shitty poems."

The wheel starts turning without stopping to load. We head toward the top again.

Determined not to appear like the lust sick teenager I feel like, I say, "If they're about you, they're bound to be crappy."

He lets out a laugh that turns into a bright, sexy smile that shines through the shadows, and I swear my heart lurches.

For a magic lipped ass.

Chapter 17
Gabe

The echo of the highway thuds under us, mixing with the music from a local rock station while April, all prim with her legs crossed and feet tucked under the seat, pretends to read some book about psychology. I'd call bullshit, but I'm aware that kiss freaked her out. Therefore I let her pretend and just drive.

But fuck.

I want to pull this piece of shit truck over and devour her, tear her book away and her clothes, then put my mouth between her legs.

Fuck. I'm getting hard all over again.

My phone vibrates from its spot in the open ashtray—my truck is old enough to have one— jingling the coins under it. April glances at it and gives me a pointed look.

Fine. I should answer the damn thing. It will at least get my mind off fucking the chick next to me. Hopefully, it's not Kristy. By number of voice messages she leaves, the girl doesn't seem to be getting that I'm not interested anymore.

I yank it out of the ashtray without checking the name on the screen. "Yeah," I answer, my sexual frustration coming out in an irritated tone.

"Ah, hey Gabe, this is Allie, just calling about tomorrow. I'm sorry but something has come up and I can't meet with Sharon and Todd to move the stuff into the apartment. I'm really, really sorry," she adds. "Unless we can do it later?"

Shit. I draw in a deep breath. I'm not going to my old man's to get my stuff. Last week we almost came to fists over where my truck was parked on the street. And there is no way I can cancel my weekly session with Joan, my therapist, or band practice. "No, Sharon has to be to work by five. She has to drop it off before then. No problem though, one more night on Sam's couch won't kill me."

"Oh, you're making me feel guilty, maybe I can get—"

"Seriously, don't worry about it. I can meet her the following day."

"You sure? I might be able to get a friend from art class."

"To move my shit in? Not necessary. We'll do it Thursday."

"I can help then."

"No need. I don't have much. Just need two people to move the bed. Sharon can't lug that thing up a flight of stairs."

"All right, I'm really sorry."

"No problem." I toss the phone back in the tray. I'll call Sharon later about the change of plans.

April lightly clears her throat and shuts her book. "Um, excuse me for being nosey, but it's hard not to sitting so close. Um, while eavesdropping—not on purpose—I got the idea that you may need some help moving."

I shake my head. "No, there's not much to move…unless…" I shake my head again. "Never mind. Dumb idea." I glance at her slim frame. "You have to be like five two and one hundred pounds."

"Try five five and definitely far more than a hundred pounds, but if Allie was going to move your stuff, why can't I?"

"Wow, you're pretty good at that eavesdropping stuff." I can sense her glare from across the cab. "It's not a big deal waiting one more day."

"Doubt that. You have to be sick of Sam's couch, and I'm guessing you've been staying there to keep away from your dad?"

"You getting psychoanalytical on me?"

"No, that was just obvious."

I tap my thumb on the top of the steering wheel. "Yeah, I'm trying to stay out of trouble, and living with him tends to turn me into a ticking time bomb."

"Good thing you're staying away then." She unzips her book bag. "But seriously, I can meet Sharon and Todd."

I'm having a hard time imagining her prim, little, proper self, lugging a mattress and bed frame up to the apartment.

She dumps the book in the bag. "I moved all my stuff into my apartment with one other girl, so I'm sure Todd and I can handle it."

She sounds so proud of herself that I give in. "Okay, Tough Chick, just move the bed. I'll have Sharon leave the boxes in the truck. I'll get them after practice."

"Tough chick?" she says with a light, tinkling laugh. "I kind of like that." She glances over and smiles at me.

And I almost run off the road.

Just from that smile on her gorgeous face.

Damn. I haven't been this wound up in…well, never, and definitely not ever from something as simple as a smile.

***

I drive Sharon's old Corolla into the parking space Allie said went with the apartment. Practice went smooth tonight, so smooth we finished an hour early. Now that things have become serious, the band's over the bickering and ego bullshit that has plagued us. Not that I seriously participated in their stupid arguing, other than telling them to get their shit together and just play. We're all about work now, about getting it done, and getting it done perfect. A bit of debate still happens, but it's about the music, not who is calling the shots. And I have to admit, the last month and half have been the best, as far as creating and learning and working together.

I truly think we have a shot at making it big.

As long as I don't fuck it up.

I go up the stairs, planning on putting the bed together, then getting my truck, along with the rest of my shit, from the bar Sharon works at. But when I get to the top of the stairs and push open the door, I'm startled to see April standing on a chair and stretching toward a cupboard above the refrigerator. Her rounded ass takes up most of my vision.

"Hey—" is all I get out because she whips around, sees me, and teeters at the edge of the chair. Shit! In one second, I cross the few feet separating us and catch her right before she hits the floor, which leaves me crouching on the floor and holding her in my arms, while she stares at me with wide ocean-colored eyes.

"You okay?" I gently ask.

She nods and scrambles out of my arms as fast as she fell.

Damn. Now that I know she's all right, I wanted to check out all the curves that had basically landed in my lap.

"What are you doing here?" she asks, a hand on her forehead as she plops in the chair.

"I believe this is my apartment." I stay crouched, keeping us at eye level.

She drops her hand onto her lap. "I mean this early."

"We finished early. But what are you doing here?" Wanting to touch her, I brush back a few erratic strands of hair across her cheek.

"Putting stuff away," she says slowly, watching my hand.

Comprehension sinking in, I stand and notice the mostly empty boxes surrounding my feet on the floor. "You didn't have to do that. You should have left them in the truck."

Her cheeks turn pink. "I didn't have anything else to do and I wanted to help."

My first instinct is to be an ass and say something about her wanting to see my underwear or some shit, but her pink cheeks and downward eyes keep the comment from coming out. "Well, thank you. It was quite nice of you, excessive but very nice."

She smiles weakly and pushes out of the seat. "I should—"

"What is that?" I interrupt, pointing at a large, blue gift bag on the table—besides the couch, the only furniture the apartment came with.

She glances at the bag. "Oh, I wanted to get you a little something. You know, like a house warming gift since this is your first place."

I snort. "My opulent one room apartment?"

"It's still yours."

"You're right," I concede with a grin, moving toward the table.

She stands and pushes the chair in saying, "I should get going."

Screw that. She's here, and I'm keeping her for as long as possible. All night if I get my way. "Just wait a minute. Let me at least open your gift."

"Not necessary." She grabs her purse from the counter. "I know you'll like it."

"Yeah?" I ask in a challenging tone. "Let's just see."

She crosses her arms and leans on the counter.

Smirking at her, I reach inside and tug out a huge aluminum pot, which is full of tissue paper, bags of different colored dried pasta, and utensils. I cock a brow at her before going in the bag again. Next, I pull out a strainer filled with more tissue and jarred sauces: red, white, green, and even a bright orange one. I hold out the orange one, raising my brows in question at her.

"Butternut squash." She lowers her chin. "I figured on variety over picky with your appetite."

"Good figuring there. You're right. I like it. You definitely got the idea I'd eat anything, huh?" She nods as I set the jar down and turn to her. Dressed in jeans and that flannel with a tank under it, instead of her usual preppy shit, she looks extra sexy. What I'd like to eat at the moment is her.

"You." I take a step toward her. "Should." I take her purse and set it on the counter. "Stay." I grip the counter near her hips. "For dinner."

"Um…" She blinks at me, hopefully confused by my nearness.

I lean closer, not touching her, but allowing her to feel my warmth, and I'm hot. Hot for her. "Let me cook for you at least."

"Um…" She draws in a deep breath. I have to stop from leaning forward and drinking in her release of air.

"I'd like to show you my appreciation after you've worked so hard," I say, my tone smooth.

"Ah, I'm not sure…" she says hesitantly, but never finishes the thought, her gaze on my mouth.

I can almost hear her brain at war with her libido. Hands on the counter, I trail my thumbs on the skin of her waist, right above the line of her jeans. I bend near her ear. "You can relax and I'll do all the work."

She lets out a soft gasp, and at the noise, I'm instantly hard.

Damn. I hope I'm reading her right because I can't keep talking shit while my mind has one thing pounding across it. My hands slide to her waist, spraying across her back and pulling her from the edge of the counter. My mouth lightly brushes the line of her jaw. "And I hate eating alone."

Her eyes are wide as I face her again.

I bend toward her mouth, stopping centimeters from it. "So please stay."

A slight shudder goes through her. "Okay."

As far as I'm concerned, the question and that answer had nothing to do with pasta. I close the short distance between us, yanking her by the hips to me. "Good choice," I say against her lips before covering her mouth.

She grabs my hair and kisses me back without restraint, melding her body closer to mine, standing on tiptoes to reach me. She's sweet, wild, want under my mouth and hands. The kiss is so hot, that without thinking I lift and set her on the counter. Her legs wrap around me and I gasp into her mouth as my cock hits the hot center of her.

Fuck.

I break the kiss, only to kiss her hard and fast, again and again.

I want to taste and touch all of her at once.

Now.

I don't know where to start, what to touch first, I just want.

All of her.

My hands glide. Over her ribs. Along the sexy curve of her hips. Down to the sharp points of her knees. My mouth slides. To the corner of her mouth. To suck on her bottom lip. Along her chin. My fingers grip. Her skin. Her curves. Her hair. I tug the silken strands, force her head back, and expose her neck. My mouth follows the line of her throat, nipping and sucking and tasting velvety skin, which leads me to wanting so much more. After releasing her hair, I slide my palms under the back of her shirt. My fingers find the clasp of her bra.

Her chest rises in harsh breaths. Somehow, lost in the feel and taste of her, I force myself to pause, my fingers gripping the closure. I wait for her to realize my intent, give her time to stop me if that is what she wants.

Her fingers dig into my shoulders, and that's all the encouragement I need. With my mouth above the line of her tank, I release the clasp and my hands are on her beautiful tits in two seconds, molding to their shape, caressing the soft skin, and brushing her hardened nipples until she's panting above me.

The sound is so damn sexy.

My phone vibrates in my pocket.

No. Fucking. Way.

My thumbs brush back and forth over nipples.

Her legs clench around my waist. Her grip on my shoulders tightens.

I drag the edge of the tank lower with my teeth.

And my phone starts vibrating again, like the person called me back right away.

I'm about to toss the phone in the freezer. Who the hell would keep calling? Who the fuck would I stop for in the middle of this?

Then it hits me who it might be.

"Fuck!" I say, stepping from April and dragging out my phone.

Shit, it is Sharon.

"Sorry," I say to a dazed eyed April before I answer the phone with a, "Hey, Sharon."

"I need your help," she says in a frantic tone. "Your dad's here at the bar. He won't leave. He's getting argumentative and I'm afraid he might hurt himself."

I snort. "More like you or someone else. I'll be there in ten." I've tried to get Sharon away from my dad, stayed at the house longer than I should have to keep her safe, and even offered to share an apartment with her. However, she won't leave him—claims she loves him and he needs her, though I've questioned that and her countless times—and I can't stay any longer or I'll forever be caught in the cycle.

"Please hurry up!" she says as I hang up.

April's already jumping off the counter. "Where are you going? Do you need my help?"

"No!" I say a little—maybe a lot—harshly at the idea of her anywhere near my father. I run a hand through my hair. "I've got to go."

"Okay…should I wait?" she asks in small, confused voice.

Though ecstatic that she would ask to wait, I shake my head. "This may take a while. Sorry. Really sorry. Sorry for you and me. I owe you dinner," I say, shutting the door and not looking back. If I look back at her tousled form, at her swollen kissed lips, or her blue confused sexed eyes, I won't be able to leave.

Chapter 18
April

I sit across from Dr. Medina as she flips through my folder. This date for our meeting had been looming in my head since mid- August when I applied to the Clinical Counseling Program. Now near the end of October, I'd almost forgotten about it. If it hadn't been on my phone calendar, I would have missed the meeting. She has asked several questions already, but I'm getting the suspicion that were moving on to my group therapy—more like group agony.

She closes the folder. "Well, April, I talked with Jeff last week and he assured me that you were progressing nicely. Naturally, he wouldn't give me any particulars, but I trust Jeff." She takes off her reading glasses and lays them on the folder before folding her navy suited arms on the edge of the desk. "So I'm more than happy to inform you that I think we should go ahead and schedule your interview with the board of Psychology professors."

Relief comes over me. Finally. "Thank you, Dr. Medina."

She smiles. "During our call, I also asked for Jeff's permission to tell you a bit about him." She sits back, hands in her lap. "Jeff was one of my…I suppose favorite students. Not that I pick favorites, he just has such an unconventional way of working with people, that as a professor I couldn't help being intrigued. Though he is competent in the current strategies, he tends to adapt therapy to each individual group." She smiles at me again, though this time it is more of a compressed smile. "Your approach is very by the book, April. Nothing is wrong with that per say. But along with facing your own issues, I wanted you to perceive how therapy should be about individual needs, and not only what the texts say is obligatory. I hope you have gleaned that from Jeff's sessions."

"Um…" I say, stalling because I haven't gleaned anything from those torture like sessions. "Yes, I suppose he does adapt to our groups needs, though I probably wouldn't have been able to express it as clear."

Nodding, she picks up her glasses. "It's always good to understand and remember that all those textbooks are starting points. People and their needs can transform all those philosophies into true counseling and therapy."

"Quite true," I say numbly, feeling like she just tossed three years of college out the window.

After scanning the schedule on her computer, she assigns me a date for the interview. I thank her and leave, actually rush out of her office, feeling bewildered at her praise of Jeff and on the edge of embarrassed by her opinion that I'm rigid.

Out of the psych department offices and in the hall, I'm startled at the sight of Riley and Romeo waiting by the entrance to the stairs. Until seeing them, I had forgotten telling Riley about the upcoming meeting. Of course, they would both be here to offer support in case it didn't go well.

"Hey," Riley says, coming up to me, her expression growing more worried with each step. "Are you all right?"

I nod, even force a smile. "Yes, my interview is in about four weeks."

"That's great, April!" Riley says, hugging me.

Romeo watches me with lowered brows. When Riley moves away, he asks, "Then why do you look like someone just kicked your ass?"

Because I just learned what Dr. Medina really thinks about me, but instead of revealing that, I shake my head, as if I'm shaking off an emotion. "I don't know. It's been a stressful morning, a couple of months."

"Then let's go to lunch and celebrate!" Riley says, moving toward the stairwell.

Crap. Along with everything else, I'd forgotten about Riley's earlier plans about lunch since none of us have Thursday afternoon classes. "Yeah, sure," I say, not wanting to let her down and forcing yet another smile. I feel so much like a damn cheerleader with their fake toothy smiles that I'm getting on my own nerves.

The three of us head to the parking lot and her car. Some fans of Luminescent, two girls and a guy, spot Romeo as we walk across the campus. The guy asks for an autograph on his notebook. Always aware of the importance of fans, Romeo signs the notebook and talks with them a bit while the girls eye him in awe. Riley, having grown used to this, just stands to the side with me and grins.

In Riley's car, not wanting to discuss the interview, I keep the conversation about her gig on Saturday night, asking about their music set. Luckily, she spends most of the ride describing why she choose each song.

As she pulls into the parking lot of the bar where Sharon works, panic erupts in me at the realization Gabe may be here. I'm still in shock over the other night, especially at my response to him. Between the interview shock and my lingering lust shock, I'm not emotionally prepared to face Gabe.

"What are we doing here?" I blurt.

Riley smiles over her shoulder at me in the back seat. "Best burgers ever. Unless you don't want burgers?"

"Um...burgers are fine." I mumble, wanting to ask about Gabe but not daring.

Inside, the place is half-full of people eating. My eyes scan the room while I follow Romeo and Riley to a table. So far so good, Gabe's not in sight. After my stressful morning and awful meeting, I don't want to deal with the feelings he evokes. Or face the fact that we've come to a fork in the road in our friendship, because although I'd been certain he didn't want anything to do with me in that way, the other night clearly proved my opinion wrong. But I'm still utterly confused about our mutual desire, as in what does he exactly want? A fling? A one-night stand? A relationship? More importantly, what do I want? Because even the thought of anything semi-serious freaks me out. I have a plan, have had a plan for years. And it has never included anything like the fire between Gabe and I.

Riley hands us all a menu from in between the ketchup and mustard, then asks me, "So are you dressing up on Saturday?"

I pause glancing at the short menu of burgers and sandwiches. Though Sunday is Halloween, the gig is in celebration of the holiday. "I'm not sure. It's not really my thing."

"Me either," Romeo says.

Riley elbows him in the ribs. "You're dressing up."

He groans.

"Your band is dressing up?" I ask Riley.

She nods. "You're going to have to wait and see as what."

"The suspense may kill me," I say with a touch of sarcasm.

Riley laughs. "Well, it is going to be awesome."

Sharon steps up to our table, holding an order pad. The sight of her reminds me of Gabe again, since she called while we were in the middle of hot and heavy. I push the thought away, I'm not going to be rude or standoffish to this woman because I'm slightly—very—mortified by my—really my body's—behavior.

She smiles wide and takes a pen from her apron. "Hey, guys. How's everyone doing?" Petite with brown hair shot with gray and deep laugh lines, she appears older than my mother, though I'm guessing she's around the same age. Yet Sharon's smile and bright eyes are far more welcoming than my mother's polished look.

"Awesome," Riley says. "And you?"

Sharon shrugs. "Working a double, so tired but paying the bills." She turns toward me. "Thanks a bunch for helping move Gabe's stuff the other night, April. Without you, he probably would have lived out of those boxes for months."

I flick the edge of the plastic menu. "It was no big deal."

Sharon shakes her head. "No. It was very nice of you."

I can't help a blush, looking down at my menu. When I look up, Romeo is watching me with a critical expression. Great. Sharon's revelation probably put more ideas in his head.

We all order burgers, and then the onslaught comes. Riley asks question after question about the meeting. Knowing she is interested in my life as a friend, I answer as honest as possible, but I gloss over anything related to my group therapy or Dr. Medina's comment. Neither are topics I'm prepared to confront with anyone, except maybe Gabe...well, at least before we almost had sex on his kitchen counter.

Romeo mostly listens and watches, which makes me aware that he knows that something is off. Although, I present my perfect self to him, he knows me quite well. When Riley takes a break from her interrogation and heads to the restroom, he raises his brows and waits patiently.

I play with my straw bending it back and forth, then let out a sigh. "Near the end of the interview, Dr. Medina made a comment basically saying that my counseling style is paint by numbers from textbooks."

He leans over the table, his eyes intense. "Who cares what she thinks? She is only a professor, probably hasn't counseled people in years. You got the interview for the master's program. And I for one know, have seen on several Sundays, that you're not paint by numbers. You care, you care a lot." He sits back. "So forget her."

I tilt my head and nod. "I guess you're right."

He smirks. "I'm always right."

I let out a "harrumph."

He leans forward again. "So what is going on with you and Gabe?"

My gaze narrows on his knowing look. I do not need to go into this today. "I already told you we're just friends," I say in a low voice.

His expression stays skeptical.

Riley plops down.

"So," I say in a conspiring tone. "Have any ideas what I could dress as?"

She certainly does, enough to fill the rest of the time between burgers and the bill. And unfortunately, after all her brainwork, it looks like I'm going to have to dress up.

Ugh. It already seems like I'm dressing up as someone other than me every damn day.

Chapter 19
April

I feel lost, adrift on a sea without a boat, about to drown. Everything is twisting, doing one eighties, changing, and transforming before my eyes and behind my back. I've been lying around my apartment since having lunch with Romeo and Riley, more than eight hours ago. I can't get a handle on anything: not myself, nor the situation with Gabe, and definitely not my education or future. Though I know Dr. Medina didn't intend to, her comment has me second-guessing everything, especially my capabilities.

The meeting ruined my confidence, not only in what I have learned the last three and a half years, but also in all of my plans for the future. I'm suddenly wondering if I'm a square peg trying to fit in a round hole. Certainly, not everyone ends up in the career best suited for them. Yet if I'm not cut out for counseling, it could hinder people who need help, and that's the last thing I want to do.

So I've been trying to figure out how big the space is between reality and my desire, my need for the career. I've laid on my bed or the couch. I stare at the walls or ceiling and think, but I'm having a hard time seeing past my want to reality. I have planned and wanted this career for too long. So long, it has become part of who I am, who I need to be, and I can't imagine giving it up and walking away.

Somewhere past eight at night, I'm lying on the couch, staring at the ceiling when a knock sounds at the door.

Oh no, that has to be my other problem.

Gabe.

I close my eyes, wishing him away.

The knocking grows louder.

Not wanting to deal with the dilemma, I roll into the couch, smashing my face in a cushion.

"April! Open the door!" he yells, knocking the loudest yet.

I finally get off the couch and go whip open the door.

He grins at me.

His stupid, lovely grin deflates some of my anger and serves as a huge warning sign. I cannot resist this man. Those giddy bubbles that his mere presence produces rise up inside of me, even with the last hours of depression. My response makes me more depressed. Obviously, I'm nowhere near conquering my infatuation.

"I'm sleeping, not feeling well, going back to bed," I say, shutting the door.

He stops the door with his foot. "You sick?" His eyes are troubled as they roam over my wrinkled shorts and T-shirt.

"No," I sigh, not being able to lie to him. "Just in the head."

His head tilts in question.

I lean on the edge of the door. "It's about school, and I really don't want to talk about it."

"Well then," he says, pushing a bottle of wine into my hands. He picks up the pot that I gave him. "A little dinner and booze might get your mind off of it." He breezes past me.

I shut the door, none too gently, and follow him to the kitchen. "Did you hear—" I pause both speaking and moving to stare at him. He's dressed in a slick pair of designer jeans frayed with holes, a wide black belt, and a long sleeve, white button up shirt. The sides of his hair have been pulled back into a small ponytail, which should make him look like some sort of mafia douchebag, but instead it reveals his harsh lined jaw and cheekbones. Though he always looks good in his normal jeans and white T-shirts—kind of like a modern surfer James Dean—he looks good like this too, real good.

"What are you wearing?" I finally ask, stunned with his presence in my little kitchen.

"Oh, yeah, thanks for reminding me." He reaches for the top button of the shirt. "We had a photo shoot. Hate those things, but with Peyton behind the lens"—I've learned from Riley that Sam's new girlfriend Peyton works for the school newspaper and went on the summer tour with the guys—"they're not as bad as usual." He peels off the shirt to reveal a tank top.

Oh, hell no. I can't be around in him in that thing. His lean, hard muscles take up the entire kitchen. I can see the indentations of his damn six-pack through the worn material of the tank. My fingers curl with a sudden, strong want.

He holds the shirt out with one finger. "Got a hanger? It's Justin's, and would probably cost me an entire paycheck from the garage."

"Sure," I say, keeping my eyes from the sight of his body. I set the bottle of wine on the counter and take the shirt, careful not to touch his hand. I hang the shirt in the hall closet. When I come back to the kitchen, Gabe is at the stove, facing away from me.

The tattoo on the back of his neck is crossed drumsticks. Outlined and shadowed, they almost look real. Thinking of how important drumming must be to him, I'd like to touch the ink, maybe even trace the lines with my tongue.

Where the heck did that come from?

He glances over a muscled shoulder at me. "Hope you like pasta," he says with another panty melting grin before going back to stir whatever is in the pot.

I lean on the counter that encloses the kitchen, worried about my sanity. "I'm not very hungry."

"Did you already eat?" he asks in a tone that says he didn't think of the possibility.

"No."

"Then you're hungry." Without asking me, he starts searching inside the cupboards and takes out two short glasses. After setting them on the counter, he twists the cap off the bottle of wine and pours. He comes around the counter and hands me a glass.

"I'm not much of a drinker," I say, thinking that if I lose any of my inhibitions, I'm going to attack him.

He lifts his glass and clinks it with mine. "It's strawberry wine."

My brows lower. I turn the bottle around. Yup. Cheap strawberry wine. "We're not splitting that bottle," I say in a tone of disbelief.

He lowers his glass. "And why not?"

"Because...because," I sputter, taking in his sculpted chest and warm brown eyes and his sexy full upper lip. My gaze comes back to his and his expression changes from light and carefree to dark and ominous as he watches me. "It's not a good idea."

"Why not?" he demands in a silk shot tone.

"Because... " I mutter, backing away.

"Because why?" he demands, following me, staring at my outfit in an entirely different way than earlier, and definitely noticing my braless state.

I back up faster. "It's just not."

"Why?"

My back hits the wall next to the bathroom.

"Why?" This time the demand is harsh.

"Last time I drank, I hit on you!"

He comes within inches from me, his eyes blazing into mine. "What's stopping you now?"

"Um..." It's really, really hard to think with him so close.

He puts his hands on the wall, one on each side of my head. "I won't stop you," he says in a low tone that hits me in the gut. His lips hover above mine, and I'm tipsy from just his mouth and body so close.

I blink at him. "Ah..."

His eyes bore into mine.

Damn. I want him. Those eyes. Those lips. That body. I want all of him. Other people do this. All the time. Why can't I? His eyes are telling me I can. My body is telling me I should. My brain is trying to tell me something else. Lots of something elses.

He lowers his lashes and leans closer but waits.

My body yearns, definitely buzzes at his close proximity. He waits and I want him so bad, lust hits me like a gust of hot wind.

Screw my brain.

For once, I'm taking what I want, especially after all the despair of the last hours.

Leaping at him, I grab his jaw and kiss him with all the desire that's been building inside of me for over a month, and he kisses me back just as fierce. With his hands on my back, mine twisted in his hair until it's free and clutched in my hands, the kiss is long and deep and sexily messy. When we come up for air, it doesn't last long. Gabe practically slams me onto the wall and we go for round two.

I refuse to think. I just go with the sensations. The muscles under my palms. The hard body flush on mine. The taste of his lips. His hot hands on my skin. His thick desire against my stomach. His harsh breath in my mouth.

I feel wild. Uncontrollable. And free.

I feel alive.

Something I haven't felt in ages.

He kisses my jaw, my ear, my neck while my palms learn the landscape of his muscled back and hot, smooth skin. When he sucks at my neck, my response is to yank him by the waist even closer, pressing against him. At the contact, a four-letter word is huffed on my collarbone.

Then he's kissing me again, moving his hands under my shirt, skimming my ribs and breasts as he raises the shirt. He breaks the kiss to yank the shirt over my head and drops it to the floor. The wall is cool on my back as I grasp his hips to steady myself. He leans back, his gaze caressing my skin from stomach to face.

His eyes lower to watch his fingers trail around the piecing at my bellybutton. "You're so damn beautiful, it almost hurts." He continues watching his hands skim until he's cupping my breasts. "So fucking beautiful," he sighs, and that sigh hits me between the legs.

When he lowers his mouth and covers a breast, my fingers dig into his shoulders. The sensation of his mouth is amazing. My memories, mostly awkward and self-conscious, of teenage groping are nothing like this. Gabe flicking his tongue over my nipple feels right, so dang right that I groan.

Wow. His lips are magic. Everywhere. They're melting me in a pile of lust goo.

In the next second, he has my legs wrapped around his waist, his mouth on mine, and my back off the wall. His lovely, magic lips drain every last brain cell to the point that I'm startled to find myself lowered to the bed. Body humming, I wait and want with a catch of breath.

Leaning over me, Gabe raises a hand to fan out my hair above me. He drags his fingers over my ribs to my waist, then leans back into crouch, taking my shorts with him. He pauses above me, his eyes wandering over me, a sexy lock of hair almost obscuring his view.

I'm still, letting him examine me in the soft light—the only source coming from a small lamp on my dresser. Obviously, he likes to look. Slowly. My feminine pride should be screaming at being objectified, but the warmth and lust in his gaze keeps my body humming. The intensity in his eyes has my breath hitching. He leans forward, hands on my thighs, sliding up and pushing them apart. I'm not sure what is hotter, his gaze or his touch.

His eyes grow scorching as his hands slide to the top of my thighs and both his thumbs brush me. "So wet," he murmurs in a hoarse voice. "Just for me."

His touch, holy hell, his touch is hotter! My breath hitches more at both his words and his caress.

He comes back over me, hands skimming my ribs, his mouth finding a breast as fingers slide into me.

"Ahhhhha," Comes out of me in a scale of awkward notes.

His mouth and hands play my body like an instrument, and I do lose my mind, twisting and turning and thrashing in the messy bed. I grip and pull at his shoulders, astounded at the response he gets from my body, astounded that I can feel so much passion, so much want. Dry, boring me, on fire. Though I'd like to stay under his touch forever, it doesn't take long before I'm melting into the tangled sheets and gasping into the room. Opening my eyes, I'm not surprised to find him watching me.

I do surprise him—if the slight widening of his eyes is an indication—by tugging at his tank. "Take it off," I demand in a hoarse voice. I'm done with the wanting. I've become determined to have it all.

Though his face stays intense, a cocky grin curls his mouth as he pushes up on his knees and sheds the shirt in one quick swoop.

"The pants too," I say in a low tone, drinking in lean, hard muscle, my fingers itching to touch.

His gaze narrows as he flicks open the buttons.

Button fly jeans. Hot, hot, hot. Thank you jean makers somewhere in the world.

My mouth turns dry as he stands at the end of the bed, shedding both pants and boxers, then plucking out a condom from his wallet.

Like him, I revel in the naked sight in front of me. He's beautiful long, lean, sculpted muscle from shoulder to thighs, and his evident desire for me…marvelous. I haven't seen a penis in the flesh since— well, never, and it seems that I've been missing out. On a lot.

He rolls on the condom—and whoa, him holding himself is so hot that my toes curl in the sheets—then he kneels back on the bed over me, and my heart and lust go into overdrive.

This is happening. Now. I'm having sex. With Gabe.

Amazing. Incredible. Insane.

My hands grip his biceps. Oh, how I want this, have secretly wanted it for longer than I'd admit, even to myself. And now it's finally happening.

He settles over me, his hands on each side of my head, the tip of him sliding between my legs, making me musically gasp once more.

"Do that again," he demands in a hoarse voice, sliding over me, and without trying my throat complies. "Damn," he hisses. "I could probably come at just the sound you make."

He kisses me hard and fast before positioning himself at my center. I drag in an anxious breath and lift my hips. Closing his eyes, he plunges forward.

"Ahhh…owww," escapes me in a long wail at the burning sensation. My nails dig into the skin of his arms. I'm not a total idiot. I knew it was going to hurt, but after so much pleasure, the pain is foreign.

Gabe braces himself above me. "What the hell, April?" he says harshly. "You're a—a virgin?" His tone makes the world foul.

Wiggling my butt, hoping to find an angle of relief, I wince instead of answer.

"Fuck!" He shakes his head as his arms begin to tremble. "We can't do this." He shakily pushes up.

I wrap my legs around him, ignoring the pain. "I want this. I've wanted this. Don't stop."

The skin along his cheekbones tightens as he draws in a deep breath. "Okay, okay," he says, and I'm not sure if he's talking to me or to himself. "I'll try to take it slow." He draws in another gulp of air and gently lowers himself.

Besides the fact that the pain has dimmed, I'm ready for the burning throb as he moves within me. I keep my breath even as he lowers himself on his elbows and takes my face in his palms.

For several long seconds, he studies me in the dim light, his expression filled with wonder. Finally, he kisses me, slow and sweet and intense. When he begins moving again, the pain is a back note to all the other sensations. The length of his skin aligned with mine. The heat of him. The incredible slide of him inside of me. I'm caught between the passion and the wondrous sense of being this close to someone. I never imagined it would be this intimate. In this moment, it feels like he knows me. I know him. Every little piece.

I open my eyes to find him watching me. Strain and concern etch his face. The concern brings a soft smile to my mouth. He releases a relief filled groan, then lowers his head and slides a hand between my legs. With his mouth on my breast and his fingers moving between us, I can't concentrate on the lovely intimacy. The building passion takes over once again. The pain is just a small nuisance as I grip his back, raise my hips, and follow the pounding rhythm he sets until I unravel beneath him, sighing out another long music like breath, my thighs clamping around him.

"Fuck!" he whispers, his mouth over my heart, his body shuddering, his clutch on my shoulders tight.

I wrap my arms around him and bask in the intimacy of him orgasming in and above me.

He lays there breathing hard for over a minute, then pushes up, his eyes fiercer than ever. "What the—why wouldn't you...how the hell were you still a virgin?" he demands in a harsh tone.

Chapter 20
April

"Well, ah…" I say, trying to collect my thoughts, while becoming hurt he isn't on the same cloud nine I am.

Suddenly, a loud blaring horn sounds from inside the apartment. For a split second, we stare in surprise and confusion at one another. Gabe is the first to realize what is going on and scrambles out of bed. Finally understanding the blare is coming from the smoke detector, I quickly wrap a sheet around myself and follow.

The blare of the detector grows as I get in the main apartment.

In the kitchen, inside a cloud of smoke, naked Gabe has the pasta pan under running water in the sink. I get the broom from the side of the stove and knock the alarm down from the ceiling, keeping a tight grip on the sheet. With the loud blare gone, the smoke hanging in the air becomes the next major annoyance. After tightening my hold on the sheet, I open the door and with one hand on the broom, fan air outside.

I'm still fanning air out when Gabe, wearing just his jeans, comes into the living room. "Here let me," he says, taking the broom.

I rush off to the bedroom and slip on a pair of yoga pants and a T-shirt. Back in the main apartment, the smoke has dispersed to a slight haze and a strong, burnt smell hangs in the air. The door is closed but Gabe is opening the window above the bookshelves.

The pan of burnt food lies in the kitchen sink full of water and burnt gunk. Knowing Gabe's huge appetite, I go to the fridge. The idea of cooking seems refreshingly normal after the lustful bizarreness of the evening.

"You like omelets?" I ask over my shoulder.

"You don't have to cook for me, April. Especially after...I...ah, burned a pan of pasta on your stove." His tone is harsh. I read his underlining thought, *and took your virginity.*

I keep piling stuff on the counter. "It's not a big deal. They're easy to make, and you haven't had dinner." I get a cutting board, a knife, a bowl, and a pan. I'm trying to stay busy, not dissect what happened between us in bed. I want to dissect that later. Alone.

He comes into the little kitchen. "Just let me order something in."

"This is healthier," I say in a tense tone, unwrapping a carton of mushrooms. I concentrate on my task, not the chaotic emotions beating through my head.

He steps next to me. "Let me do it then."

Apparently, the loss of my hymen has made me an invalid. "Gabe—"

"Sit down," he says roughly. "You are not cooking."

His tone and the hard lines of his face, tell me arguing is futile. I go sit on a stool at the counter, fuming a bit at his control.

Gabe brings the cutting board over to the peninsula, pours me a glass of wine, and begins slicing mushrooms. Becoming more irate by the second, I glare at him, then the wine. Well, that pill has already been swallowed. I take a large gulp. It's awful.

He clears his throat and glances up. "So…why me? Why now? Why wouldn't you have told me before? I—what the hell, April?" he repeats in the same tone as he did in bed less than an hour ago, hacking a mushroom to mush.

I gulp more sickly sweet wine down instead of lashing out at him.

He pauses chopping to stare at me. "April—"

"Stop it!" I blurt, smacking a hand on the counter. "You're ruining it! It was passionate and spontaneous and wonderful. Quit trying to label it with regret." I pick up the wine bottle. "I don't and won't regret it."

Apparently collecting his thoughts, he stares at me. Ignoring him, I fill my glass to the brim, hoping that the wine will moderate my ire. He pushes away from the counter, then comes around the corner to take my jaw in his hands. Worry lines his features.

"It was more than wonderful and spontaneous and passionate." He lightly kisses me. "It was—you were amazing and hot and mind blowing." He kisses me again. "Better than I'd ever imagined, and I have been imagining." Another soft kiss follows. "I'm sorry. I don't mean to be an asshole. Anger is always my first response." His thumbs caress my skin before he releases his hold on my face. "It was just a shock finding out about your lack of experience in the middle of my mind being blown by you."

All warm and fuzzy from his descriptions, I can only nod at his apology.

He goes back around the counter and pours some of the wine in his glass, then smiles at me, raising the glass. "To sharing a bottle of shitty strawberry wine."

I clink my glass with his, though the list is kind of mute at this point. I got the interview, but I don't want to talk about that mess right now. The reminder of it has me taking another sip of wine.

Gabe starts cutting a red pepper, his strong hands moving methodically as he cuts.

His apology and sudden patience prompt me to share a bit. "I only had two boyfriends in high school. One for about two months of freshman year, and the other for half of junior year. Perhaps if that relationship had continued…" I watch the pepper become a pile of diced cubes as I reach for the bottle of wine. "I had other hobbies, so boys and relationships were always second."

"What about Romeo?"

I snap up. His eyes stay fastened on the pepper he's cutting, but from his tone, I get the sense that he has thought about me being with Romeo a lot. I suppose his assumption that the relationship was sexual is natural.

"Romeo and I were never—there wasn't a spark there." I take a long drink then set the glass down with a clunk, recalling how much Romeo reminds me of my father. That should have been my first clue that things wouldn't work. "We get along so well, I think we both expected a lot more than we got. At first, we both chalked up the awkward goodnight kisses as something that would pass as we got more comfortable." I shake my head at the memory, and my openness—I'd say it's the wine but being with Gabe brings out my honesty. "They didn't, and although hanging out together was fun, we did not connect romantically, at all. Eventually, we decided to just hang out."

He pauses cutting an onion in half to smirk at me. "So I give you that spark?"

My lids lower. "Apparently."

He smirks wider before concentrating on slicing the onion. "Since high school you've only dated Romeo?" he asks a touch of incredulity in his tone.

I shrug. "I've been on a few other dates, but college has always been about my future and career instead of partying or dating."

He chops with a precision that conveys he knows his way around a kitchen. "What were these hobbies that kept you from being a normal boy crazed teenage girl?" He pushes the onions into a neat pile next to the mushrooms and peppers.

"Lots of stuff."

"Like?"

"Like music," I say, deciding it's really not a big deal if he knows I can play.

He pauses cracking an egg at the edge of a bowl. "That guitar in you room?"

"Yeah," I say, my grip tensing around the glass.

He starts beating the egg whites with a fork. "You should play me something. You have to play something for me."

"I don't play anymore," I say stiffly.

"Never?"

"Never."

"Why?"

"Because I don't." My tone is icy, but I can't help it. The reason is off limits. Even in my head. For my own sanity.

He takes a long swing of wine, then cuts butter into the pan and turns on the stove.

"You were good?" he asks, grabbing a spatula.

"I don't want to talk about it." The words come out embarrassingly like a plea.

He glances over his shoulder at me.

I look at the counter, at the bright, red rings from the wine and force my mind away from the memories he is bringing up.

When I glance up, he is adding the yolks to the bowl. I take a long gulp of the strawberry wine. Only a teenager would dream of drinking this horrid stuff, but it is making my head feel deliciously light, after all the emotion over the last few days, and especially the last few hours.

Gabe rims the pan with the spatula.

"How'd you learn to cook?"

"My dad cooked at work. He didn't like coming home and doing it." He drops veggies into the center of the pan. "Learned by necessity, and eggs are cheap."

I don't like thinking about his childhood. It angers me, and because my head is starting to feel like a wad of cotton, I decide to watch him cook. I like watching him. The precise way he moves. The intensity of his gaze while he concentrates. The masculine perfection of him. I sigh, putting my jaw in my hand. He is just so lovely.

I take another drink of wine. It's actually not that bad, just sort of bad.

Gabe continues cooking, his muscles moving, his face stoic with concentration, and his movements so meticulous, I wonder in another life, one where he wasn't raised with his father, if he could have had a future in some sport, or maybe the wine in me wonders such things. He adds cheese and flips the omelet over before cutting it in half and serving it on two plates. My eyes are on the huge portion as he sits next to me since the small dining table is covered with notes for my upcoming poster board presentation, handing me a fork.

"It looks awesome, but I can't eat all of that."

"Then I'll finish it," he says, pouring a bit of wine in his glass, then finishing the bottle off in mine.

With an off kilter nod, I dig the fork in and take a bite. Wow. Best food ever. "This kicks my would-have-made-omelet's butt."

Chewing, he grins closed mouthed at me.

I take another bite. Delicious. "How'd you get it so fluffy?"

He takes a sip of wine. "Beat the whites, then fold in the yolks. Saw it on some cooking show once like at three in the morning on PBS—no cable at my house—or some shit and it stuck with me."

It's quiet for several long minutes as we both stuff in food. Me like a caveman, him slow and meticulous.

"What else can you cook?" I ask, during a breath of air, not food, thinking of inviting him over more, just to cook, unless…

He taps his fork on the edge of the plate. "Meatloaf, chicken and rice, goulash, homemade mac and cheese, butter and noodles, sloppy joes…cheap shit. My dad tended to spend more on beer than food."

"Hmm…" Whenever he talks about his dad, I want to punch something—like his dad's face—especially after more than half a of bottle of crap wine. I concentrate on cutting another piece of the best omelet I ever ate, while mumbling, "Your dad is an asshole."

Surprisingly, Gabe laughs. "He is."

"And that's funny?" I ask, gawking at his laughing mouth.

He shakes his head. "Don't think I've ever heard you swear."

"Ah, my mother drilled that into me, expected me to act like a lady—her vague yet extensive scale." I wave my hand in exaggeration at the last word, forgetting there is a large chunk of food on my fork. I drop the piece of omelet on myself. Half goes down my shirt, the other half rolls across my shirt and onto the floor.

Now I laugh. "Oh, I think I'm a bit tipsy." I stand and try to shake the food out of my shirt. "And greasy," I add, scrunching my nose at the sensation of slimy bits across my front.

Laughing again, Gabe bends to pick the pieces off the floor. "Go clean up. I'll get this."

Grossed out, I nod, then rush to the bathroom. Tipsy and uncoordinated—I'm like a mix of exhausted and buzzed—it takes me two tries to get my shirt off. I almost fall over, removing my pants. Afraid I might break something, like an arm, I take a shower slash bath sitting and kneeling on the bottom of the tub, gripping my body wash and body scrubber. It takes forever to put on my robe that always hangs behind the door, and longer to brush my teeth. When did getting toothpaste out of a tube become challenging?

I practically stumble out of the bathroom into my bedroom, but stop short in the doorway at the sight of Gabe sitting on my bed.

"Hey," he says, standing. "I was getting worried you passed out or something worse in there."

"Ha," I reply in a wince because he's not that far off. "Um...you staying or something?" I blurt, confused about him in my bedroom.

Almost to me, he stops and runs a hand through his hair. "Well, I've been drinking and... I don't know. I—I just want to hold you." He says the last sentence like it's being torn from him.

I want to roll my eyes. I'm guessing he feels guilty. Men and the prized gift of virginity. Yet, even using the door frame to hold myself up—beyond the wine, I'm guessing stress, and probably sex, has me bone tired—I somehow realize that showing my irritation would not be a good idea. And though the idea of sleeping with him feels weird, I also find it intriguing. I've never slept the whole night with anyone.

"Okay," I say, and push into the room. Gabe grabs an arm and helps me to the edge of the bed.

"Got an extra toothbrush?" he asks as I plop down.

I try to think. The image in my head of my bathroom drawer is empty. I'm not very good at thinking right now. "Just use mine."

By the time, I realize the bed has been made, tug back the covers, and somehow stick my feet and legs between the sheets, he is back helping me and fluffing pillows behind me.

Oh, for frickssake.

I lay back, keeping a calm face. After removing his pants, Gabe slides under the covers, curling his arms around me, turning me halfway over, and molding his body to the back of mine. Well what do I know? Nothing. Because this is not weird. It's marvelous. It's cozy. It's intimate. I like it.

I like it a lot.

I lay there full of tired, buzzed wonderment until a startling concept has me halfway awake. Maybe I like it so much because it's Gabe, the angry drummer I've recently become friends with, who I'm starting to respect and really, really like. And now he's acting all weird because I was a virgin. Although the sex was surprisingly wonderful, and I really, really wouldn't mind—actually would love —doing it again, I don't want to lose him as a friend.

My hands grip the arm around my waist. "Gabe?"

"Hmm?" The sound is a breath on my shoulder.

"I…I don't want tonight to change anything. I want to stay friends. Just like we've been. Okay?" I ask in heavy whisper.

There are several seconds of silence. Finally, he says, "Yeah, okay."

Relieved, I whisper, "Goodnight," then fall asleep imagining his arms tightening around me and his face burying into my shoulder.

Chapter 21
April

I promised myself that I'd never wear a tiara again.

Yet here I am, my head sparkling, entering an old theater, heading toward the bar, next to Marilyn Monroe—Chloe. Heads turn. Lots of male heads. More for Marilyn, but several check out Audrey Hepburn—me—too.

The venue for the Halloween bash is near Detroit, almost two hours south of where we all live. It's a big venue. A venue that Luminescent Juliet has played for the last two years, which is why Shush got the job, basically from Romeo's recommendation. In the mist of cutting another album and working out a record deal, Luminescent Juliet passed on playing the usual gig, but every member is here to see Shush, and we're all staying in a hotel less than a mile away.

I'm sharing a room with Chloe, Riley's best friend. I would have preferred my own room—nothing against Chloe, I'm just used to being alone—but she needed someone to split the bill with since Riley is staying with a band member. Of course, she brought costumes—Riley told her to. And of course, in the midst of all my drama, I forgot to bring my own.

I'm dressed as Holly Golightly from *Breakfast at Tiffany's*. Tight black dress, pearls around my neck, long black gloves, and hair in a ridiculous bouffant twisted into a bun topped with, yes, a tiara. Chloe's choice, definitely not mine. Much, much too attention getting.

Chloe winks at a guy gaping at her chest as we pass.

Well, at least not that attention getting.

Everyone else is here already. According to Chloe and her text from Peyton, they're about halfway into the crowd on the left. The section roped off near the stage isn't big enough to fit all of us. Once we get our drinks—gin and tonic for Chloe and a Sprite for me—we head off into the crowd.

Loud conversation, the Door's "People are Strange," and an excited buzz fills the room as I follow Marilyn. But the noise stays faintly in the background because I'm filled with a nervous buzz. I haven't seen Gabe since the night we slept together. When I woke yesterday morning, he was gone, leaving a quickly jotted note on my counter. *Had to get to work. Still owe you a real dinner. Your friend, Gabe.* The 'your friend' had bothered me to the point it turned into a conundrum. Had he wrote it to indulge me? Or was it meant sarcastically? After agonizing over it for most of the day, I texted him that evening with, *Everything's okay, right?* About half an hour later, he texted back a mere, *Yeah, everything is fine,* which did little to ease my apprehension. I'm totally oblivious about how to act after…well, sex with a friend. Now, with my stomach in knots, I'm heading toward him.

We step onto the main floor, then head to the left, squeezing between people as Chloe flashes them a sultry smile and pushed up cleavage encased in a white flowy dress.

Allie, dressed as a pirate, is the first to spot us. She waves frantically. Next to her, Justin is also dressed as a pirate. Peyton and Sam are dressed up as Princess Leia and Han Solo. And at the back of their group, leaning on the rail between the sections, are Romeo and Gabe, both in their normal attire, jeans, boots, and open button ups over plain T-shirts. Well, Romeo is wearing a bandana pirate style on his head, along with bigger silver hops in his ears than he normally wears. His form of dressing up for Riley. Both holding beers, they're in the midst of a conversation as Chloe and I join the group. The whistles and cheers from everyone as we get to the group brings Gabe's gaze in our direction.

His eyes widen on me, but Allie wraps me in a hug. "You look amazing!" she yells in my ear.

"Thanks!" I yell back, trying very, very hard not to glance Gabe's way, wondering—hoping like an idiot—if he's staring. "You look awesome too!" And she does in a leather bustier that shows off the blue swirling tattoo that winds around most of her left arm.

Blonde Princess Leia—Peyton—clinks her plastic cup with mine, but before she says anything, a ripple of noise trickles through the crowd. It sounds like a mix of awe and excitement.

We all turn toward the stage as the sound grows.

The members of Shush are taking the stage. Except for the singer who wears a long white ragged dress, they're all dressed in torn black clothes from tights to tattered up tank tops. Their faces are pale, while their eyes are hollowed with black make up, giving them all a ghoulish appearance. I'm guessing they're supposed to be zombies until Riley hits the cymbal and the guitar player breaks into the opening riff. It takes me a few moments to recognize Rob Zombie's "Living Dead Girl." The crowd goes wilder when the singer hits the refrain, understanding the costumes. The song isn't super heavy on drums, so Riley adds several stick twirls.

Though caught in the band's performance and the crowd's enthusiasm, Gabe's presence behind us won't let me release the edge of apprehension, especially as Shush rolls through the same set they did at the bar and U-Palooza. The familiarity of it has my brain wandering to the man behind me.

I'm being an idiot. He said everything was okay. Yet it doesn't seem okay. In between songs, I talk with the girls around me, while Gabe stays in the back, three people over. It's like he's ignoring me. Or I'm ignoring him. I feel middle schoolish. I want to strangle myself with the pearls around my neck. But even logic can't keep my nerves at bay.

Shush close out their set with "Crush" by Garbage, which is another song that is a perfect fit for the night. Especially the line, *I would die for you.* Since the beat is a touch slower than most of their other choices, the band stays with Riley for the entire song too. And the singer's tendency toward strong and loud vocals works perfectly with the song.

The crowd goes crazy when they finish and say good night. Whistles, claps, and shouts for more go on for several minutes. Fortunately for Shush—they probably don't have anything else ready to play—there are two more bands scheduled for the night, and a bunch of stagehands come out immediately and start changing over the stage. The Pixies "Where is My Mind" comes over the loud speaker and people start moving toward the bar and bathroom.

"Need another?" Justin asks loudly, lifting his empty beer.

I shake my head. "I'm good."

Everyone but Gabe, Romeo, and I head for the bar at the back of the theater.

Romeo grins at me. "How'd Chloe get you to wear that?"

I can't help a frown. "Remember? Riley practically begged I dress up."

He gestures to his head. "Me too."

"Yeah, well I forgot to bring something simple, and Chloe brought several costumes. This"—I sweep a hand down—"was the least revealing."

"Then," Gabe says in a cool tone. "I'd like to see what else she brought."

Romeo looks between us as my eyebrows rise. I ignore him, watching Gabe take a sip of his beer, his top lip over the plastic rim, and suddenly I'm remembering every kiss and touch from two nights ago. Quick flashes—his lips dragging over my skin, a moan in my ear, him above me—blink in my head, turn the nerves in my stomach to those bizarre fluttering butterflies. Ignoring my reaction to him, I lightly say, "Feel free to check out our closet."

His eyes narrow and though he doesn't say it, I read his mind. *I want to check them out on you.* He forces a smile. "Something I could wear then?"

The forced smile hits me hard. Everything is not okay. I can sense it. Tension hangs in the air between us, even dims the lustful memoires hanging at the back of my mind. "Um…" I stall, wanting to ask him what is wrong, why he looks on the edge of angry, and what I did to get this frost that seems to shoot out at me.

Romeo clears his throat, but before he can make a comment, which I'm sure would be totally asinine, Riley appears, jumping on him in a leggy embracing tackle.

Both Gabe and I look away as they hotly kiss.

Seconds later, everyone returns, including the rest of Shush. I stay on the perimeter amid the congratulations and cheering. In between the cheering, Riley comes over and twirls me around, exclaiming that Chloe out did herself. Chloe beams. But there isn't time for much else because people from the crowd come over, recognizing the opening band and wanting to get in on their tiny slice of fame for the night until the next band comes out.

When the next band does come out, everyone's back to hip rocking, head bouncing, and arm swaying concert going robots. The band is loud, fast, and on the edge of heavy metal. They also border on sucking, but the half-drunk, wild crowd loves them.

Of course, the singer of Shush is all over Gabe again, but now the bassist is hanging on his other side. At each smile, each hip rub, each touch, I see out of the corner of my eye, I want to rip the women away from him. A dark, angry coil of jealously wraps around me. My gloved hand nearly crushes the empty plastic cup in my grasp. I shouldn't feel this way. I have no right to feel this way, but as Riley, Allie, and Peyton sway with their boyfriends, I'm suddenly jealous of practically everyone surrounding me.

The poorly played music and shouting singer grate on my ears. The flashing lights are irritating. The Shush guitarist swaying closer and closer to me—after he hit on Chloe, who likes to flirt but is quite committed to her boyfriend—has my skin crawling. In a rush to get away from everything—mostly my ugly jealousy—I whip around and start pushing through the crowd. Since the music is also too loud at the back of the theater, I go into the lobby.

Standing to the side amid empty plastic cups on the floor, I simply draw in deep breaths for several minutes. The taut line of my body finally loosens and the pounding jealousy reduces, but lingers. When I try to get myself to go back in the theater, my feet refuse to move. The thought of seeing Gabe with those women brings on an anger and dejection that borders on overwhelming.

I'm turning into a complete mess. Nothing is making sense. Gabe and I are supposed to be friends but it seems in the blink of an orgasm our friendship has changed, and even I can't handle my emotions.

I turn toward the entrance. I wanted to leave early. Guess I'm leaving extra early.

At the coat check, I'm digging out the ticket from inside my left glove as Gabe comes up to me.

"What the hell? You leaving?" The question comes out from a sneer.

I concentrate hard on appearing unruffled. Plucking out the ticket, I shrug. "It's late. I'm tired. I really only came to see Riley's band."

He crosses his arms. "Thought we all came to see the band and hang out."

I hand the ticket over the table to the attendant watching us. "I'm not much for hanging out." It comes out snottier than I intended, given that I wanted to say hanging on people.

"Too good for us?" he sneers again.

My brows lower. I'd like to wipe that sneer off his face. "You still going there? Grow up," I huff.

The guy across the counter holds my ticket, watching us.

Face stern, Gabe gestures to my head. "Can see why you choose that outfit, Princess."

"You forgot ice," I say through clenched teeth.

"I sure fucking did," he says, his lips curling into a snarl.

"Why are you being such a jerk?" I snap.

His entire face becomes a sneer. "Maybe because you're being a cold ass, uppity bitch."

My mouth drops open, closes, and opens again. Tears threaten the corner of my eyes. "Get my coat!" I grind out to the attendant, who appears as slacked jawed as me. Next, I turn my fury on the person who induced my rage. My gloved finger taps on his chest. "You are a cold ass, slutty bitch! Two days ago you were with me, even spent the night! Tonight you were flirting with two women right in front of me. Slut!" I angrily repeat and continue tapping his chest.

After staring at me in open mouth wonderment, Gabe grabs my hand, pressing it to his chest. "You're jealous."

"Not," I say, tugging at my hand.

The attendant comes back, holding out my short jacket. I didn't know I'd be going to the concert in a dress. Gabe grabs it and yanks me by the hand to the other side of the room.

"Let me go," I hiss. "He needs a tip."

Gabe draws me closer until I'm inches from him.

"You're jealous." His tone is full of fact.

"It was disrespectful," I counter.

"You're jealous," he repeats, this time the slightest grin curving his lips.

"It's natural to be hurt by your carousing so soon after the fact," I tactfully argue.

"You're jealous and pissed." His tone is full of wonder.

"Your flirting made me feel cheap."

"Super fucking jealous."

"Like the only thing between us was a one night stand."

The smirk on his lips dies and he grabs me by the upper arms. My coat falls to the floor. His face creases with tension. "What do you want from me, April?" he demands, his face inches from mine.

Confused by the plea in his eyes, I look down at his chest. "I don't know."

"Because the other night you begged to be just friends," he says harshly.

His bitter tone has me blurting, "What do you want?"

"I don't know either." His grip tightens on my arms. "I...this started because I needed to feel—in control, but then, well, I liked being with you"—this warms me up, even with his tight grip on my arms—"and I do want to be friends."

I try to yank out of his grasp. "Is this how you treat friends?"

He lets go of my arms and takes a step back hitting the wall. "No." He bumps the back of his head on the wall. Twice. "But then I don't have a shit load of friends."

"Me either. That's why I'm not very good at this. I've heard that—that sex can mess everything up, and I don't want it to mess us up." I let out a sigh. "I'm pretty sure it is." I go to bend for my coat, but he beats me to it.

Sighing, he holds my coat for me to get into. "I encouraged those two to flirt with me. I was hoping you would get jealous. But I don't want anything to do with them."

Putting an arm into a sleeve, I blink at him. "Why? Why would you do that?"

He looks away. "I—girls like you tend to use guys like me."

With all the uppity, preppy comments he has made in the past, it doesn't take much for me to figure out what he means by girls like you. "I'm not like that. The other night…things just seemed to happen."

"I know you're different, but it's hard for me to accept. And maybe—no, tonight when things felt weird, cold," he elaborates, "between us I just…when you asked to be friends, I assumed that was the reason."

He draws in a deep breath and it becomes obvious he is forcing himself to explain. That he believes I deserve an explanation, even though it appears to be torture for him, helps me empathize with his twisted view. He expects to be used and treated like crap because obviously he has been in the past. After being told physically by his father that he is nothing for years—and probably verbally—it's easy for me to understand his fear. My heart weeps and beats—that he is confused about us as I am—for him.

My fingers find his jaw and turn his gaze from the floor to meet mine. "I meant it. I want to be friends. Still mean it. It's not that I don't…"—I need him to understand that I think he is more than good enough for me—"couldn't imagine wanting something more from you."

In reality, touching him, glimpsing the conflict and hurt in his eyes, I want him with a fierceness that frightens me, and it's not just the sex, although I want that too. I want to know everything about this man, his past, his dreams, what's in his glove box, his favorite bands, his …just everything. I've never felt this way about anyone. And the depth of my want scares me. Even though I've been more honest with him than I've been with anyone in a long, long time, I'm hiding my scars. And they're not like his.

I deserve mine.

I drop my hand and my gaze. "Even if—well, I don't think either of us are emotionally ready for anything other than friendship. We're both messed up, and you need to stay focused on music right now and controlling your temper, and I need to stay focused on my education." I finally look at him. "Being friends is really for the best…"

He studies me for a long, uncomfortable silence, perhaps recognizing I'm withdrawing into my shell and debating on calling me out. A tremble fills my insides. Outside, I'm motionless, hoping he'll let me retreat. I'm not ready to dissect whatever is going on between us. My brain needs to catch up with my emotions.

He finally says, "You don't have to go because of me."

And my hope wins. I shake my head. "I have to get up at five to get back by eight. Someone is covering my shift at the Family Center until then."

"Can't take a day off?"

"Not usually, plus Romeo is taking the day off."

He lets out a sigh. "You have to wait for the shuttle?"

I nod, digging in my glove for a tip.

"Then I'll wait with you."

"You don't have to."

"You're not waiting outside by yourself," he says in a stern tone.

I resist rolling my eyes, give the coat attendant a tip, and let Gabe follow me outside.

We talk about safe things as we wait in the cool night air. How school is going for me, how the new album is coming together for Luminescent Juliet, how his new apartment is coming along, and other mundane items while we wait. The hotel shuttle is supposed to come around to the venue about every forty minutes. Luckily for Gabe and me, it comes within fifteen minutes. Or else all the tension and want floating in the air between us may have unraveled into something that would make a bigger mess. I somehow keep my emotions—that seem to be all over the place—at bay during our trite conversation.

As the shuttle pulls up, Gabe moves closer to me. "I'm sorry for being an ass, April." He lets out a puff of fog from a deep breath. "And yeah, being friends is probably the best for us."

I force a close-lipped smile and nod. "Sorry for losing it too." I step around him, but say over my shoulder, "See you at group."

And then I'm in the bus, swallowing and trying hard not to cry.

Oddly, it feels like I just lost something that I didn't want to let go.

Chapter 22
Gabe

I try not to think about her, but she comes to me at night in dreams or during mindless activities—like breaking down a carburetor or when I'm practicing some song that I've played for ages. The floral scent of her hair, the soft feel of her body, the depth of her aqua eyes, the curve of her cheek, the sweetness of her smile…fucking silly, romantic things that I've never thought about a woman before. They assault me at the oddest times.

Yet in group, as she sits quietly across from me, it's impossible not to think of her. Her presence looms no matter where I look. The other idiots in group have become shadows. April sucks up all my vision. Like right now as Jeff drones on, she stares at her hands. I know this even as I stare at the floor, because for every second of group, I'm completely aware of her every move. I was hyper aware of her from the moment I joined group, but lately I'm consumed with her for the entire hour.

It's been over two weeks since we slept together, weeks of wishing it never happened because I'm addicted. At the same time I'm wishing for more that should never be. She's right. After life with my pop, I'm fucked up to the point that I can never be twisted back into right. And while I'm more screwed up than her, she's depressed, or maybe guilt ridden for some idiotic reason, over her cousin's suicide to the point of obsession. She carries it with her like a hidden badge that shines between the layers of polite perfection if you can get close enough to look.

And I've gotten close. Too close.

Besides all of that fuckery, the mere idea of seriously being with someone like April fills me with an unfamiliar anxiety. My past girlfriends, chosen for their empty minds and open homes—the more I could be away from my father the better—never expected much, other than lots of attention. *You're hot, hot, hot. You make me want to fuck, fuck, fuck.* And yeah, she does that to me too. More than any of the ones before her. Shit, just peering across the circle at her has me rearing to go. But in those quiet moments of day to day life, my subconscious dares to imagine more.

Me.

Having a real relationship.

With her.

As if fucking possible.

Like my pop would say, *Shit for brains, Gabe.*

Pissed that I'm in this predicament, I need to get over her. Learn how to deal with it. Move on. Maybe and truly just be friends.

Fortunately, these last few weeks have been busy. The band has become a writing and practicing machine, rehearsing four times a week and almost six hours the last two Saturdays. We have two recording sessions coming over the next two months. One over Thanksgiving break and one after Christmas. Romeo is determined to finish out college, Sam wants to also—just not as bad—and Justin doesn't give a shit. The rest of us have to follow Romeo's lame ass schedule so he can get what he wants, a degree. Therefore, we're cramming practice in between school schedules, work, and my fucking never-ending therapy, which keeps me busy—while the want of April hovers like a desolate ghost lodged in the back of my head—most of the time.

But here in group, my obsessed mind can't get away from her.

Once Jeff finishes his wrap up and excuses group, April and I are in the parking lot sharing our usual nonsense about day to day things—or more precisely pretending to be friends. While we talk about bullshit, I plan to drop the bomb. The bomb that is the first step toward mending our friendship. And maybe mending her.

Somewhere along the way, I truly began to care about April, so much that my care is a tight knot in my chest that I carry throughout the day and sleep with at night. My own little coil of April anxiety. I want to help her get over her crippling sadness, free her from the guilt that is holding her back, and loosen that knot so maybe I can at least sleep.

"Hey, can I talk to you for a few?" I ask, keeping my tone level as we veer toward her car.

"Ah…I believe we are talking right now," she says, her smile a touch sardonic.

Damn. She's so beautiful it hurts to look at her sometimes. "About something important."

Her brows rise a bit, but she nods as we come to her car.

"So the band's going to L.A. over break." Her expression turns confused as she hits unlock on her key chain. My feet shuffle as I concentrate on a way to explain my idea. "And I was wondering if, well, we fly out on Friday, but if you were going to miss class on Monday or Tuesday, you could fly out on Wednesday. Plus we don't have group that week either."

She leans back, staring at me with wide eyes. "Why would I fly out?"

"Shit," I say, thinking my dad is right. I can't do a damn thing correctly. "I'm not explaining this very good. I emailed that actor, the one your cousin wanted to meet."

Her pretty winged brows shoot up. "And he agreed to meet?"

"Not yet, but he will."

She blinks at me, then slowly asks, "Why are you so sure?"

"Told him we wanted to interview him for a video."

She pauses, her hand above the door handle—her escape. "What video? Romeo agreed to let Michael Thomas in your video?"

"No. It's just an interview." I lean a hip on the door, stopping her from opening it.

"Thomas will be pissed when nothing comes of it."

I shrug. "Don't care what some washed up teeny bopper actor thinks."

"Um..."

"Do you seriously care what this guy thinks?"

"Well, no, but it's rude..."

"Never know, maybe we will use him. Anyway, we all have our own rooms for once. Sam said I can stay with him, so you can have your own room. I mean…"—fuck, I do not want her thinking I'm hitting on her, that's not what this is about—"I'm not trying to set something up with you. I just—you just—the list is almost done. You should finish it."

She searches my gaze with her conflicted one. "I don't need to finish the list, Gabe. My interview for the clinical program is right after Thanksgiving. Jeff gave a good report and Dr. Medina recommended me weeks ago. Once this semester is over, I'll be done with group too."

I bend closer, almost over her. "You should finish the list for you."

She looks past me, drawing in a visible breath. "I—"

"And for me. I think I need closure on that fucker," I add, like the dickhead that I am hoping to sway her with my needs.

Her expression becomes more conflicted.

I stand up. "Just think about it. I can get your plane ticket."

Her eyes grow huge. "You don't have to do that!"

"Think about it." I turn toward my car, but say over my shoulder, "I'll text you in a few days."

I don't look back, and by the time I get to my car, she's gone.

Gone. Gone. Gone.

The way it should be.

But I still feel like punching my hood.

Chapter 23
April

I haven't been to California in almost three years. I Skype with my father once a month, but I've used school as an excuse not to visit. There is no escape from music with him. It's in my face twenty four seven whenever I visit. Yet Gabe's plea that I finish the list for him swayed me more than any of his other arguments. However, I didn't want to take his room or be trapped with him for five days. It would be too much for my emotions and hormones.

Of course, my father was thrilled when I asked him if I could come for Thanksgiving. Of course, he picked me up from the airport. Of course, we're at his house. He has always been more of a teacher or a friend, but my father cares for me deeply. My mother is not happy. She expected me for Thanksgiving. That I'm staying with my father has her quite upset. Yet Gabe's plea hit me harder than even her persistence.

So here I am at my father's house in Malibu, standing next to a grand piano overlooking the sunlight ocean, as he makes me a latte on his imported machine in the kitchen. The waves roll in, the piano beckons, the sound of cream being steamed sounds. Unable to resist, I lay my fingers on the cool wood of the piano at the far end, away from the keys. Though silent, I imagine the instrument humming for me.

My father holds a cup in front of me and nods at the piano. "Would you like me to play something for you?"

No! I take the cup. This is why I've stayed away. I don't want to hurt him. Turning my back on music is like turning my back on him. I can't hurt him, so I can do this. I will do this. At least it's not a damn guitar.

"Sure, please," I say and take the cup, my hands faintly shaking.

He looks at me oddly for a long second, then sits on the bench. I imagine him flipping out the tails of a suit coat, clearing his throat, and raising his hands over the keys in a pretentious fashion. Instead his hands find the keys with a subtle poise, and instead of a tuxedo he wears worn jeans and a faded T-shirt. And rather than crazy gray hair flopping as he plays, his brown hair is short with only hints of salt.

My father was trained to be a classic pianist from an early age. My grandparents had big plans for him. In college, out from under their thumbs, he spread his wings. Quit college and joined a rock band. Lived in a rat-infested apartment. Wore spandex on stage. And beat the crap out of guitars. Eventually he found a path half way back to their ideal as a composer for pop and rock acts, but it took a long time for my grandparents to forgive him.

However, he still plays many of the compositions he competed with from age twelve to seventeen, like the one he is currently playing, Beethoven's "Moonlight Sonata." The notes fill the house, as my father's expression turns serenely concentrated. The piano vibrates with his beautiful playing, a perfect backdrop to the scene of treetops and roofs slanting toward the ocean.

I internally sigh as the music of my childhood tugs at my soul. My father appears so complacent while playing that I'm jealous. Of my own father. But I sip coffee and keep my features smooth. Inside I want to scream at him to stop or hug the notes and dance around the room with them. Unfortunately, the composition is almost fifteen minutes long. I sip my coffee, tap my foot, and try to appear elated to hear him play. It gets hard as the pace picks up and he rolls out the notes in fast succession.

I smile and sip.

Yup, this is why I stayed away.

My father is music. All types, in any form. On countless instruments. He has never been married, nor will he ever get married. This is his wife, his love, his life.

And he passed his love to me. Through not only genetics, but also through his teaching and his coaching—*April, learn piano first, play all kinds of music: Spanish, folk, blues, jazz…never stop learning…don't just play, feel the music, let it roll into your soul…*

And I did until thorny guilt tore at the essence of me.

Internally, I'm becoming a tangled mess as he plays and memories float over me. Away from my father, I can pretend, even believe I'm meant for something else. Here with him and the music of my childhood, it's very clear I'm living a lie. But those tearing thorns leave me bleeding and prepared to live the lie out.

I finally give in. Set the coffee cup on a nearby table and lay both of my hands on the piano. Close my eyes. Let the notes flow through me, mathematical precision turned into sound as emotional art. Fine. I will always love music to the depths of my soul. Thorns entangle and tear. I bleed. I take a deep breath. Not embracing. Just relishing. The thorns loosen but stay clamped in.

My father finishes and I open my eyes. "No one plays like you."

He smiles warmly. "From you, I'll take that as the highest compliment."

I go around the piano to the bench and sit opposite from him, then throw my arms around him in a desperate hug. "I've missed you." The words are muffled in his shoulder.

"Missed you too," he says, hugging me back.

Damn. I feel like crying. I hug him tighter, hoping to absorb all of his peaceful energy.

"Everything okay, April?" he asks, his tone edging into worry.

"Yeah," I sit back, drawing in air before I do start crying. "Getting sentimental in my old age, and your playing brought back memories." I've gotten so good that the twisted truth comes out of me effortlessly. *April the exceptionally skilled liar.*

He laughs. "Old age. If I could be twenty one again…"

My phone rings with an annoying chirp. I try to ignore it as he pushes off the bench. "Go ahead, I need to call Eddie about dinner on Thursday."

When I asked to come, I told my dad that I had friends in town. He didn't mind. My father is the epitome of laid back. I think the endless music in his life keeps him calm.

I tug my phone from my pocket unsurprised at seeing Gabe's name on the front. His text reads: *Told you. The douche agreed to meet tomorrow for lunch at some place called Leaf. 2 okay? Need directions?*

I groan. Leaf is a hotspot for stars to have lunch. Meaning the paparazzi stalk the place. This guy is a douche. I text back that I know where it is and that I'll be there at two. He doesn't reply. Gabe is like me, not much of a phone aficionado.

I hear my father talking on the phone about turkey and sweet potatoes to his longtime girlfriend, Eddie. If they're still together. Even when they are not a couple, they remain friends. My father is not into drama. The exact opposite of my mother.

Turning around on the bench, I can't help but notice the gleam of white ivory keys.

No embracing. Just relishing. I remind myself as I stand and quickly move from the instrument.

Chapter 24
April

Leaf is oddly decorated in bright floral prints and loud colored furniture. You'd think, being a celebrity hang out, it would be modern and sleek and cool, but no, it's loud French country on crack. I've actually been here a few times before. My mother used to fly with me back and forth for the summers until I was fourteen. She'd stay for two days at the beginning and the end, so we could do some sightseeing. One of her must stops became Leaf—my father would never want to come within one hundred feet of the paparazzi—and I was never sure if it was to glimpse at celebrities or to feel like one.

When I come in, I ignore the photographers hanging out on the sidewalk and checking me out to discern if I'm anyone worth a lift of their camera. There inspection though is kind of creepy. Although I'm early, the hostess, obviously recognizing me from a description, leads me to a table on one of the patios. Michael Thomas is not here. But Gabe and Romeo are. I'm suddenly flustered, wondering why Romeo is here. What did Gabe tell him?

Romeo smiles when he sees the hostess gesturing me to a table. Gabe's expression remains stoic, making me think that he is aware that I'm not okay with the situation. I force myself toward the table.

"Hey," Romeo says as I sit. "How's your dad?"

Startled, I give him a questioning look before I recall that he has been a fan of my father for years. I'm a little off kilter because of his presence. "Good, he's working on a sound track for an independent film right now." I glance, maybe more like glare, at Gabe, who reads his menu. Ah, he knows I'm upset. "Hello, Gabe," I say in a flat tone. He appears tired with scruff heavier than usual on his jaw, which oddly adds to his normal surfer look, giving it a hot edge.

Holding his menu, he waves at me with two fingers. "Hey, April, how was your flight?"

His expression is pure innocence, his tenor monotone. I can't help a scowl from forming. "Fine." Luckily, our server brings me a water and takes my order for a lemonade. Once the server is gone, I pick the menu up, trying not to obsess how Gabe got Romeo here or why. I'm also a bit irritated with myself for caring. "How's the record coming?"

Romeo sighs, twisting his glass of water. "It's getting there. Still ironing out some rough spots. Transitions, beginnings, and endings, you know the shit that can make or break a song."

Gabe crosses his arms. "He's being the usual perfectionist asshole."

I don't comment. Romeo grins.

Ignoring Gabe, I ask, "You guys working tomorrow?"

"Yeah," Romeo says. "We want to get done with at least half the album this trip. Finishing is more important than a turkey dinner."

I nod again like a puppet. I'd been toying with the idea of inviting the band to my father's house for Thanksgiving. Home cooked meal and all that. Now upset, the invitation is sour on my tongue. I clear my throat. "Well, if—"

"Romeo," Gabe says in a tight tone. "Could you please give us a minute?"

Romeo pauses lifting his glass of water, glancing between us. He sets the glass down, his eyebrows raised and his look at me pointed.

I tap my menu on the table. Romeo must assume I was lying to him about there being nothing between Gabe and I, which I kind of was. "I don't think that's nec—"

"For a few minutes?" Gabe interrupts.

Romeo pushes away from the table. "Yeah, sure."

Gabe leans forward as soon as he leaves. "I should have called or texted." He runs a hand through his hair, then grabs the back of his neck. "We've been busy, but Romeo agreed to help when I explained we've been working on your cousin's bucket list. He is far better than I am at this business bullshit. And damn, April, he knows about your cousin right?"

He looks so stressed out at upsetting me, it takes me several seconds to say a simple, "Well, yeah."

He lets go of his neck and drops his hand. "It's not like I told him you were in group."

"No, but he thinks there is something going on between us."

Gabe stares at me, then lets out a gruff laugh. "There's a lot of shit between us, April. Does it matter what Romeo thinks? Why is it that at one moment you don't care what anyone thinks, then in the next you're freaking out about it?"

My mind whirls at his question. Of course, keeping my issues close keeps people out of them, but here in this restaurant where my mother pretended that her career as an actress didn't dead end with lying across car hoods in rock videos, I'm not so sure. I'm wondering if all her social rules about outward appearance did seep into me over the years.

"Hey," Romeo says, interrupting my internal breakdown. "Look who I ran into."

I blink at the boy—well, man in a wavy swooped hair doo over his sunglasses and boy clothes—standing at our table.

Romeo gestures to the open chair next to me.

The man pushes the sunglasses on his head and baby blues twinkle at me, obviously thinking I'm star struck.

Maybe about ten years ago, I'd swoon over him, and that's a big maybe. Today, not so much. I glance across the table at Gabe, his mahogany eyes hard, his scruffy jaw even harder as he glares at Thomas who appears to be checking me out. Yeah, that face is swoony. I could be imagining his jealously, but it makes me warm inside, which is very wrong.

The server practically runs over to our table as soon as the movie star's butt hits the chair. Thomas orders a water with lemon and lime slices.

After Romeo introduces everyone—me as a close friend—Thomas leans back in his chair. "I listened to the track you sent me. Though a bit old fashioned"—apparently rock is old school to this guy—"I liked it. So about this video…"

Though Romeo looks to Gabe, he stays silent. Romeo reluctantly turns back to Thomas. "Well, nothing is, ah,"—he crosses his arms so that the silver rings on his fingers shine in the bright sun—"totally figured out yet…we're"—his side glance at Gabe is murderous—"just trying to line up everything at this point. We were thinking of something like…well, one of Aerosmith's nineties videos with shots between a band and the story of a wild couple."

Huh, Romeo's improvising isn't too bad. No wonder Gabe wanted him to come.

The server brings the water and sliced fruit then we all order different variations of their fancy sandwiches, except for the movie star. He gets a fancy salad. Romeo only has to BS a bit more because Thomas shares his proposals while we eat. He suggests several directors and actresses that star in major motion pictures regularly. I almost snort and spit out a fry, at one of his suggestions, being that the actress won an academy award last year. He also suggests ridiculous locations like an expensive hotel in Beverly Hills and a swanky nightclub known to cater to high rolling rappers. He even wants a posse of guys to follow him into a club in one of his imaginative scenes.

This guy is a douche.

The idea of fifteen-year-old Rachel meeting and having her dreams dashed by this guy sours my stomach.

After he finishes half his salad, he pops his glasses back on, then announces that he might be interested, but they need to go through his agent when they're ready. And then, thankfully, he's gone.

"Holy fuck, my head is pounding with all his bullshit," Gabe groans, pointedly looking at me. "Any remorse on using that guy?"

I drop my napkin on my half-finished sandwich. "None," I say, then smile extra sweet.

"Four to go then."

It takes me a few seconds, while Gabe finishes off the last bite of his prosciutto BLT, to realize he is talking about the bucket list.

My mouth makes a thin line as I imagine getting a tattoo or going on a stage.

Romeo pushes his empty plate away. "The day I let that asshole in one of our videos hell will have frozen over."

I wince. "Thanks for coming and leading him on."

"No problem," Romeo says then lets out a laugh. "I kind of got a kick out of his ego."

I look to Gabe. "And thanks for setting this lunch up. I appreciate it."

He shrugs, then frowns. "I wanted to kick his ego, like in the face."

A laugh escapes me. "Well, you two can get back to work. I can get the check. It's the least I can do after breaking up your recording time to listen to all that."

Gabe's lovely lips twist. "I invited you. I'm paying the bill." His tone is like steel.

I push my plate to the edge of the table instead of arguing with him like I want to. "Then let me get the tip."

He shakes his head.

This time Romeo wiggles his brows at me as the server sets the check down.

I restrain an irritated sigh as Gabe puts money in the little folder. "If the band does have a big enough break tomorrow, my dad's cooking a full meal. We should be eating around four. He never minds extra company."

Romeo's eyes light up. "Man, I'd love to meet your dad…"

Gabe taps his thumbs on the table. "Like you're going to take a break."

Romeo shakes his head. "Yeah, it's probably not going to happen. However, we might be doing a short set at the Whiskey a Go Go Saturday night. You want to come if that happens?"

Gabe frowns at Romeo, then takes the sunglasses from the edge of his T-shirt and slips them on.

Romeo leans toward him to catch my attention. Dang, I was staring at Gabe, speculating if the invitation upset him. "Sure, I always wanted to go there," I absently say, mentally kicking myself in the butt for being absorbed with Gabe. "How'd you get a gig there?"

Romeo leans back in his chair. "Our manager—"

"You have a manager?"

"Kind of. We're letting him do some promotion and stuff. Since the band that night isn't going on until eleven, we might go on at ten. Get some more exposure. I can send a car to pick you up if it's a go."

I shake my head. "My dad lives in Malibu. I can just meet you."

"All right, let's hope it's a go," Romeo shoves off from the table.

Gabe is already standing.

I stand too. "Good luck with the album."

"Yeah, we might need some luck," Romeo says with a laugh.

Gabe shakes his head. "We don't need luck. We have Romeo." He gives me a forced smile, bending to pick up a bag that I hadn't noticed next to his chair. He sets the shopping bag on the table in front of me. "Here. You'll know what to do with it."

Then they're gone.

Confused, I open the bag and find a white paper floating lantern.

First the lunch, and now the lantern. Though Gabe's actions continue to tell me he cares about me, when we're together, the easy camaraderie that grew between us seems almost non-existent. And I can't imagine ever getting it back.

Staring at the lantern, I'm more confused than ever.

Chapter 25
April

The Whiskey a Go Go is old, musty, dirty, and quite awesome. Everything is dark, except for the red vinyl on the booths, and the black and white photos on the walls. The place drips with rock history. Among others, The Doors, Guns N Roses, and Led Zepplin have played here. I should have come early to wander around and check out all the memorabilia hanging on the walls. But I almost didn't come, contemplating making up some lame excuse.

The last few days, visiting with my dad, walking along the beach, staring at the ocean, even releasing the paper lantern, have given me too much time to think. Everything goes by in a whirlwind at home. Here time almost stands still for me. All I've been able to think about is the tangled mess between Gabe and me. He cares about me. Obviously, since he set up that ridiculous lunch. We're attracted to one another—if only booty call was an option for us. But that one night has thrown us several steps back and we can't seem to find a way back to being friends. And whenever I'm with him, I'm stuck in a state of confusion.

Yet here I am.

Mostly because most Saturday nights at my father's house turn into an impromptu jam session. He cooks a huge dinner in the outside kitchen by the pool, and everyone in his circle is always welcome. A variety of musicians with an assortment of instruments and styles show up. I loved Saturday nights at my dad's since the age of eight when I first experienced it, and even joined in around the age of twelve, then loved it more while participating with my guitar. Now, it would be pure torture to sit there among such talent and not play. Thus I picked the lesser of two evils. Or I'm hoping I picked the lesser of two evils.

Right now, the band is waiting to go on stage. Romeo met me out front and after we did a quick tour of the place through a packed house, so it wasn't much of a tour. Then we met the rest of the band in the back room. Unexpectedly, Justin and Sam appeared happy to see me. Guess a familiar face in a strange place is always good. Gabe just gave me a nod.

Standing on the side of the stage, the guys are reviewing the set and talking over the change ups. I'm excited for them to go on, especially since one of the new songs is in the set. I hang back and listen while they argue about a transition from song to song.

Having been to many of their shows before they went on the summer tour, I'm a bit surprised to see that Romeo isn't making all of the decisions. He always did in the past. But it's evident that the band is making decisions as a whole, instead of letting Romeo lead them. The realization has me more excited to hear their new song. I'm expecting it to be a mix of all of them.

The music beyond the stage lowers and someone announces, "We have a bonus band tonight!" A murmur, a few yells, and a slight ripple of applause follows.

The guys stop talking and all seem to take a deep breath. Gabe suddenly appears pale.

The announcer continues, "An up and coming band who toured with Brookfield this last summer. Luminescent Juliet!"

Justin leads the way while a few more shouts and another flat ripple of applause sounds.

Gabe is the last to leave the dark hallway. He takes a deep breath and rolls his shoulders, then glances back at me.

I smile. "Go blow their minds."

He studies me for a long second, his gaze almost wistful before his lips form a quick grin and he goes out on the stage.

I step closer to the small stage, close enough to see half of the skeptical crowd out in front. Once Gabe sits and is situated behind his drum kit, Romeo breaks into a loud riff.

The first song is "Midnight." I've heard it countless times and could probably grab a guitar and strum the melody out, even though I haven't played the instrument in years. Luckily, I know this song. If it were the new one, I wouldn't have paid much attention.

Because as they play, I'm only aware of only Gabe.

I've seen Luminescent Juliet play lots of times, but being fearful of wanting to play music, I never zone in on them individually playing instruments. As I stand on the side of the stage, Gabe is too close for me to ignore.

My hands curl around the edge of the wall as I watch him.

He moves around the kit, hair flying in his face, brows low, lips twisted in absorption.

It's obvious when he plays he is in his own world, delivering every ounce of his energy and focus. On one hand, I'm jealous, knowing how it feels to be caught in the music. On the other hand, the concentration on his face, the intensity of his expression, adds to his allure.

He is sexy and powerful and graceful all at once. My insides warm and melt and vibrate to the beat he sets.

They practically roll right into "Gone Baby" next.

My want for him increases exponentially as I watch Gabe pound out the rhythm. I swallow tightly. If I had observed him this close last year, I would have been infatuated with him since he joined the band. The universal picture for musical elegance tends to be either a violin on a shoulder or a person gracefully reaching for the strings on a harp. But Gabe pounding from drum to cymbal—his hair swaying, his jaw hard, his elbows raised—so fast the picture is almost gone before you can see it, becomes my image for musical elegance.

The song ends and seconds later Gabe sets the beat with his sticks and they roll into "Blood on Snow," a faster song, edging on the line of punk. I know this one too. Not only is it good, but it heavily features the drums. My nails dig into the wooden edge of the wall as Gabe transitions into a spastic drum fill.

I draw in several long breaths, trying to control the want, both physical and emotional, rolling through me. I need to get a grip. Like now. I look over the other band members then the crowd, who seemed bored at the start but now press closer to the stage, watching with a rapt attention while head bobbing.

Shutting my longing down, I focus on the crowd's attentiveness. I'm guessing most of them are seasoned rockers who can spot talent when they see it, and from the look on their faces, opened mouth awe, they are seeing it. Even I, who swore music off, can't stay far from Luminescent Juliet. I've always known they had enough talent to make it big. Yet there are so many factors to the business end of this industry. Things have to line up to make it, and they look to be lining up perfectly for the band.

At the end of the song, the crowd goes nuts, whistling, clapping, shouting, and raising drinks.

Justin grins widely, then he shouts out a, "Thank you! This next one is going to be on our new album. We hope you like it."

A rush of excitement hits me as Justin steps back and Gabe hits his sticks together. Romeo, Justin, and Gabe break into the music hard and fast.... Da-ta-ta-dum follows a hard riff three times over, then the heavy drums fade into a pulsing beat and Justin steps up to the microphone.

"And so it starts again..."

The song is a definite mix of all four band members. I can hear Romeo in the melody. Sam's influence in the bluesy under beat. Justin in the wide-open chorus of the vocals. And Gabe's influence with the almost thrash metal sounding drums at each transition. It's good. It's eclectic. It's different in a twisted way, and from the look of the crowd, it's going to be a big hit.

They finish the song and the crowd goes absolutely nuts. They end the short set with "Inked My Heart." It's their most popular song thus far. A few people in the crowd wear expressions of surprise, probably recognizing the song.

I lean on the wall and try to keep my eyes—and longing—from Gabe. It's a huge challenge.

After the set, amid huge shouts and thunderous applause, Sam lifts his base over his head. Romeo gives a big wave. Justin fist bumps or shakes hands with people in the front of the crowd. Gabe pushes his sticks in his back pocket and walks of the stage.

I shuffle back as he comes toward me. His face is still tense, his body rigid. He stops feet from me and I blurt, "You guys were awesome. You played awesome. It was the best I've seen you play."

He stares at me with an intensity that is similar to the look he had as he played. The expression has me nearly melting into the wall. Gaze becoming more intense, he comes closer and air bubbles inside my chest from the want he always inspires.

The rest of the guys come off the stage, piling behind him.

Gabe's mouth tightens to a thin line. He murmurs a "Thanks," and moves past me.

Romeo bumps shoulders with me. "You going to come celebrate with us?"

"Sure," I squeak as we proceed down the hall toward the tiny room we waited in before their short set.

Fist bumps, high-fives, and the plethora of excited cussing fills the room from their exhilaration at how the crowd reacted. A bucket filled with ice-cold beer waits and they're soon passing bottles around. Justin tries to hand me one, but I shake my head at the brown bottle. As the stagehands pack their instruments and load them into a rented van, Romeo calls Riley, Justin calls Allie, and Sam calls Peyton.

Gabe and I are left smirking at one another.

"Sure you don't want a beer?" he asks.

I shake my head.

"Something else?"

"Nope, I'm driving."

He nods as if understanding, but takes a sip of beer and glances away.

We stand there in uncomfortable silence, listening to the half conversations around us as stage hands trudge through the room with the band's gear. Once the van is loaded behind the venue, Justin waves their Town car off, telling the driver they will call when they're ready for a ride. Exiting across a hotel parking lot, we walk down a couple blocks, then cross the street to the Viper Room. The band's new manager, an older bald man, waits up front so that the bouncers let us in. Instead of going to the main floor, he leads us into the basement bar and a table in the back corner. He's all congratulations and back slaps until the waitress brings amber colored shots of what looks like whiskey.

The manager raises his glass. "Expensive stuff, probably should be sipped, not shot, but I've learned there is a time for everything." He downs the amber liquid. Following suit, the guys drain their glasses too.

Luckily, old Baldy—managers leave a bad taste in my mouth after all of the stories from my dad and his friends—didn't get me one. Another round of drinks is ordered. I order a ginger ale.

There is lots of talk of the upcoming album, how it is over half finished, and possible bands they could tour with come spring. I sip my ginger ale and mostly listen—next to each other Romeo and I talk about the performance in intervals between everything else—while I try not to let Gabe draw my attention. But he does, even in my peripheral vision, which leaves me feeling desperate and morose. I can't handle my father playing piano or looking at my guitar case or being real with people. Dealing with whatever—lust? friendship? something more?—is between Gabe and I is way beyond what I can manage. And at this moment, I'm more aware of it than ever.

After about an hour of listening, I turn to Romeo and softly tell him, "I think I should get going. Don't want to worry my father." My father trusts my judgment, but it sounds like a good excuse.

Romeo nods thoughtfully. "I can walk you out."

We stand and Mr. Manager looks at us with surprise. "Where are you two off to?"

"Be back in a few," Romeo says in a tone that says, screw you, you don't get to ask me where I'm going.

All eyes are on us. Gabe's are narrowed to slits.

Baldy puts a palm up. "Didn't mean to offend. It's just that Lennings should be stopping by any second. It was a surprise, man. I knew you wanted to meet him."

I almost laugh. I know Lennings. He is one of my dad's pals and a renowned—at least to people who pay attention to that kind of music—jazz and blues guitarist. I smile at the new manager, then Romeo. "It's okay. You don't have to walk me out. My car isn't that far from here." Since all the parking lots were full by the time I got here, I parked on a street about two blocks over and one block back from the Whiskey, and paid the ridiculous meter fee.

Romeo looks indecisive until Gabe pushes from the table. "Dude, just sit down. I'll walk her out so you can meet the big, badass guitar player of your dreams."

Great. Exactly what I need. Being alone with Gabe. But I'm not about to argue in front of everyone. "Have a good night. You guys did an awesome job. It was amazing," I ramble while Sam and Justin grin. Then I take off ahead of Gabe.

He catches up with me outside, matching my brisk gait.

An uncomfortable silence sits between us, cooling the warm night air. The wall between us bothers me, eats at my conscience as if I did something wrong.

It becomes so uncomfortable that I attempt to make small talk as we walk. "So the album is going good?"

"Yeah," he responds, hands in pockets and face forward.

"I'm imagining you guys put in twelve hour days."

"Sometimes more."

"Whoa, like how much?"

"Fourteen. Fifteen."

I turn the corner. His one word answers are beginning to grate on my nerves. "Is the label giving you guys creative freedom?"

"Pretty much."

My teeth clench at his short response. "That's good. Some labels try to take over and change a band."

Unsurprisingly, he doesn't comment, but I continue on. "Think you'll be able to get the album done during the next recording session?"

"Probably," he says, his voice sounding robotic.

That's it. I whip toward him. Calmness gone. "What is your problem?"

"Problem?" Though his hands are in his pockets, he taps his thumbs on the outside of his jeans.

"You're being a jerk," I blurt.

His brows lower, and I'm aware it isn't from the couple scowling at us as they have to split up and go around us. After a shake of his head, he runs a hand through his hair. "You know, I don't think we can be friends. You're driving me fucking crazy."

My head jolts back. "I'm driving you crazy?"

He sighs, but I spin back around and march to my dad's Range Rover.

As I dig in my pocket for my keys, he comes behind me. "Running away again, April?" he mocks, grabbing me by the arm and turning me toward him.

"Stop it," I say, trying to tug out of his grip.

He grabs my other arm. "This is part of why you're making me fucking nuts. Every other thing sets you off."

"That's..." I pause, realizing that it is true, though it's not in the way that he thinks. I'm not going to argue with him. Arguing won't diminish the gap between us. I sigh. "Maybe you're right. Maybe we can't be friends."

He leans closer. Too close. I can smell the whiskey on his breath. And sense the warmth coming off his body. See, under the glow of the streetlight, the dark brown speckles in his eyes. All these things bring memories that I'm constantly trying to suppress. Stupid. Stupid. Stupid. April.

He drags me closer, his gaze pained so much that my chest tightens. "That's the thing. I don't want to be friends. That's the other part. I want more. Even though I'm not good enough for you, even though you don't, I want more."

Shocked, I blink at him. He wants more? Like a relationship?

The notion of more is sending a stark, cold fear through me as he lowers his head and kisses me hard. His mouth pulsates over mine, driving the fear out of me, driving everything but the sensation of him away. On his tongue, whiskey tastes wonderful. My hands find the firm curve of his chest. His palms slide up and his fingers press into my back. I stand on my tiptoes and let him drink me in like he did the whiskey, only this isn't a quick shot, it's a slow, slow sip, that leaves a burn for more.

Laughter from someone on the sidewalk and a, "Hey, get a room!" has Gabe drawing away.

Staring at each other, we're both breathing hard.

Gabe is the first to break the silence. "I'd say sorry, but I'm not, even if I should be."

My forehead wrinkles as I try to process the last five minutes but my brain is sluggishly slow.

"Get in your car. Go home."

"Gabe." His name comes out of me in a pleading tone.

"Just get in your car and go home. Now."

"Gab—"

"Before I get in your car with you and fuck you a block from Hollywood's Sunset Strip, April."

My stomach flips in eagerness at his words, but his harsh tone has me digging in my pocket for my keys. "You said—"

"Get in your car," he says sternly.

I move around the front of the car. "I think we need to talk."

He stiffly nods.

Eyes glued on him, I go around the car. The moment my butt hits the seat, he stalks back toward the Strip.

Mind whirling, breath still harsh, I watch him until he disappears in between the people on the sidewalk, as that cold fear begins to bubble back up at the idea of more. My imagination had never even gone there. I had never truly considered us as a possibility.

But I'm very aware that more with Gabe isn't a simple more.

It would be everything.

Like no more lies.

Like no more hiding.

Like finally sharing the truth.

Chapter 26
April

Fear pounding in my chest, I sit in my car outside Allie's tattoo shop and watch the upstairs windows. A shadow has passed by a lit window twice, so I know Gabe is inside. Yet I grip the steering wheel and try to dredge up enough courage to get out of the car. It's been over a week since California. Over a week since he said he wanted more from me. Over a week since he kissed me. But he hasn't answered any of my calls or my texts.

The car is getting cold, the night darker, and my fear heavier with each passing minute, but still I sit. I think of all the things I need to say. I've been thinking all week. Over thinking until my brain and heart ache. Both are going to explode if I don't get out of this car.

Before I can change my mind, I quietly get out of the car. I keep my tread light on the stairs. I want to surprise him. Or maybe not allow him time to send me away. Or maybe not run away before he knows I'm here. My knock is heavy but quick. Then I hold my breath and wait.

Steps sound. The blind in front of the window shifts. His face appears and his brows rise. We stare at each other through the glass.

Fear pounds but I offer the slightest smile. His eyes narrow. Yet the knob turns.

"What are you doing here?" he asks across the crack in the door.

Strong. Tough. Persistent. Like Gabe. That's me. Right now. For as long as possible. "Obviously by the amount of times I called and texted you, I'd like to talk."

"You should know by now that talking isn't going to work."

I want to agree, then take off, instead I pull out the big guns. "How many times have you barged into my apartment?"

He gives me a long look, then sighs and opens the door. "Fine, but I have to work at seven tomorrow morning."

I force myself to breeze past him before he changes his mind, even though it's still early in the evening.

After shutting the door, he leans on the back of it and crosses his arms. "Okay talk."

Nothing like just getting to the point. I drop my purse on the table and take a deep breath, preparing to confront the elephant in the room that we've both been dancing around. Although I've rehearsed this in my head multiple times, it comes out as a jumbled mess. "I'm not good at this." I point a finger at him then me. "I rarely date, and I always assumed…well, at first I thought you pretty much hated me. I couldn't seem to see past your original dislike of me to realize that you might want—"

"April, this isn't nec—"

"Just let me finish, please," I beg because if I stop I won't be able to continue.

His jaw tightens, but he stays silent.

"And, well, as you know, I'm a bit of a mess." I bite my bottom lip. "Maybe a huge mess, so much so that I consider myself too screwed up for you."

He opens his mouth.

I put my palm out.

He shuts his mouth, though his body entire is tense, as if he is holding back words.

"I mean, you're screwed up too, but not like I am." I draw in a deep breath. "More than screwed up, I'm…well, I've—I'm just really an awful person." He is staring at me like I've lost my mind. "Can we sit down?" I say, sliding into a chair. "I—this is hard to explain. I've never told anyone, and"—I take another gulp of air—"I need to sit."

My announcement and erratic behavior gain his full attention. The taut lines of his face change to a soft wonder. Perhaps he is guessing what is coming, though he has no idea how horrible it actually is. He silently moves across the room and sits next me, which feels too close. His gaze and expression are patient, so patient I want to cry because that gaze is probably going to change.

My hands clench together in my lap. "You've never asked about my past, about her. Why haven't you ever asked?"

He shrugs. "People always want to know about me, my dad and shit. I always spit it out. Get it over. So I don't pry, no matter how much I want to. And I did ask, well I kind of asked that day we walked through the drive thru. You shut down."

Biting my bottom lip, I want to shut down again. Instead, I release my lip and start anew. "You said you wanted more. I think—no I want more too, but I'm afraid once you know the real me you won't want

220

more." I let out rush of air and he tries to grab my clasped hands. I yank them back. "Don't. Just wait. Just listen."

He nods slowly, twisting sideways and looping an arm on the back of the chair. He waits, his face devoid of expression.

I rub my temple. "I'm not sure where to start."

He waits.

I sigh and drop my hand back in my lap. "Back in high school I was different. Different than now and different than the other kids at my private school. I didn't care what they thought. My whole world was centered around music. I played both the piano and the guitar, but mostly the guitar. I had a band, a retro"—a sad laugh escapes at the word—"nineties grunge band. Most of the time I looked the part, wearing ripped up jeans, flannels, combat boots, and a knit beanie, but they all believed I was the coolest girl around. Probably because I couldn't have cared less what they thought. Although I didn't hang with any clicks, everyone knew me. People paid attention to me and respected me. And I knew that, even then I understood how my fellow teens paid homage to my confident-could-not-care-less-attitude."

Although he appears confused, his countenance is the picture of patience.

"I was completely wrapped up in the band my senior year, using almost all my free time to practice, to write, or to teach them what they didn't know. So when my step sister—"

He cocks his head at that.

"Yeah, I've kind of made a habit of lying. You should be aware of that. Internally, I claim it's to make things easier on myself, and in a way it is, but your comment about me caring what people think made

Jean Haus

me realize I'm probably doing it for my image too. If the issue was forced, it seemed less messy, less personal to refer to her as my cousin." I draw in a deep breath. "Yet we"—my voice cracks and I draw in another breath since it is so hard to talk about Rachel, especially since even remembering her brings on acute guilt and sadness—"were step sisters. Really practically sisters. Our parents married when I was four and she was two. We shared the last name, Tanner, since my mother changed mine to my step-father's."

I wipe an escaped tear from my cheek. Other than that, I refuse to give my tears attention. If I do, I won't make it through this. I will become a sobbing mess, and I don't want Gabe's pity. I don't deserve it. I draw in a deep breath. I started this and I'm going to finish it, no matter how many wounds it opens up.

"At first when she began having problems with some girls in my class bullying her, I offered my support. It started over a boy. Some jock, some football star that the girls in our school treated like some sort of god. He was dating a girl in my class but messing around with my sister. As far as I know, they would text or talk on the phone and even met at a couple of parties. I thought the whole thing was stupid. I told Rachel to quit talking to the guy if he had a girlfriend and ignore the girls, then I talked to the girlfriend, told her it was over and to leave my sister alone. And she did at first.

"Though I loved my sister, I considered her a drama queen and thought that she shouldn't have messed around with the guy in the first place. Obviously, I didn't love her enough because a few months later it got worse. The weekend before—before it happened was her weekend at our house. All that weekend, she begged me to do something, just talk to the girls again, try to get them to stop bullying her. She was positive they would listen to me once more. I agreed to talk with them to get her off my back. I wanted to get her out of my room and get back to my music. But I was busy and angry at her. Why did she keep letting this guy—who had a girlfriend—reel her in and use her? At least that's what I questioned then. Now I realize that she craved, maybe even needed, attention."

Still sitting sideways in the chair, Gabe rubs the scruff on his jaw.

My lips press together, as though I'm unconsciously trying to stop the next part from coming out. But I'm determined to finish this, finally determined to bare all. "Thursday night of that week, at her mother's house, she took her own life." Though there are millions wanting to break free, only one more tear escapes me. I don't wipe this one away. "Pills. A whole bottle. Right before bed. She simply went to sleep forever." I look above his head and add, "I never did talk to those girls. I was too damn busy, and too damn angry. Too busy while people were demeaning my sister, calling her slut and cum dumpster and thot at school, on Facebook, even her phone was full of degrading texts. Though I was totally unaware of it before it happened, the girlfriend got all her buddies and then some to attack my sister in retaliation of the rumors going around about my sister and the boy together at some party."

Gabe turns then leans forward, elbows on his thighs and a hand half covering the frown on his face. I can see the wheels turning in his head, my past making him re-think everything.

"You know," I say, my tone flat and my anger at myself renewed. "I had to look up some of that awful stuff. Like a thot is some ridiculous slang for a ho, as if ho do isn't misogynistic enough." I finally wipe at a cheek with my knuckles. "Of course, I was furious with those girls, even sucker punched the girlfriend the day I returned to school, but in time, I realized I was to blame just as much as them. In fact, I was worse. She was my sister, and stuck in my selfish bubble of music love and angry over her actions, I let them torment her to death." I draw in a shaky breath. "And you know, looking back, Rachel was probably bi-polar or something since she fluctuated between super happy and depressed from about the age of twelve. But she was never diagnosed. Had she been, I may have listened better. As if someone has to be diagnosed with a disorder to listen to them," I say in a sardonic tone, wishing as always that I could go back and time and do something, anything different.

He leans forward more and sets his palms on my knees. "April," he says in soft, pacifying tone. "You made a mistake, a terrible mistake. And though you believe it, your intervention may not have changed anything, and you were young, shit, still in high school."

Instantly furious, I jump up, knocking my chair over. "Don't say that! My age does not vindicate my selfishness! Don't you think I've tried that excuse? It doesn't work!" My arm furiously slashes the air. "She's gone and I didn't do anything to stop it!" My chest rises in deep breaths as if I'd been running. "I just sat in my room tinkering over fucking notes while disgusting words drilled holes in her heart."

He stares at me for several long seconds, as I tremble with indignation aimed at myself, then he slowly sits back against the chair, crossing his arms. "You're right. You screwed up. Big time. You should never play music again, should become a counselor, and help those in need like you didn't your sister." His eyes shoot exasperation at me. "Guilt should drive you to sacrifice your life as compensation for such a mistake." He drops his hand, smacking his jean-clad thigh. "Besides, that is the only way to help others, especially considering your talent, it's the best way." A hard sarcasm laces his tone.

A despondent laugh bursts from me. "You think I gave up music? You think it's possible for me to be that good? That selfless?" A harder, cackling laugh escapes me. "I want to play. Every. Single. Day." I pick the chair off the floor and plop onto it. "I can't. At first, after she was gone, I wallowed in depression for months. Eventually I picked up my guitar, and the sound was flat, emotionless, technical, precise crap. I tried again and again but it was no good. I'd lost my soul and my music." I let out a harsh breath, deflating in my chair, feeling worn and broken. "Now, I'm trying to get one half back. The music is gone."

He rises slowly, then stands in front of me. Dread welling up within me, I watch him with lifeless eyes, but suddenly he's kneeling in front of me. "It's not gone." His fingers lightly tap the center of my chest. "It's just locked in here by grief and pain and guilt. And your soul is there too, though weary and full of shame, I've seen the beauty of it several times."

I grasp the hand pressed to my chest, probably squeezing it too hard. "Why are you arguing with me? Aren't you repulsed? Why aren't you kicking me out right now?"

His slight smile is sad. "I've made mistakes. A life of them. I've felt shame—"

"It's not the same if others make you feel that way," I whisper.

He nods. "Sometimes it was others, and sometimes it was my doing, enough that I've grown tough as nails to the world, wearing a chip on my shoulder that like an ass I can't always break past. I've done things…gotten so angry…physically hurt people." Staring at our hands clasped together, he shakes his head. "I have no right to judge you." He wipes the wetness from my cheeks that I wasn't aware of. "There was a time when I thought you were perfect, cold, untouchable. And while I wish with every cell in my body that your sister was still here, the person I believed you were isn't someone who could ever want or understand someone like me." He presses both our hands to the center of my chest. "But this person is."

My lip quivers as emotion engulfs me until I burst into loud, gulping, messy sobbing.

"Hey," he says softly, pulling me off the chair and into his arms. "I thought you wanted more too."

My face is buried in his chest, but I nod against his soft T-shirt. "I do," I say into the cotton before another sob escapes. Wrapping my arms around him, I add in a tiny voice, "I just don't deserve you."

I feel him shake his head as he shifts his arms around my body, then carries me across the room. He settles on the couch and just holds me, his fingers a soft whisper in my hair. "Not sure I'm worth deserving."

"Oh, you so are." And I hold him back, for once not feeling alone.

Chapter 27
April

We sit holding each other for quite some time. Much later after my sobbing stops and my breathing evens, I drag away from his chest to look at him. His expression is gentle as he brushes a strand of hair from my face.

"You sure you want to try this?" I ask referring to us, my voice raw and hoarse from crying.

"Well," he says in a dry tone. "The last couple weeks have been completely fucked up caught between what I should do and what I want." His gaze roams over my face, telling me without words what he wants. "It's like I've been leaning on the edge of a knife, either waiting for it to cut me or wanting it to cut me to escape in the pain. And now, except for a tiny part of me that wants to save you from me, knowing you want more, I feel relief." His fingers graze the side of my face. "And wonder." His palm slides down my neck. "And hope." Fingers trace my collarbone. "And that I'm the luckiest bastard on the face of the earth."

He is such a beautiful soul, a blend of sweet and tough and resilient. I trace his upper lip like that night months ago. His skimming fingers pause. His eyes bore into mine, obviously remembering that night too.

I let out a contented sigh. "I'm the lucky one here."

He starts to shake his lovely face, but I push up, grasp his jaw in my hands, and catch those beautiful lips with mine, kissing him softly. Hands holding my scalp, he kisses me back. Again and again. His tenderness burns through all of my doubts. Everything fades away, except his touch, his lips, and hands on me. When gentle, warm kisses turn demanding, he sits back, his eyes concerned.

His thumbs rub strands of my hair. "We don't have to rush things. You've had an emotional night." He slides his hands to my waist and attempts to pull me back into his lap, but I twist myself up until I'm straddling his lap and holding onto his shoulders.

"This isn't about rushing." After weeks of confusion, I'm filled with an emotion that borders on euphoria because I can be with him. "This is about need. I need this. I need you."

Tension creases his forehead. Anxiety fills his lovely eyes and hardens the lines of his face.

I draw in a breath and try to explain that wonderful feeling of intimacy that I remember with him. "It not about the sex, though I want that too. It's about being close to you. Not knowing where I start and you end."

The lines in his forehead deepen until he lets out a, "Fuck," puts a hand on the back of my head and slams into me, his mouth a bruising force.

This intensity, this desperation, this is what I want from him. His fierceness sends music into my veins, the notes a fast, rhythmic crescendo that exposes his need for me, and drives my need to equal the wildness of his. Together, we're a flying, building tempo, our sensual energy changing to prestissimo—the fastest tempo—in an instant.

In between hot nips and rough bites and gripping hands, I lose my sweater and jeans, Gabe his T-shirt and belt. Within the storm of another kiss, I'm blindly working on the button of his pants when he breaks our kiss, flips us around, and kneels on the floor in front of me.

My underwear hit the floor as I grasp his intent. "Um, I'm not sur—"

"Shhh. I've wanted to taste you forever." He lifts my legs on his shoulders and my hands hit the bottom cushions of the couch.

Between his eyes on me and his words, a wave of heat hits me, but I'm still a bit mortified. "Um—"

His hot, wet mouth touches the center of me, and all words are lost. I nearly melt into the couch. My hands find his shoulders and grip tight before I do dissolve in the cushions. Mortification dies. With his hands cradling my butt and his tongue on my hot skin, this is the second most intimate moment of my life. After I practically bend off the couch, sing like an alley cat, and nearly tear Gabe's hair out, I slowly open my eyes to find him leaning on my thigh staring at me.

I'm mortified all over again. And not just a bit.

He shakes his head, brushing his scruff on my inner thigh. "Don't look like that. You were beautiful. That was beautiful."

Mortification dies at his words.

He stands and holds out a hand for me. Dressed only in a bra, I let him take me by the hand around the couch toward the bed. Along the way, he flicks off the lamp, leaving the light above the kitchen sink to illuminate the apartment.

As he unclasps my bra, I undo the button of his pants. I push his jeans and boxers down, and he kicks them off. Curiosity mixed with a fierce lust has me reaching for him. Standing motionless, he watches me with slitted eyes as I learn the contours of his hard, hot skin. Too soon, he's setting me on the center of the bed, then rolling on a condom before he follows.

We lay on our sides for a long moment staring at each other in the shadows.

He grips my shoulder. "I've been thinking about this, all the time, nearly every second of the day, since that night," he says softly, his breath a whisper on my lips.

"Me too," I admit, as every cell in my body buzzes with anticipation.

"All that waiting has me wanting to go slow, make it last."

I nod, thinking I just want it to start. As in now.

Gabe moves first, sliding his palm from the side of my breast over my hip to my thigh, causing my skin to buzz as much as my cells. He leans in and kisses me softly as he wraps my leg around his hip. Then he shifts closer, sliding into me, hard and hot and smooth.

A moan escapes me at the marvelous feel of him.

His lips form another smile against mine as he drives deeper. We're soon breathing hard, our kiss a press of open mouths as we move together. My calf grips his hip. My fingers wrap around his biceps. My heel digs into his buttock. Closer! my body screams, along with faster, but Gabe keeps it slow and meltingly torturous, his face a rigid, sexy picture of holding back.

Sweaty, muscles straining, and glued to him, I'm truly not sure where I end and he begins. And he does make it last and last until the leisure tempo ends in a fury, our interwoven bodies becoming a mass of shuddering, sweet trembles.

We lay glued together for quite some time, allowing our breathing to calm. Later Gabe draws the covers up and over us, pulling me to his chest.

"Someday, I want to hear you play," he says into my hair.

My full heart tightens. "I wish I could but it's gone."

He shakes his head and kisses my temple. "You'll play again."

His certain tone has me sighing and softly saying, "Maybe."

Even though I don't believe it.

Chapter 28
April

I wake to a sensual dream. Spooned against Gabe's hot, hard body. His mouth on my neck. His hand between my legs. Half asleep, I'm floating on a warm cloud of lust, and I wiggle closer. When he enters me from behind, the cloud soars amidst panting and straining. A bite on my shoulder sends me tumbling in pleasure from the cloud back into Gabe's bed.

A tinkling bell sounds somewhere from the floor.

"What is that?" I ask, coming down from the amazing wake up sex.

"My phone. Alarm," he says in a harsh puff of breath that whispers on my back.

"How long has it been going off?"

I feel him shrug.

Worried for him, I try to squirm out from under his warm body. "You're going to be late for work."

He draws me close, still breathing hard. "Don't care. This is where I want to be."

"Gabe—"

He kisses my ear. "I'm getting up but you sleep."

"Huh?" I say groggily.

He scoots out of the blankets. "I want to imagine you here in my bed while I'm at work and know it's not a fantasy."

I giggle, then sigh dreamily at the notion of him imagining me.

After another kiss, this one on my shoulder where he bit me earlier, he rolls out of bed.

I lay in bed content to fill his imagination while he works, listening to him getting ready. Shuffling in drawers. Showering—that has my half-asleep imagination wandering. Opening the fridge. His footsteps coming back to me and another kiss landing on my forehead.

"Dinner? Tonight?"

"Yes, please," I say, smiling into the pillow.

I hear him chuckle prior to the sound of the door opening and closing.

Bone tired, it doesn't take long for me to fall back to sleep and fulfill his fantasy.

***

When I wake again, the apartment is bright from the sun. I stretch with a smile, thinking of the night before and the early morning. The slight tightness of my body reminds me of Gabe. Wanting him, I roll onto the far pillow, breathing in his scent. A warm happiness fills me at the familiar smell until a nagging guilt hits me.

I shouldn't be this happy. I don't deserve it.

I flop back over and stare at the ceiling as tears threaten to fall.

I don't deserve them either. And I definitely don't deserve Gabe.

This is where I want to be.

My hands grip the edge of the sheet.

Though I don't deserve him or the happiness he brings me, I don't want to hurt him.

In all the confusion of the last few months, I never anticipated this bone wrenching guilt, never imagined this happiness.

Because I never thought we would be together.

My head and my heart churn in a dark whirl.

I need to get out of here. Get my head on straight. Perhaps ignore my heart, and the warm feelings.

After flying out of bed, I quickly find my clothes strewn all over the room. Dressed, I detangle my hair with my fingers, then search for my shoes. I find one under the table and spot the other under the couch. I'm slipping on a flat, when someone starts banging at the door and turning the handle. Muffled shouts come from outside next.

I quickly grab my purse, as the wrenching grows louder. "Just a minute!" I yell, wondering who it could be. Gabe, who forgot his key? Romeo, who somehow saw my car parked outside?

The open door reveals an older man wearing crumpled clothes. His face is red and angry with a purple vein raised along his temple under messy brown hair.

His brows lower. "Who the hell are you?" he asks in a mixture of a growl and sneer.

Totally baffled, I merely blink at him.

"Jim!" Someone cries from behind him, and I notice Sharon, trying to push in front of the man. "That's April. She's one of Gabe's friends."

Wobbling into the apartment—forcing me to step back—he pushes her back on the porch. His bloodshot eyes roam over my disheveled appearance. "Ah yeah, more like a fuck buddy."

My mouth falls open as a red-hot blush hits my cheeks.

Lips in a sneer, hands fisted at his sides, and swaying a bit, Jim quickly inspects the one room apartment, then marches over to the kitchen and whips open the cupboard above the fridge.

"So sorry, April," Sharon says quickly as she comes in. She goes to Jim and tugs at his shirt while he throws everything out of the cupboard, items crashing onto the floor. "He said he didn't take it. Just wait until he gets here!"

"Little fucker's been a liar since he was in diapers," Jim mumbles.

Jim must be Gabe's father, I realize as he furiously tears out the contents of the next cupboard. Cereal boxes, crackers, and jars thud to the tile.

Standing next to the door, I'm frozen. Part of me wants to flee. The other part doesn't want to leave Sharon alone with Gabe's irate father who I know is dangerous, and is probably drunk—at ten in the morning.

"Stop it!" Sharon yells. "You're destroying his apartment!"

Jim turns around, his eyes drilling fury at Sharon. "The damn gun didn't just disappear."

Gun? Alarm bells go off in my head.

Plates begin falling and smashing onto the floor.

Sharon keeps pulling at his shirt and telling him to stop. My purse falls to floor as I wring my hands. My mind is blank. I have no idea how to deal with this.

Suddenly, Allie comes through the door. Her eyes widen on me before she turns to where the racket is coming from. "What the heck is going on up here?"

Sharon glances over her shoulder.

Allie looks to me.

I point to Jim. "Gabe's father. He just showed up. He thinks Gabe has his gun hidden here."

Allie's expression turns alarmed as she faces Jim and Sharon. "You need to leave. Now."

Jim opens another cupboard and Sharon's whining grows frantic.

"This isn't your property," Allie says firmly. "You need to leave now."

"Fuck you," Jim says.

"All right then, I'm calling the police," Allie says, before rushing out.

"Jim!" Sharon wails. "You heard her! We have to go!"

He keeps yanking items out of the last cupboard. The floor in the kitchen is littered with destroyed food and broken dishes.

Sharon starts feverishly yanking on his shirt and arm. "Jim!"

He turns, then grabs her by the neck, yanking her on her tiptoes. "Shut the fuck up."

I finally quit the hand wringing and race across the room. "Let her go!" I heave on his hand wrapped around her neck.

Sharon wheezes.

"Let her go!" I scream, frantically tugging on his arm, clawing at his skin.

When I scrape his arm, his blood shot eyes spit fury at me, but he lets her go. She falls against the counter. For a split second, I'm relieved, then a meaty hand covers my face and violently shoves me back.

I'm falling. Arms flailing. Some yells—an angry roar that fills the apartment. Leaning on the counter several feet from me, Sharon's face twists in distress. I'm about to splat on the kitchen floor covered with spilled food and pieces of broken china. Muscled arms catch me inches from landing on the broken shards. Strong hands lift me and set me on a chair.

"You okay?" Gabe hoarsely asks, leaning over me.

I can only nod.

After assessing me with a long look, rage creates deep lines around his mouth and he flies across the room, taking his father with him. He slams his father against the wall. Twice.

Jim shakes his head, dazed from his collisions with the wall.

"I told you! I told you!" Gabe snarls as he draws his fist back. "You don't hit women! Especially her! Never her!" He hits his father hard and fast. Once. Twice. Three times. Then more. In the face.

Blood drips from Jim's mouth.

"Gabe!" Sharon yells, pushing herself from the counter.

I get up too. Though my legs are wobbly, I grab Gabe's arm as he pulls it back. "Stop! He's not worth it!"

Gabe's arm tenses, but he doesn't release another punch. He just stands there, staring furiously at his father, and breathing hard.

Jim starts sliding down the wall.

Gabe's fist contracts.

"Leave him alone!" Sharon wails, rushing toward Jim.

I grip Gabe's shoulder. "You have to stop," I say as loud and calm as possible. I lean closer to him, trying to get him to hear past his rage. "I'm fine. Sharon's fine. Just leave him alone."

Gabe steps back. He stares at me, but I can tell that he isn't seeing me past the rage in his eyes. He weaves as if drunk too.

Appearing dazed, Jim lays on the floor and Sharon kneels at his side. Sobbing, she whispers in a voice full of despair, "I took the gun. I didn't want you to do anything stupid or get hurt. I took the gun."

I wrap my arms around Gabe, holding him tight and bury my head in his chest. "It's okay. It's okay," I repeat into his work shirt, waiting for him to hug me back. "I'm okay. Sharon's okay."

But his arms never rise. Instead, the door whips open and two policemen flood the room, followed by Allie.

Obviously confused and blinking in shock at the scene in the kitchen, Allie points to Jim lying on the floor. "He's the trespasser."

Sharon's still crying.

The police look from Gabe, who has blood on his knuckles, to Jim, who is passed out cold on the floor. One of them asks, "What is going on here?" While the other radios for an ambulance.

Gabe steps from me and raises his wrists. "I punched the shit out of him."

The cop who radioed for an ambulance goes to Jim. The second one studies Gabe, reaching for his handcuffs.

"No. No. No," I say, moving in front Gabe. "His father choked the woman on the floor and shoved me down by my face."

Gabe steps in front of me, holding out his wrists. "I'm already on probation for assault and battery."

At that the policeman, clinks the cuffs around Gabe.

"He was defending us!" I say.

The policeman looks to Gabe, whose face is granite. "We'll figure this out, ma'am," he says and takes Gabe.

"Gabe," I sob, but he doesn't look back as they go on the porch and down the stairs.

Allie comes and puts an arm around my shoulders. "What happened, April?" she softly asks.

I cover my face and shake my head. Since Gabe's father came through the door, everything has been surreal. But Gabe ignoring me...I drop my hands and whisper, "I don't know."

Chapter 29
Gabe

I've lived on hope for too long. Reality has raised her ugly head, and I'm face to face with her, accepting and despondent all at once. It was a good ride, but the shit is over.

Jail sucks. The food sucks. The two-inch thick mattress sucks. The idiot who snores like a bear in the bunk below me sucks. The boredom sucks. But what has sucked the most the last three days—because this is my third offence and possible felony so I had to wait for a court arraignment for bail to be posted—is the shit whirling in my head.

The possibility of prison. My father knocked out cold. Sharon hiding guns. My spot and future in the band. But mostly April. I can't get the sight of my father shoving her by the face to the ground out of my head. My brain plays the image on repeat over and over again until I want to punch the shit out of the cement wall next to my bunk. If she hadn't been with me, the fucker would have never touched her.

Now Monday morning, I'm dressed in my orange jail finery and trussed up like a hog in chains that loop from my wrists to my feet as they take me from the jailhouse to the courthouse. As a guard opens the door to the courtroom, I catch a glimpse of Romeo, Justin, and April sitting in the front row.

My jaw hardens. Why the fuck would they bring her? The sooner I get over that shit the better. For both of us.

I stare straight ahead at the far wall as a guard removes the chains from my wrists and from my feet. Without looking at anyone, I proceed to the table where Justin's lawyer waits. The same lawyer we used when I beat the shit out of Allie's ex.

The judge comes out and within less than twenty minutes, the facts are laid out—including my past misdemeanors. Each time the prosecution adds another layer to the proceedings, it's like a punch in my pride. The list makes me wonder how I can have any pride with a rap sheet like this because there's more. There were times the police weren't called. Many times I got away with the release of my temper.

My head hammers as the prosecutor drones on about how I've proved I'm a danger to society. And because I'm such a danger, he tries to add my juvenile rap sheet to the proceedings. Justin's lawyer argues. The judge doesn't let that two pager in.

Once the prosecutor is done, I plead guilty in a matter of fact voice, and my bail is set.

The sentencing will be forthcoming within a month.

Yesterday, during his visit, the lawyer tried to talk me in to pleading not guilty, and talked and talked and talked. He believes it's the only way to get a reduced sentence. I refused. I did the shit. Like I can stand here and act like it didn't happen or that I had a blip of insanity. My pride may get me killed one day—probably sent to prison on this one—but I'm not a lying actor.

They chain me back up—I stare at the wall—and transport me back to the jailhouse. Knowing Romeo or Justin is posting my bail— more money that I'll owe—I don't get too comfortable, just sit on the top bunk with my back against the cement, ignore the idiot trying to talk with me from the bunk below, and try not the think how prison is going to suck way worse than this.

Within the hour, the guards are processing me for release. In my mechanic clothes once more, I walk out with Justin, who is giving me the third degree about being stubborn and pleading guilty.

I am guilty fuckhead. Seeing as how he just bailed me out, I keep the retort behind my teeth.

My head about explodes as I realize whose car is waiting for us in the parking lot. Just my luck.

April drove.

Jaw tight again, I get in the backseat with Justin. April turns around with a soft smile and a, "Hi." I nod and turn toward the window. I can almost hear her disappointment, certainly sense it coming from the front seat.

Justin continues droning about my guilty plea, explaining how I need to help the lawyer with everything possible at my sentencing, so I get the least punishment possible. I stare out the window. Justin starts pleading, reminding me that a third offence can warrant two years prison time. I stare out the window. Romeo joins in, tells me to get my head out of my ass and listen. I stare out the window.

There's no fight left in me. I can't turn the tide on my inevitable future any longer. A fucked up life and prison should have been stamped on my forehead the minute I was born.

Justin and Romeo are both shouting at me as April parks in front of the tattoo shop.

I finally turn to Justin. "How is my father?"

His frustrated expression changes to a mixture of surprise and blankness.

April twists in the front seat toward me. "He got out of the hospital yesterday. A concussion and broken jaw," she softly says. "Sharon and I have been in contact over the past few days. She....well, she feels responsible since she hid the gun from Jim in the first place."

Fuck.

I close my eyes, drawing in a harsh breath as concussion and a broken jaw reverberates through me. As a kid, I never truly wanted to hurt my father. The only thing I wanted was for him to leave me alone, then leave Sharon alone. Instead, I put his ass in the hospital because I couldn't control myself. I let the air caught in me out in a fast rush, escape out of the car, and fly up the stairs to my apartment.

Inside, I lean forward across the counter and press my forehead on a cupboard.

This morning, during the arraignment, and even the trip home, I believed in the illusion that by giving up and giving in, I could ride this out. That illusion is falling to pieces. I draw in breaths, trying not to imagine my father in pain with Sharon going nuts by his side.

The image crashes into my skull again and again.

A knock sounds on the door.

I. Cannot. Deal. With. This. Shit.

The knocking grows louder, more persistent.

I beat my head against the cupboard, wishing I could knock myself out.

She starts yelling, "Gabe!"

Hissing every swear word known to man, I push away from the counter and whip the door open.

"Hey," April says, her face twisted in worry.

I lean on a kitchen chair. I can't seem to stay upright without help.

She comes in shutting the door, troubled eyes sweeping over me.

My gaze roams the apartment, anything but on her. Then I'm noticing how clean it is. My head snaps back to her. "You?"

She nods. "And Allie." She steps closer. "Gabe…"

I run a hand through my hair, resisting the desire to pull the strands out, then hold the back of my neck, trying to squeeze the tension out of myself. She stands mere feet from me, wide eyed and worried, beautiful and perfect. So perfect, it's starting to hurt to look at her.

"Listen, April," I say to the floor. "I don't think things are going to work out between us."

There's a long pause of silence before she says, "Don't do this." She comes closer forcing me to meet her gaze. "Don't equate letting me go with doing the right thing. It's not right."

I drop my hand and laugh despondently. "The right thing? Didn't you hear? I'm dangerous. Being with me is dangerous. And I'll soon be a convict. I'm no good for you. I know it. You know it. The whole fucking world knows it."

"No." She shakes her head as her expression grows imploring. "That's not true, even Romeo admitted this morning that we should be together."

The warmth in her pleading eyes almost has me grasping for her.

My jaw turns hard, harder than it felt in court. Though a tight knot forms in my chest, I ignore it. "Romeo? Who the fuck is Romeo in all this? What does he know? You think with all the shit going on in my life, I can deal with you and your shit? Your fucking whining over your sister?"

She blanches, as if I punched her. The whiteness of her skin, the shock in her expression, and the pain in her eyes, make me want to take the words back.

But I don't. I can't.

I cross my arms and sneer, deciding to put the last nail in the coffin, before I'm on my knees begging her to take me back. "You're a good fuck. Maybe the best fuck in my life. A fuck that I wanted to keep around, but the fucking ain't worth dealing with the guilt ridden baggage you bring. Baggage that might be worse than my own shit."

My words are like bullets from the gun of my mouth. They hit her hard until she doubles over, trying to gulp in air. I harden my resolve and ignore the anguish her visible pain brings me.

She finally stands, her look raw and full of accusation. Without saying a word, she stumbles to the door and slams it shut.

The knot in my chest feels like it's going to explode. I want to punch every surface in the apartment until my knuckles are raw.

Seconds tick by until I can't hold all the pain in any longer. A chair flies across the room. The wall gets a punch. The front of the refrigerator takes a hit. My knuckles are raw and blood drips on the floor. Then before I destroy the entire apartment, I grip the counter, plant my face on a cupboard, and just breathe.

Chapter 30
April

My last group session. Two days from now, I graduate. I could have skipped the session, since a week after my interview I was accepted into the clinical program. However, this may be my only chance to see Gabe. Though I know deep down that he was trying to push me away, it took a few days for me to get over his cruel words. He nearly shattered my heart with his cruel words, but as I gradually acknowledged his intent, I have become determined to make him see reason. I've called him, texted him, and even gone to his apartment. He has not answered my calls, my texts, or his door. I have considered going to the garage he works at but that would be the last resort. Yet, I'm hoping he will show up at group.

I know what it's like to shut people out. I'm a pro at it. And now I'm being shut out. Though I deserve a broken heart and definitely don't deserve him, I can't help thinking that Gabe needs me. Ironically, I had been leaving his apartment on the day of the fight not sure if I could handle being with him. Now faced with the possibility, I'm desperate to be with him. The thought of his absence in my life overrides my heart crunching guilt at being happy. But his sullen demeanor is slicing at my heart, slowly tearing it to ribbons with each text and call and knock he doesn't answer. However, I'm determined to be as stubborn as he is and refuse to give up. Though there are times, several times a day actually, when the loss of him leaves me unable to breathe as sorrow and tears threaten to overwhelm me.

But of course, we are fifteen minutes into the session and still no Gabe.

Instead of letting that tear at me, I force myself to concentrate on the group. It has changed over the last month. Misha has ceased giving me the evil eye, though her glare still carries contempt. Chad continues to be upset about his stepfather's rules, but is also not as nasty as he was in the beginning. And Jason has been contributing a little more each session, if only opinions.

I previously considered Jeff a quack but I'm slowly comprehending how he subtly gets us to talk and keeps things moving by forcing us to share, causing us to be more comfortable with one another. And I imagine within a few more months the group members will learn to trust one another. Reflecting on past group sessions, I can't say I totally understand how Jeff did it, and that worries me. As someone who desires to be in his position one day, I should be able to see how he is maneuvering us. Some of his machinations, like forcing us to share something each week or do something outside of group, are clear to me. However, not all of his actions are comprehensible to me, which once more leaves me wondering if I'm pushing myself into a mold that I'll never fit in.

Jeff is droning on about how helping others not only builds self-esteem, but heals us too. Perhaps, the droning is his secret, leaking into our subconscious and gradually changing our view of the world. Though, at the moment, just Jason appears to be intently listening to Jeff. Misha stares off into space. Chad stares at Misha. And I'm preoccupied with staring at the door.

However, even if Gabe doesn't show, I've decided to come clean. It seems that if one of us has the balls to speak, it opens up new doors for everyone. Knowing I haven't contributed much to this group, I would like to give something before I leave it. And I'm slowly coming to terms that hiding my past isn't solely about keeping me from depression. It has also been about being afraid of how people view me.

So when Jeff asks me first if I have anything to share, I draw from a well of courage deep down inside of me that I didn't know existed until recently, and start a condensed version of what I shared with Gabe over a week ago.

About a third of the way through my rendition, the faces around me turn shocked, half way through, they turn absolutely stunned. I'm almost finished and feeling wrung out when a light knock sounds at the door. No one notices except for me. Instead, my pause gets their attention. When another knock sounds Jeff reluctantly gets up. The sight of Gabe's stony face causes my heart to accelerate. Jeff quickly directs Gabe to his seat, sits down, and gestures for me to continue.

But my attention is drawn to Gabe. He sits with his arms crossed, looking at the floor and ignoring all of us. Every cell in my body yearns, to the point of pain, to go to him, get him to look at me, get him listen.

Jeff clears his throat and I snap out of it, reluctantly continuing. Though with Gabe here now, it's much harder than before. Once I'm done, everyone stares at me dumbfounded, even Gabe—I suppose he didn't expect me to share with anyone else.

"Well," Misha says, her tone shocked, "I can understand why you're here now." She looks at me normally for once—meaning without her normal malice or contempt. "I'm truly sorry to hear about your sister, but how—how do you get over something like that?"

I draw in a deep breath. "You don't. You just attempt to live with the guilt the best you can."

"And try not to hate yourself," Jason says quietly, which has me wondering for the umpteenth time why he is here.

The crease on his brow has me saying, "That's true. How—"

"It's not like you killed her," Chad blurts.

"Well, no…" I squeak then trail off, not sure how to respond to that, nor wanting to.

Gabe turns to Chad, his face hard and intimidating. "You really should shut the hell up."

Gabe coming to my aid gives me a spark of hope.

Chad leans back against his chair, grumbling, "Just trying to help for once."

Misha's pierced mouth twists in concentration. "I don't think that's going to help. I'm sure everyone questions what they could have done different after a…accident, but to have had the person asked for your help…" She sadly shakes her head. "But sometimes help isn't enough."

Gabe's brows rise at Misha or more accurately her thoughtfulness.

"That took a lot of guts to share with us, April," Jeff says when there's a lull in the conversation. "And though I do understand why you've felt guilty, you also have to have the courage to forgive yourself."

Never having considered it that way, I try to wrap my head around his idea. It almost seems too big for me to process.

"I know what it's like to feel guilty," Jason softly says, then takes a huge gulp of air.

We all turn to Jason.

Gaze on the floor, he says in an almost whisper, "When I was a kid, well eleven years old, I was over my friend's house. He—we both wanted to check out his dad's gun collection."

I cover my mouth to hold a gasp in, fearing what he is going to say next.

He draws in a deep breath then blurts out, "I accidently shot him."

The gasp comes out muffled from behind my hand.

"Holy shit!" Chad says under his breath.

Jason shakes his head, his eyes sad. "He didn't die, but the bullet went into his side and lodged into his spine. He became a paraplegic, and now—and now I visit him almost every weekend."

I can't help taking his hand as my eyes begin to tear up. "I'm so sorry to hear that, Jason. I'm not sure I even—"

"Dude," Chad says, "you were just a kid."

Jason blinks at Chad. "And he's an adult forever stuck in a wheel chair."

"You know," Gabe quietly says to Jason, "you're not helping your friend by cutting yourself off from life." He glances from Jason then pointedly to me as I wipe tears from my eyes.

Misha's head snaps to Gabe. "Hey asshole, he never said he was cutting himself off from life!"

Gabe ignores her and waits for Jason to reply.

Jason's hand trembles in mine as he asks Gabe, "But why should I get a normal life?"

Gabe's forehead creases. "You're stuck in guilt and your friend is stuck in a wheelchair. I'm sure those visits are wonderful."

"Gabe!" I say as Jason's hand trembles more.

He ignores me and demands of Jason, "You ever go anywhere with your friend?"

Jason shakes his head.

"Ever do anything other than visit him at his home? Go anywhere?"

Jason shakes his head.

"Do you ever do anything?"

"Not really," Jason practically whispers.

"So you're both invalids. One bullet. Two lives ruined." Gabe sits back, shaking his head.

I release Jason's hand to point at Gabe. "And you're not just throwing the towel in on yours? Refusing to play in the band? Refusing to talk with the lawyer?" Romeo has been keeping me up to date, or more accurately, keeping me up on how Gabe has cut himself off from everyone and everything.

Gabe's top lip curls. "April," he says roughly. "I don't believe I was the one sharing. My shit is not part of this group discussion."

I let out a huff of anger and sit back, while his irate eyes drill holes in me.

Jeff, who had been calmly listening, leans forward, probably hoping to diffuse the sudden tension. "Jason, first of all I want to commend you for your bravery for sharing that with us. It must have been difficult, but like April, it took a lot of courage. However, I think Gabe might be right, though said crudely. Maybe we could help you think of things you and your friend can do."

Jason sits up fully as if getting ready to listen.

Surprisingly, Chad gets the ball rolling. "Maybe you could go to a game like baseball or basketball like the Pistons?"

Jeff nods. "That is a terrific idea, Chad."

Misha says, "I've seen paraplegics at the bowling alley. That could be fun."

Spitting mad at Gabe, I mumble, "The movies." Lame but it's all my angry brain can come up with.

Gabe says, "How about you research some shit, like Google it."

We all stare at Gabe, obviously offended at how rude he is being.

After a long lull of silence, Jeff studies his watch. "Okay, well then, we're over our hour by almost thirty minutes. But this has been a very productive session. I want to thank April and Jason for their bravery, and let's all think of something that could help them for next time." He closes his binder. "So we'll see everyone next week, before our two week break for Christmas."

Gabe is out the door as soon as Jeff finishes. I rush out to catch him, cooling my anger each step of the way.

"Hey, can I just ask you one thing?" I loudly ask when we're both on the sidewalk.

He spins around. "I'm getting tired of this shit. Romeo and the rest of the band are up my ass twenty four seven in between you blowing up my phone and rapping incessantly on my door. When will you people realize I just want to be left alone? I don't owe any of you fuckers anything."

Ignore his words. Ignore. Ignore. Ignore. I chant in my head, reminding myself he's spouting hurtful things as a defense mechanism. But his spiteful words have me blurting out, "Don't you miss me?" This wasn't what I'd planned to ask him. I wanted to ask him something similar to what he said to me over a week ago; if his soul is still there, though weary and full of shame. Unable to stop myself, I add, "I miss you. So much."

His hard, twisted expression falls for a quick second, and I glimpse behind the mask of resentment he has been showing the world. The stark hopelessness I see slashes at my insides and tears at my heart, but in the next second, his face twists back into a mask of ire.

"Excuse me," someone asks from behind me. "Excuse me, April?"

Jason, I realize and turn.

He offers me a shy smile. "Could I get a ride?"

My heart does a little flip and I nod. "Of course—of course you can get a ride." By the time I turn back around, Gabe is marching toward his truck.

I watch him until he gets in the truck, longing a knot in my chest, then turn to Jason. "Ready?"

He glances past me at Gabe. "You sure?"

254

"Jason, I've been asking you for months," I say with the warmest smile I can muster. I want to follow Gabe, want to beg and plead and throw myself at him. But I want to be there for Jason too. I dig my keys out of my purse. "I'd love to give you a ride, especially when it's this cold." Then I turn my back on Gabe and walk Jason to my car.

Chapter 31
April

I stare at the rolling ocean. It's a strange sight on Christmas day. I've never been at my father's for Christmas. I always spent the holiday with my mother and flew out a few days later for New Year's with my father—except for the last three years when I didn't come at all. My mother completely flipped when I told her I was swapping the holidays around this year, but even her flip out couldn't stop me. I needed to get away, and the calmness of my father and California seemed like the perfect solution.

And it had been. Between graduating and both of my parents coming in for commencements, I had stayed busy in Michigan. Then traveling to Malibu, getting the house ready for Christmas with my dad, and doing a bit of shopping, I stayed busy here. Last night we went to a Thai restaurant on the beach. This morning his girlfriend came over and we opened presents, then we made a huge breakfast.

Right now people—mostly musicians—are streaming into the backyard below me. Like always, the special moments of my father's life are surrounded by music. They will soon be having an impromptu jam session.

When the sun began to set, I came upstairs to the living room and took a selfie of me by the tree with the sun setting over the ocean. Keeping my vow not to give up on Gabe, I call and text him every day, even if he never responds. Though I typed out, Merry Christmas! Wish I was with you, next to the picture, my finger hovers over the send button.

This is starting to kill me. His stubbornness is breaking my heart.

I'm trying to stay strong but I seem to be breaking down a little more each day. I fall on the couch, wipe tears from my eyes, and draw in calming breaths. More than wanting to be with him, I'm worried about him, distraught that he might be lonely, might be fearful of going to prison, or might be depressed. But he won't let me in. And the last time I talked to Romeo—about a week ago—he still won't let anyone in. Their album has even been put on hold.

After I give into a few more tears, I push send and go to the kitchen.

I'm going to be strong. I'm not going to give up.

This is my daily mantra.

Since my dad will start grilling soon, I pull out trays of steaks and start seasoning them. Though I'm determined to be strong, I'm a little too melancholy to be around people on Christmas day and don't want to gray up their day. I'm wrapping potatoes in tin foil, when the front doorbell rings. It must be someone new. Someone who doesn't know you just go around the house to the unlocked gate in the back.

As I open the door, my heart jumps into my throat. "What are you doing here?" I gasp at Gabe as shock has me questioning the sight of him in long shorts and a tank on my doorstep. His mahogany eyes are conflicted. I peek behind him, wondering what the heck is going on.

He buries his hands in his pockets. "I need to talk to you."

Yup, it's him, I realize before I pinch myself. Then I almost snap out a sarcastic remark, seeing as how he had to come across the country to talk with me while I've been trying to talk to him for weeks while we were mere miles apart.

He runs a hand through his hair. "Can I come in?"

"Um…" I step back on wobbly legs. "Sure, yeah…" I shuffle farther into the foyer and sit—before I faint from the surprise of seeing him on my doorstep—on the bench across from the door. Scenarios are rushing through my head. Some good. Some awful. Why is he here? "Why are you here?" I ask, blurting out my thoughts.

He shuts the door with a trembling hand. Why would his hand be trembling? What is going on? I'm not emotionally ready for whatever he is going to dish out.

"Romeo talked—guilt tripped—me in to finishing the album. We flew in this afternoon." He comes to stand a few feet from me. Everything I want is so close yet could be a world away. "I have to meet with my probation officer next Tuesday, and I'm not supposed to leave the state. Therefore we decided to start today and get another half day in."

"Oh," I slowly say, trying to understand his words past the emotional storm rolling over me. "But why here? Why aren't you recording?"

He comes closer, standing inches from me.

A lightning bolt of anxiousness strikes along my spine at his closeness.

"Since we started a couple of hours ago, I couldn't do shit, played like shit. Maybe because it's thousands of miles away from home and Christmas day, I keep thinking how I'm only miles from you. How much I'm hurting you." He kneels, setting his hands on the bench next to my thighs. "And no matter, how wrong I am for you"—I start shaking my head at that, but he continues—"How being with you makes me feel brand new as if none of my past matters."

My head stops shaking and I simply stare at him. Okay, okay, okay, that was good. So good astonishment is starting to melt into a warmth that is slowing spreading across my limbs.

He looks above my head, then back to me, drawing in a deep breath. "But mostly how much I'm in love with you."

In the following silence, a new shock hits me like an electrical zap as he gazes at me with a mixture of desperation and longing. My bottom lip trembles while I attempt to let his words sink in. They feel impossible, the thought of someone—Gabe!—loving me. I do reach out and pinch my thigh. At the sharp pain, shock, mixed with relief, has me bursting out in tears.

"April," Gabe gently whispers, embracing my face with his callused hands. "I'm sorry. I've been a complete ass. I believed I was doing the right thing. I tend to get angry and over react. But when Romeo handed me your address less than an hour ago—"

Craving physical proof of those words, I stop him with a kiss. Within seconds, he kisses me back, long and deep and soft.

He pulls away, brushing the tears from cheeks with his thumbs. "You forgive me then?"

Still feeling out if it, I let out an unlady like snort. "I think my actions said more than any words."

He shakes his head. "I always seem to fuck things up."

I lean back on the wall, shaking my head. The thoughts that have been swirling in my mind over the past few weeks have me saying, "I think we're both...scared. Neither of us believed anyone could love us...couldn't see what was happening..."

"I'm not sure what's happening should be," he says in a tense, sad tone, releasing his hold on me.

I sit up, refusing to let him be the martyr. "We're both screwed up. You helped me confront the past, but my guilt is always going to linger. I did wrong, and no matter what you say, it's the truth. And though I'd give anything to, I'll never be able to erase your father's abuse. That pain will always linger too. But together, we're less screwed up. Together we're stronger, better people, like you said, brand new." I let out a crazy laugh. Yeah, still in shock here. "Guess it's true, being in love can change a person."

The contemplative look on his face changes to wonder.

I grin—I'm kind of drunk on shock. "I think I've been in love with you since you made me dance in the rain." The truth, I realize. I just never admitted it to myself until now.

After a second of open-mouthed bewilderment, he kisses me hard, plastering me against the wall. I like being between him and the wall, in fact I love it.

Someone clearing a throat, then saying, "April?" has us wrenching apart.

I glance up to find my father. "Hey, Dad."

He raises his brows instead of asking.

On a giddy high, I introduce them, explaining Gabe is one of the band members from Michigan recording an album here. They shake hands and give each other a quick greeting.

Though my dad appears confused, he returns to the kitchen. Unlike my mother, he doesn't try to mess with my life or tell me what to do. Guess he got enough of that from his parents.

Gabe sighs. "I have to go, but…Merry Christmas."

I lean on him, looking into his soulful mahogany eyes. "You've just made it the best one ever." He smiles as I wrap my hands around his shoulders. "With everything in your life right now, I get why you're hesitant, but promise me two things?"

"Two?" he says cautiously as his hands find my waist.

"Don't shut me out."

"Don't think I can anymore."

"And work with the lawyer."

His hands tighten on my waist.

"Whatever happens, if you go to prison, I'm not giving up on you. I'll visit you. Write to you. Wait for you." He winces at that, but now that I have his attention, I'm determined to help. "But don't you give up. The truth isn't going to destroy your pride. People may pity the boy you were, but trust me, they will be astounded at the man you've become, because of all that boy has been through. I know because I am."

He stares at me with an expression of confusion mixed with awe. "You shrinking me again?"

A sad laugh escapes me. "I'm not much of a shrink. I just understand you, like you understand me and the whole guilt twisting my perspective thing." He nods but I persist. "Promise me."

"I'll talk with the lawyer," he concedes.

Understanding that's all I'm going to get, I hug him tight. "When are you getting back to Michigan?" I ask into his chest as his arms come around me.

"Late Wednesday night."

"How late?"

"About one in the morning."

"Is that too late?"

"Hell no."

Chapter 32
April

Allie gave me the extra key. I sit and wait and watch the clock for over an hour as it ticks closer to one a.m. A nervous flutter rolls through my stomach every few minutes while I wait, but the flutter will not stop me from taking another leap into my past. When the sound of the door handle turns, my stomach threatens to do far more than flutter, yet the sight of Gabe walking into the apartment has me ignoring the nervous tsunami in my midriff.

I launch myself at him from his couch. Though it was two days ago, I shout, "Happy New Year!"

Startled, he drops his bag and catches me. After a long, hot kiss, he closes the door.

"The album done?" I ask, leaning back to look at him.

He nods. "Except for final mixing and mastering."

"Congratulations. Feel good about it?"

"Yeah, it's good, maybe great."

"Oh, from the one song I heard, I'm sure it will be great." I move back, putting my wringing hands behind my back. "I have a surprise for you."

His brows rise and he grins as he sheds his winter coat. "More than that attack welcome?"

Nodding, I step to the side. My guitar case is on the table.

At first, he blinks at it, then lifts his gaze. "You don't have to do this."

"I want to," I say, going to the case, appearing calm, although I'm anything but. I drag out the guitar. "Or maybe I need to."

Gabe silently watches me for a long moment before moving to the couch. "All right, play something for me."

I drop on a chair across from him. "I haven't played in almost three years, so expect a few, or maybe more, slip ups."

"It will be better than anything I could do."

"Well it's not the drums," I snort, attempting to appear calm. I settle the guitar in front of me with trembling hands. I'm scared, actually terrified, but the instrument feels right, the cool wood in my hands like a forgotten friend that I hadn't realized how much I missed. This friend and I need to become reacquainted.

I draw in a deep breath and begin. Slow, soft finger picks, paired with changing cords changes into a fast rhythmic progression of higher chords, then it repeats though the cords change slightly. I keep my attention on the guitar, fearing if I glance at Gabe, I'll forget the memorized notes. The pretty melody builds and drops again and again. I mess up on a few chords, the timing during a couple of transitions, and the finger picking during the faster parts. There was a time I could practically play this instrumental in my sleep. Although I remember the notes, timing and finger motion need practice. Yet, it doesn't sound flat. I'm startled—more like elatedly shocked—to find there's emotion behind the music. Something I had believed I would never get back.

Finished, I draw in another breath, cradle the loved instrument in my grasp, and meet the stunned gaze across from me.

"What was that?" Awe fills his tone.

"Mozart's Lacrimosa from Requiem in D minor, changed a bit for the guitar though. I used to do it much, much better."

Gabe's brows nearly hit his hairline. "Better?" He stands up, towering over me. "That was insane." He takes the guitar from my grip and sets it in the case. "And sexy, unbelievably sexy." He grabs my hands and pulls me up. "We could never be in a band together."

"Why not?"

"Watching you play, I wouldn't make it through one practice. I'd want to do this." He brushes my fingertips with his lips. "And this." His lips find the other set of fingertips.

I never thought the whisper of lips on my fingers would be hot, but I'm practically panting.

"And this," he says before kissing me.

"Is that all?" I ask a bit breathlessly when we come up for air.

He tugs me by the hand toward the bed. "Nope. The rest of the band would get quite the show."

"Show me then."

He grin is too sexy as he pushes me onto the bed. "Oh, I plan to."
****

Gabe's harsh breath is in my ear. My leg is around his waist. Water is pelting us. My hands grip the slick, hard muscles of his shoulders. I'm going to have tile marks in my back. Shower sex. Best way to wake up. Ever. Who would have thought? He lifts my leg and changes the angle of his entry. Oh, good move. Quite, quite lovely. A few thrusts later, I'm releasing one of those melodious sighs that he loves.

After the wake up sex that leaves me tired, he wraps my limp body in a towel and helps me from the shower. "Other than a two o'clock appointment with my probation officer, I have the day off. Want to go out for breakfast?"

It takes me a few seconds to find my mind. "I'd love to, but call your lawyer first."

He gives me a level look.

I give him one back.

"He's actually Justin's lawyer."

"Call him."

His fingers lightly slide across my shoulder then up the line of my neck, sending little, hot shivers through my body.

I step out of his reach. "Call him now."

He lowers his hand. "Fine."

I smile sweetly. "Excellent."

While I dress on one side of the apartment, Gabe calls from the other side. Wearing just jeans, he leans on the counter and crosses his bare feet.

It's quite the yummy sight, and has me questioning if I should even bother with clothes. I try to give him some privacy by going back into the bathroom. Done putting my wet hair in a bun, I step out into the apartment to find Gabe leaning front ways on the counter, his back muscles tensely bunched.

"What's going on?" I ask, my tone fearful.

He slowly turns around. "The hearing is on Friday."

Coming toward him, I almost trip. "This coming Friday?"

He nods.

"How?" I expected a few more weeks with how slow the legal system usually works, but this is too fast. We've just finally found each other.

He shrugs but his jaw is rigid. "I already pleaded guilty. Guess it should be quick."

My fingers curl into his belt loops. "Three days…"

He leans down, resting his forehead on mine. "I wanted—I wanted to…do so much with you."

The sadness and fear in his gaze is breaking my heart. I don't want his possible last days of freedom to be dark and full of trepidation. Knowing my gaze probably reflects his, I force a smile to my lips. "Let's make it the best three days ever."

****

We sit on my couch after dinner. Gabe in the corner. Me lying with my back against him. I went shopping—bought everything the male population is known to love, from steaks to potatoes to mushrooms—in the afternoon while he met with his probation officer and then lawyer. After we ate, I offered to play the guitar. Gabe said to wait or we'd be in bed before eight. We've been talking about anything and everything. How Riley helped him become a better drummer. The huge crush I had on my piano teacher when I was twelve. How Gabe is always nervous prior to a show whether on the major tour they opened for this past summer or at a local venue here. My one show in a teenage club basement with my retro band. He talks about some of the good times with his father. I even share some humorous moments from when Rachel and I were children. Then we talk music. He likes the harder stuff, but doesn't mind my favorite era of grunge.

Gabe breaks the lighthearted conversation by announcing, "The lawyer wants my psychologist to offer a recommendation to the judge."

His frustrated tone has me twisting around. "You don't want him to?"

"Her. And fuck no." His fingers tighten their hold on my waist. "Isn't that shit confidential?"

I turn all the way around until we're face to face. "You can tell her any specifics that you don't want her to share, but no one's going to think any less of you."

"I know. I know. It's just…it was hard enough telling her, but to hear it back out of her…"

"Like reliving it?"

"Something like that."

I brush a finger over his top lip, the one that I find so sexy. "Part of me doesn't want you to have to deal with that, actually all of me doesn't want you to deal with that. Yet you could be trading one hell for another." Though I'm imagining, or maybe hoping, if it happens, he would go to a minimum security prison with less restrictions. However, being locked up would be awful no matter where. I'm very, very scared for him, but I'm trying not to darken our short time together and be brave for him.

He draws in a harsh breath and lets it go, touching my face. "Because of my promise to you, I'll probably agree to it tomorrow when we meet."

"Do it for you, not for me."

"I'll do it for both of us."

I shake my head, before falling on him for a hug.

All this talk of lawyers and psychologists has me wanting to bury my face in his shirt and hysterically cry. Instead, after several minutes of collecting my emotions, I push up and ask, "Ready for me to play?"

"More classics?"

"Current classics."

He tilts his head at that.

I push off him to stand. "I know a few thrash songs…like say…" I reach for my case on the table. "Metallica."

His brows go up, but he smiles. "I'm always ready for you to play." He stands and tugs me by the hand. "But you should play in the bedroom. We're going to need the bed."

****

When I get home from work the next day, Gabe is already at my apartment. Of course, I gave him the extra key. He is sitting on the couch, appearing relaxed with an ankle resting on a knee and an arm wrapped behind the couch. But the glint in his eye, the hot smoldering look, exposes what is truly on his mind.

I kick the door shut, whip off my coat, and practically dive at him. He catches me and within a few hot kisses, our clothing is loosened and a condom unwrapped. He enters me and hisses out a, "Hello."

"Hi," I pant, straddling him.

"Work good?" he asks, head tipped back, fingers digging into my ribs.

"All right. This is better."

"Yeah?" He forcefully surges upwards.

My head falls back. "Oh, yeah, much, much better."

He keeps it slow with deep, hard thrusts that have my body striving to go into overdrive. Unintentionally, I try to speed the rhythm up.

His hands grip my hips, slowing me down as he lifts his head and presses his mouth to the center of my chest. "I'm trying to hold on to these moments. The feel, the scent, the sound, the beautiful sight of you. I may need them to last a couple of years."

Forcing my body to slow, I wrap my arms around his shoulders. "I'm holding on to the fact that a couple of years are nothing compared to forever."

He nods, his mouth brushing the clasp of my bra. "A couple of years is nothing compared to being with you."

****

My bedroom is dark except for the faint shine of the lights in the parking lot out the window. I'm lying sideways on the bed. Gabe's naked stomach is my pillow. His fingers play in my hair. The motion is sweet and comforting, yet melancholy hangs over us. Tomorrow morning is his sentencing.

I want to cry and just let him hold me. But I won't. I will be strong for him. I'll cry later, buckets into my pillow.

"I'm not going into the graduate program," I blurt out filling the silence, wanting to share and wanting to dissipate the fear hanging in the air.

His hand pauses near my temple. "Because?"

I turn, my cheek sliding across his skin, to look at him in the shadows. "Because you were right. Guilt has been driving me, but I don't think I'm cut out to be a counselor, no matter how bad my remorse drives me to be one."

"Guilt can make people blind to the truth. Look at how I tried to push you away."

"Yeah, but that only lasted weeks." I let out a sigh. "For almost four years, I believed sacrificing my life as payment would somehow pay my debt, somehow let me look in the mirror again without hate. I finally get that I'm going to have to accept myself, even with the horrible wrong in my past. There's no erasing it by helping people."

"There's nothing wrong with helping people."

"When you're doing it for yourself there is."

"You're too hard on yourself, April." He scoots down and turns both of our bodies until we're face to face. "But then you're always trying to be a better person. And you know what I've learned from you?"

"What?" I ask, surprised anyone could learn anything from me.

"That the trying is what makes us better, even if it's twisted fuckery. It might not get you to the finish line, but it gets you closer."

"Huh. Well, you've taught me a lot too."

"Like what?"

"Like how being brutally honest, especially with yourself, strips all the...fuckery away."

"Ha! How immature. I love it when you swear. It's so dirty coming from your pretty mouth. Don't ever swear and play guitar in public because I'll be tearing your clothes off you in seconds."

A snort of laughter escapes me. "I've been thinking about that."

"Me tearing off your clothes in public?"

"No, but maybe now. However, I've been thinking about playing in public."

There's a slight pause of silence before he softly says, "You should. You're so talented. To play like you do after years of not playing…"

"I'm not sure. I'm considering it."

"You know punishing yourself by not playing isn't solving anything."

"I know."

"Okay, just wanted to make sure you weren't reverting to your fucked up ways." The hand on my hip slides to my waist as he sighs. "I may end up losing the chance of a lifetime here, my ticket out of the shithole I was born in."

He's referring to Luminescent Juliet. And though all of the band members would want to take him back, after two years another drummer would become part of the band.

"And at this point," he adds. "I can't berate Riley for taking my spot."

"Riley might fill in, but I'm pretty sure she'd never rejoin. She doesn't want that type of fame. They would have to find someone else."

Silence fills the room for too long a moment.

"Gabe," I say, stalling before referring to the worst possible outcome for tomorrow. "Two years would still leave you a lifetime of chances. You're more than talented. You have an edge to you when

272

you play, an intensity that is visible to the crowd. Maybe—maybe LJ won't be an option but trust me, I know a lot about the music business from my dad, other doors and possibilities will be there. Things that you never imagined…"

He buries his head in my shoulder. "I want to stay with the band. Oddly, after all the bickering and bullshit we've become close. Yet, I can't erase the things I've done or pretend I'm not guilty. I feel like I'm slowly drowning sometimes, but then somehow you always seem to show me the pinpoints of light in my tunnel of darkness."

His words—along with the gratefulness on his face—tug at me so hard, I can't help it. I start crying. He holds me tight. I hold him back just as tightly. And it's okay, because I need this in order to be strong for him.

Tomorrow might be far worse.

Chapter 33
Gabe

"I've been working with Gabe for almost a year," Joan, my psychologist, begins from her spot behind me in the front row of the courtroom.

The prosecution has already spelled out their recommendation, which is the two-year maximum prison sentence. And my lawyer has pleaded on my behalf using the facts that I have a job and am in a successful band to prove that I'm a productive member of society. Yet it seems like Joan is my one hope out of a possible two-year sentence. I like and hate Joan. During our sessions, she drags me through hell, but I always leave feeling lighter. Dreading the shit that's coming, I stay seated forward. My face is made of emotionless stone. I don't fucking want to go through this.

I think of April. And the band.

I have to go through this.

"And a picture of his life has clearly emerged from our time together. It consists of a mother who abandoned the family when he was six, a father in depression that turned to alcohol, and boy who not only was neglected but also abused."

Okay, not so bad. Just general information. I don't like the pity it induces, though it seems to be aimed at me as boy. It's always hard for me to separate my younger self from my adult self. And behind Joan, sit April, the band, and even Riley. I don't want their pity. I loathe people pitying me. A huge part of me wishes none of them were here, but strangely, another part is honored at their support.

The sound of a paper turning sounds and Joan continues, "The abuse included such things as punches in the back if he forgot to take out the trash. Slaps to the face because he wouldn't finish a burnt dinner. A kick in the stomach to send him to bed. And a vicious beating when a teacher called home about his behavior at school."

Though my expression remains like marble, my stomach reels, threating vomit. Her words call the memories back. Flashes in my mind that bring emotions that I hate: fear, helplessness, anger, and anguish. My hands curl into fists under the table while I try to keep the emotional barrage at bay.

"These few instances are a small percent of what I've learned from Gabe during our time together. I could go on for quite some time, but I don't believe that is necessary. What is necessary is for the court to understand that Gabe suffers from post-traumatic stress disorder after so many years of abuse. His symptoms include but are not limited to: intense distress when reminded of the trauma, intense physical reactions when remembering the events, a feeling of disconnection from others, being emotionally numb, a sense of a limited future, and irritability or outbursts of anger."

Yeah, that sounds about how I feel at this moment. Though I'm somehow keeping control of my emotions, I'm starting to sweat and

275

actually shake. Fuck this. Instead of screaming that, I stare at the gavel on the judge's podium.

"PTSD is different with every patient due to the different factors of each case. An important factor in Gabe's history is the arrival of his father's girlfriend around the age thirteen. She gave Gabe attention and took care of him, which created an emotional bond. And although the physical abuse hadn't broken Gabe, he had become a hard and sullen teenager. But Sharon became the one bright spot in his life. When his father began physically abusing Sharon, it didn't take long for Gabe to retaliate."

The memories of Sharon being hurt have me burying my head in my hands because the stone is melting with remembrances that bring on an acute anxiety. I had to keep Sharon safe. Still feel like I have to.

"After that, the abuse did lessen, but didn't entirely stop. Gabe had learned to live with the abuse, as long as his father left Sharon alone. He was always ready to attack if his father hurt Sharon."

My father's fists stopped hurting anything but my pride a long time ago.

"Similarly, all of Gabe's physical assaults as an adult have been preempted by a male hurting a female, a very similar situation to his protecting of Sharon."

The sound of papers shuffling sounds, but I stay unmoving.

"Though I do believe in those instances Gabe is a threat, I don't believe that incarceration is the correct solution. He has been responsive and improving in our sessions. However, faced with his father not only assaulting Sharon again, but also Gabe's girlfriend, was too much for his current coping skills. His coping skills not only need to improve, he also needs more time to come to terms with the abuse in his past. Incarceration is not the solution to either of these. Furthermore, these assaults are the one criminal issue. As an adult, Gabe does not have any other criminal history. Nor does he have any substance abuse problems. Thus, my recommendation is a complete program in a rehab facility where he can continue to heal and learn how to cope."

Still shaking a bit, I drop my hands and stare at the floor. At this point, I don't care what they decide. The memories need to stop.

"Judge Baylor," the prosecutor says in an exasperated tone. "How are we to know that the defendant's second hand account of his life to a psychologist he was court ordered to see is actual fact? This young man has viciously beat three men and broken his father's jaw. Not only is he a threat to society, he needs to be held accountable for his actions."

"It took months for Gabe to open up to me," Joan says in an unyieldingly tone. "And after, I continually had to prod him to share. I never suspected that his accounts, or anguish, were fabricated."

I hear Joan sit, and some whispering that I don't try to decipher.

The sweating and shaking and stomach reeling decrease as the prosecutor, then my lawyer make their final arguments. Their statements don't bring on flashbacks, but I continue to feel out of it, as if I've gone through some sort of emotional wringer.

The judge calls for a break to deliberate. Like a zombie not seeing anyone or anything, I go out into the hall and find a bench. April finds me. She holds my hand and I gradually begin to feel like a human again.

"This is it," I sadly say.

Shaking her head, she smiles. "This is just a short hiccup in the beginning."

Though my head is still screwed on sideways, next to April I find strength and stability, feel like I've landed on my feet. There are many fears rushing across my head right now, but the biggest one is the fear of being without her. At first, I was willing to accept whatever happened. Now I'm hoping for some sort of leniency, something that won't take me from her.

The band and Riley gather around. Conversation floats around me. I have a hard time following it. I'm trying not to consider all the possibilities that the judge will decide, but I do. Everything from two years of prison to six months of jail to months of rehab. All of it will take me from April.

After an hour, it's time to go back in and face my sentencing. Romeo and Sam offer fist bumps. They are obviously more than aware I'm uncomfortable with the pity hanging in the air. Riley and Justin give me hugs. It's been a long road for rich boy Justin and me—there was a time, more like many times, I seriously considered beating his conceited ass—but out of all the band members, I sense he feels the most for my predicament, as if he's guilty he grew up with so much while I had so little.

April tightly hugs me outside the courtroom entrance, whispering in my ear, "Just remember, there's no limit to the time I'll wait for you."

Then I'm walking back down the aisle and facing the judge and my future.

The old man clears his throat before his attention pins to me. His face is lined with tension. "This hasn't been an easy decision. Assault is a crime that has more than physical repercussions. Many of its victims deal with emotional trauma just like you. And I tend to agree with the prosecutor. You need to be held accountable for your actions."

My spine becomes steel. True. I went into this pleading guilty because I don't back down from responsibility. I do not want to go to prison. I do not want to be separated from April for two years. I do not want to lose my spot in the band. But if that's what I owe...

"Yet, I keep coming back to one thing. I'm having a hard time giving the maximum sentence to a young man that our system was completely blind to as a boy. If I could go back in time and find every person that turned their head and ignored your plight—and I'm quite sure they existed—I would sentence every one of them to a lengthy stay. But I'm left here today to sentence you. Your past has obviously impacted your present, which leads me agree with the recommendation for rehab."

An almost tangible relief fills the courtroom while I try to understand his words.

"I'm hoping that you will take this last chance seriously. You will be held in custody until the time that you can be released to a facility. No more than thirty days. You will pay for your flight and the stint in rehab. Consider this as society's debt paid back to you. A return here will not beget any more compassion." He raises the gavel, drops it, and stalks off.

I sit stunned for several long seconds. April chants my name from behind and I finally stand and turn around. I go wrap my arms around her and she buries her face in my neck. "I'm still getting locked up."

"You'll be getting help," she says against my skin.

"The band…"

"They'll wait," she says firmly.

"You…"

"Will miss you every day while I wait."

Chapter 34
April

Over Three Months Later

I come around the bend on the pretty country road blooming with spring and the airport comes into view. Nervousness and excitement flow through me at the sight. I haven't seen Gabe in over three months. I was able to visit him once while he was in jail, but he left for a clinic in Texas ten days after the sentencing. Though the visit hadn't been very private in a room full of people, we managed a few kisses and a short talk about the future.

The band was more than willing to wait for Gabe since they each had a semester left of college to graduate. Romeo had already been contemplating pushing for a later release date. Gabe's sentencing sealed the deal. The recording company they signed with wasn't happy, but really, what is two months? Plus, the delayed release helped decrease Gabe's anxiety about going to the clinic for three months.

I find a parking spot, hurry across the lot, and race up the escalator to the area where passengers come back through security. Of course, I'm early. I sit and wait as anticipation builds.

After half an hour, people begin coming out. I stand and shuffle closer to the exit. I inspect each person quickly, until finally I see him.

His hair is a tad shorter as if he just had it cut, his skin tan from the Texas sun, and his eyes light up as he spots me.

We fly toward each other. He drops his backpack to catch me. My face buries into his hard chest. His buries in my hair. And we just revel in the comfort of being in each other's arms. Nothing else. Euphoria.

He breaks the spell drawing back to look at me. "I've missed you so much," he says hoarsely, then kisses me and the spell re-weaves around us. My hands curl into his hair. His fingers dig into my waist. It takes a few minutes for us to realize that we're in the middle airport surrounded by passing people.

Gabe grins at me.

"Guess we could go to luggage," I say in a sullen tone, unhappy about the break of our kiss.

Shaking his head, he picks up his backpack. "This is it," he says as he grabs my hand.

We move toward the escalator.

"What about your kit?" The clinic had agreed to allow Gabe to practice daily because of the possibility that he could be touring days or weeks after his completion of their program. It will actually be a little more than a month before he starts touring, and I plan to be at several of those shows.

"Shipped that ground. Cheaper and less hassle than flying with it. It should be here by tomorrow."

"Oh," I say slowly, thinking I'd never be able to ship my guitar. I'd worry too much.

We exit out of the airport and I almost trip several times since all I can see is Gabe. I've been imagining this for months, three in fact. And my eyes eat him up. His eyes do the same to me. At my car, he kisses me long and hard before we get in.

"So," I say, turning the ignition. "How was the program? Worth it, I hope?"

He draws in a breath and crosses his arms. "It went well. Mostly, I learned a lot about myself, how to distance myself from my past but also accept it, and different ways how to control my temper. Tons of ways to control myself."

"That sounds good." I back out of the parking spot. "Tell me more," I ask, wanting to know, especially since we haven't talked in three months. Gabe wasn't allowed outside communication at the clinic.

While I drive, he tells me about his group, his psychologist there, his skill lessons, and even the food. It sounds like a great clinic.

After I've asked him every question possible and then some, he says, "You were right."

I glance at him and raise my brows.

"It's never going to be over. My past is always something I'll have to deal with. I'm going to keep seeing Joan. We'll just have to skype like we did on the last tour."

I nod. "I've been going to group…well, when I can. I've been spending a lot of time in California."

"How is everyone?"

"Pretty good. Jason has been going out and doing more. He and I email a lot. Misha's actually dating someone and talking it slow, and Chad, well, he hasn't grown up yet."

I pull into the parking lot behind the tattoo shop.

His brows lower. "We're not going to your place?"

I laugh. "I don't have a place anymore."

His head tilts in question.

I park and turn to him. "Like I said, I've been spending a lot of time in California, and you'd already paid Allie six months of rent, and …I liked sleeping in your bed. Was that okay?"

He grins at me. "Hell, yes. Wish I would have known. I could have imagined you in my bed all this time. But what have you been doing spending so much time in California?"

"I'll tell you later, because in about three minutes, you won't have to imagine anything."

His grin grows. We both jump out of the car and race up the stairs. At the top, I put the key in the lock and he turns the handle.

"Welcome home, Gabe," I softly say, pushing the door open.

"April, I was home the minute you entered my arms at the airport."

His words have me rushing inside, tearing off my clothes and his. Gabe is in on the disrobing too, well, mostly my clothes. But as he tears off my jeans, he pauses at the sight of the tattoo on my hip. His fingers brush the lines of the real life looking monarch that Allie created before he crouches to inspect it.

"Why a butterfly?" he asks, probably thinking if I'd do ink, it would be related to music.

"Rachel had a thing for them, even as a teenager."

His gaze rises from the tattoo to mine.

"I've almost finished the list." I draw in a deep breath. "Slept under the stars on my father's balcony. Well, I didn't sleep much. I laid there thinking of Rachel, something I've tried not to do for a long time. I cried a lot too. Mostly though, I remembered her and missed her and realized I don't want to forget her, no matter how painful the end, no matter how much sadness and guilt her memory brings me. I'll always love her."

He stands and buries his hands in my hair. "That was brave." He kisses me ear. "Very brave."

A sad smile escapes me. "I'm trying."

He kisses the skin behind my ear. "Of course, you are. It's what I love best about you, always wanting to be a better person." His hands slide down my back, sending shivers along my skin. "But there are other things I love about you."

"Oh, yeah?" I lean toward him, my melancholy dissipating at the hot look in his eyes. "Why don't you show me?"

His hands curve around my butt. "Oh, I plan to. All night."

I lean closer, until our lips almost touch. "You've got about four hours."

He rears back. "What?"

I slide my hands over his shoulders. "Dinner at Riley's."

"Fuck that."

"Everyone wants to see you."

"Don't care."

"They care about you. A lot."

"Fine. Four and a half hours. We're going to be late. I've got three months to make up for here."

I laugh. "Late is good with me."

Epilogue
April

Two Months Later

I'm going to puke. Vomit. Blow chunks.

I once thought I'd never be nervous going on stage as long as it was with an instrument.

I was wrong.

Within hours, I'm supposed to play with Luminescent Juliet. Two songs. "Ink My Heart" with some added guitar acrobatics, then one of the songs from my upcoming album. Justin is going to sing it with me. This seemed like a great idea to introduce me to their fans, but now the prospect of getting on stage is terrifying me. Since the concert is at Pine Knob, an outdoor venue outside of Detroit, Allie and Riley commandeered the tour bus while the guys were doing pre-interviews before the show.

Riley scrunches my curled hair, messy it up. "Ugh. I wish Chloe could have come. I suck at this."

Setting down an eyeliner pencil, Allie tilts her head, looking at me in the tall mirror set on the table booth. "I think she looks good. You don't like it, April?"

I don't really care what I look like at this point, keeping my lunch inside my stomach is my main goal, but I force myself to inspect their work. "Um, my hair is a little big." More like a lot, as in huge. "And the makeup is a bit dark." I don't even wear this much eyeliner in an entire year.

Riley scrunches my hair more. "In front of thousands of people you have to be a little bigger than life."

She just had to say thousands, didn't she? "Okay, yeah, then I guess it looks good." I wanted to keep my look toned down in order to showcase the music, but nerves are throwing that plan out the window. And ironically, with my jeans, combat boots, black tank, wild hair, and dark makeup, I'm a bit of a throwback to the nineties grunge look, and that grunge music has always been my inspiration for song writing.

The front door of the bus creaks open and Peyton walks in. "They're on in about twenty minutes." She glances at me and frowns. "You're looking a little pale, April."

"Yeah, I feel pale." I take a deep breath. "I think I…need a few minutes," I say before rushing toward the little bathroom beyond the bunks.

"You okay?" Riley yells.

"Yeah, just need a minute," I repeat.

Inside the tiny bathroom, I lean over and try to get my nerves under control, but fear continues to eat at my gut. I can do this. I don't want to do this. I have to do this.

For all the Rachels of the world.

My album releases in two weeks. Seventy percent of the proceeds—I wanted to go ninety but my dad talked me into seventy so

I could have some capital for future marketing—are going to three different suicide prevention organizations. This album isn't about me, even the songs, a mix of sad and hopeful and resilient, are about all those lonely people caught in the dark. Going on stage with Luminescent Juliet could be a huge springboard for the album and more awareness for the cause.

I stand up and draw in air.

I'm doing this even if I end up puking all the way up the stairs to the stage.

Though I force myself out of the bathroom, I pause in the long aisle of the bus.

Peyton, Allie, and Riley's conversation floats to me from the front. They're discussing the next three days when we'll all be staying in a swanky hotel in downtown Detroit. They sound carefree and excited, and though I'm going to the hotel with Gabe too, anxiety rocks my gut.

I begin to speculate if my acute anxiety is just about going on stage. Or if it's about the huge step I'm about to take compared to the three women up front who all have their futures perfectly figured out.

I watch as Peyton lifts her camera to take a picture of Allie laughing.

Just last month, Peyton took a job for an up and coming magazine in Detroit that promotes the city. She'll be reporting on the music scene, but other topics too, like new businesses. Though she always imagined working for a musical journal, she is beyond excited to be part of the movement to rebuild Detroit. And Sam is ecstatic about her job too. They're looking for a townhouse to rent together. Other than touring, he wants to stay in Michigan. From what I gather, he's pretty close to his twin brother, and because of his brother's issues, he makes time every month to go home and visit him in the thumb of Michigan.

Allie puts her hand out as if to stop Peyton from taking the picture and the overhead light catches the shine of the diamond on her ring finger.

Yup. Allie has her life figured out too. This coming November her and Justin are tying the knot. He proposed when the four of us went to St. Louis to catch Luminescent's fourth concert of the tour. Though they're having a destination wedding in Miami, they just bought a house not even five miles from the university. More than having her tattoo shop and working on opening an art studio, Allie doesn't want to move away because of her son. And Justin seems more than fine with that.

Riley steps in and wraps her arm around Allie's shoulders, smiling and gesturing for Peyton to take a picture.

This August, Riley is heading to L.A. Romeo will be flying out to meet her during a four day break. They'll be looking for an apartment near Chapman University, which specializes in performance degrees— including music. Riley always imagined going to school out of state and since Romeo wants to continue working on the business end of things for the band in L.A., this is her perfect opportunity.

The camera flashes.

But I'm not sure what's happening with me. Other than the album release, I have a few small gigs lined up through my dad, and that might be it. Or if things go well, I could be touring as an opening act. But everything is up in the air. And though Gabe and I spent as much time as possible together before the tour, we've never discussed the future in depth together. We've been too busy, him with practice and then touring, me with writing and then recording. Now I'm about to take a big step into the unknown, while just months ago, when I planned to be a counselor, I had everything perfectly mapped out.

"April," Riley yells down the hall before noticing me. "You okay?"

"Yeah, I'm good," I say, tugging my guitar case off a bunk and forcing a smile. "Let's get going."

We head out of the bus and toward the back of the stage, passing other busses and rows of equipment semis. After Peyton shows her pass, we go through a line of security to find the guys standing on the side of the stage. A few feet from a crowd of backstage pass holders, Gabe leads the rest of the band in a vocal warm up, probably since he doesn't do much backup vocals. Gabe finally drops his hands and the rest of the guys breathe freely again.

We wait behind the backstage fans, but Sam notices us, giving us a quick wave. He then adjusts the strap of his bass and turns toward the stage. They must be going on any second.

However, noticing us too, Gabe comes around the crowd. His eyes roam over me. "You look like a ghost," he says, his mouth tight.

I swallow down a trillion nerves. "I'll be okay."

His arms come around me. "You know you don't have to do this," he says against my massive hair. "You can just skip it and start with a smaller venue."

One hand on his back and the other holding my case, I draw in a deep gulp of air, while also drawing in the strength his arms provide. Almost immediately, the sensation of calm and safe flow through me, and nearly all of my anxiety fades away. Home, just like Gabe felt, I feel it in his arms too. I slowly realize no matter what happens, no matter where this path I'm on goes, I'll always have this.

I step back, shaking my head. "I'm fine. I'm going to do this. Plus, it's the last item on the list."

He stares at me, worry lining his mouth.

Their loud intro music sounds.

"Gabe!" Romeo yells from the stage stairs.

"Really," I say, smiling and giving him a light push toward the stage. "Go. I'll see you in seven songs."

He leans down and gives me a quick kiss. "For luck."

And then he's gone and the crowd is cheering.

Camera around her neck, Peyton goes around the front of the stage to take pictures. After handing off my case to a stagehand, Riley, Allie, and I join the backstage crowd on the side.

During thunderous applause, Luminescent Juliet start the new song I heard at the Whiskey a Go Go, and then their set is in full swing. I dance. I clap. I watch the band—mostly the drummer. I let the music flow over me song after song like I haven't allowed in years.

Too soon, Justin is announcing that they have a special treat for the night. Riley pushes me toward the stage. My nerves bubble up, but when the stagehand delivers my guitar, I pull the strap around me and grasp the neck tight. And then I'm taking my first step up toward the stage. At the top of the stairs, I meet Gabe's gaze over a cymbal. His smile is wide and reassuring. My smile back is just as wide.

Then I step out onto the stage and into the spotlight.

ACKNOWLEDGMENTS

First, I'd like to thank my awesome beta readers. Your input as always was invaluable. Also, thank you to all the wonderful bloggers for all the hard work you do. And as always thanks to every reader who gave my work a chance. You rock!

ABOUT THE AUTHOR

Jean Haus is the author of the Luminescent Juliet series, which revolves around a sexy, talented indie band from a small college town. She also writes romance for adults and young adults. She lives with her husband and son in Michigan, where she spends almost as much time teaching, cooking, and golfing as she does thinking about the romance in her books.

Visit Jean online at http://www.jeanhaus.com.

Other Novels by Jean Haus

New Adult Contemporary from Skyscape

In the Band

Ink My Heart

With the Band

Adult Romance

The Reality of You

Young Adult Paranormal/Fantasy

Under a Blood Moon

After Midnight

Snow, Blood, and Envy

Made in the USA
Las Vegas, NV
07 February 2025

17715961R00162